Love, Laodice

An Olympus Inc. Romance

Kate Healey

Contents

Content Note

*L*ove, *Laodice,* like *Ask Cassandra,* is inspired less by the myths of the Greek pantheon, and more by the darker stories of the Trojan War. This story contains violent crime and discussion of crime, including murder, gun violence, and abuse within intimate relationships.

It also includes an ill-advised workplace relationship between two idiots who are positive they can keep this to a time-limited, sex-only affair. It all works out, but it was still a terrible plan.

Chapter One

The Bride Wore Spring

LAODICE TROIADES

The sun came out the day Persephone Erinyes married Hades Kronion. The days before the couple's outdoor wedding had been stormy, but the skies cleared as dawn swept rosy fingers over the sky. By noon, the sun was shining over Ida Park, and Persephone walked down the famed rose-bordered path to meet her groom.

Her colorful gown, a closely kept secret before the wedding, drew stunned appreciation from the guests before she took a single step.

Persephone's decision to wear a multi-colored print for the ceremony was an homage to her own artistic talents and an acknowledgment of the links she and Hades both have with magazine empire (and Goddess *publisher) Olympus Inc.*

"I knew that I didn't want to wear white," Persephone confessed. "But I wasn't sure what I did want—none of the single-color dresses I saw appealed to me much. Hades suggest I start doodling, because that's what I do when I'm stuck, and before I knew it, I was sketching a gown with these huge, abstract swipes of color, sort of stylized flower petals." The colors echoed the inks of Persephone's floral tattoos—also self-designed—and

Olympus CEO Hera Rheczack suggested a textile manufacturer who could make the imagined print a reality.

For the dress design and construction, another Olympus colleague sprang into action. Penny Laconia took the printed silk and Persephone's original design sketch and created a three-dimensional gown with a corset bodice, sweetheart neckline, and a flowing skirt with a waterfall train. "Persephone was a dream to fit," Penny said. "I can't remember the last time I've had so much fun with a dress."

Persephone's spring colors allowed her mother Demeter to wear a bespoke YSL ivory suit, turning what's usually an out-of-bounds color for anyone but the bride into a background for her daughter's flair. "Color is such an interesting thing, isn't it?" Demeter said. "In some cultures, white is the color of mourning."

Bridesmaid Aphrodite Urania and groomsman Odysseus Turner shared the Master of Ceremonies role at the reception, catered by Hades's favorite restaurant, the Augean. While guests enjoyed pre-lunch drinks in the Marquee...

Laodice Troiades watched Hera Rheczack's eyes scan the copy again. She liked to think she put her best work into every wedding story she wrote, but she'd definitely pulled out some extra stops for this one, where the main players were so closely connected to Olympus Inc in general and its CEO in particular. Laodice was pretty sure she'd memorized most of the article through the constant read-throughs and careful tweaking.

And if Hera, the CEO in question, didn't stop lingering thoughtfully over that first page soon, Laodice was going to do something embarrassing, like ask if it was all right, or start gushing apologies, or maybe pee her pants.

Hera looked up. She was a short woman, and sitting behind her desk, she should have been less intimidating. But the desk was on the top floor of the most powerful magazine publishing house in the world. Laodice was a mere senior writer for the Bridal department, twenty-four floors below.

She felt her hands clench in the loose fabric of her skirt, and consciously made her fists relax.

"Cut Demeter Erinyes from the piece," Hera said.

Laodice blinked. High-profile weddings were *Goddess*'s specialty. Generally speaking, the more quotes from society matrons and celebrities she could cram in, the better. Demeter's comment had been strange, and she'd delivered it in an odd tone, but including her meant guaranteed higher sales.

Hera acknowledged Laodice's confusion with a slight nod. "Normally, you'd be quite right," she said. "Just this once, please."

And that was another sign that something had been off with the mother of the bride. Persephone and Hades had been in a state of blissful oblivion throughout the festivities, but Laodice had noticed Don Kronion, Hecate Jones, and even Hera herself keeping a sharp eye on Demeter throughout the ceremony and reception.

She'd seen it many times, at many weddings—friends and family deployed to make sure a problematic guest didn't spoil the couple's special day.

"I wondered why Demeter was wearing something that pale," she admitted. "Even with the colored gown, it seemed odd."

Hera's gaze sharpened, and for a moment Laodice was worried she'd overstepped. Then her boss's mouth twisted into a wry smile. "Demeter didn't know about Persephone's dress."

Laodice's mouth fell open. "She thought her daughter was wearing white, and she still picked that suit?"

"Yes," Hera said. "Persephone and her mother are...well, not estranged, exactly. It's a difficult situation." She tapped the printout. "But I don't want Demeter rewarded for her attention-seeking behavior by actually getting attention."

"Oh. Uh, yes, that sounds reasonable."

"This is strictly confidential, of course. However, I'd rather you know why I made the request than speculate in public." Her eyes glinted with an unmistakable warning, and Laodice mentally deleted the text she'd been composing for her group chat with her sisters.

"I'm honored by your trust," she said instead.

Hera leaned back slightly and regarded her. "You've earned it. You've been working for Bridal for...five years now, yes?"

"Yes. I started straight out of college." She'd applied for the prestigious Olympus intern program first, but the competition had been too fierce. Applying for a junior writer position in Bridal had seemed like an even wilder shot, but she'd somehow impressed Miriam, the Head of Bridal, during her interview.

"Most people who start in the Bridal section don't stay there. They transfer to one of our fashion titles, or perhaps Travel."

"Miriam's stayed," Laodice said loyally. "And Telfer Terzi has stayed for four years," she added, with less enthusiasm.

"I'm sure you've heard that Miriam is retiring. Had you thought of applying for the vacancy?"

"I've thought about it," Laodice admitted. She had a half-completed pitch deck, a revamped resume, and a list of her own accomplishments in Bridal that her older sister had bullied her into making, but she hadn't yet committed herself. It was such a huge job. Bridal was a Frankenstein's monster of a department, with two major quarterly titles, a number of special editions and supplements, and a ton of digital content. And then there was the marketing, subscriptions, vendor advertising—all of the stuff that made the magazines financially viable in a complex media landscape. She could definitely handle the editing side, but the finance aspect was much more intimidating.

"Do consider it," Hera said, and Laodice's spine straightened. If Hera Rheczack thought she should apply...

"Thank you, I will," she said.

Hera stood up, and Laodice took the cue, getting to her feet. Her head was still whirring. Hera hadn't said anything explicitly, but that was encouragement, it really was. Head of Bridal! She'd be able to choose stories, and do that Where Are They Now idea she'd been pitching. They could expand their focus past the city, maybe look at love and lovers in a wider sense—still focusing on weddings, of course, that was the bread and butter, but elopements were getting more popular now, and DIY weddings weren't going away any time soon. There had to be a way to get vendor buy-in for DIY, and she could probably attract some new advertisers.

Maybe even bring in new readers outside their audience of brides-to-be and mothers and bridesmaids of brides-to-be.

All right, yes, Telfer Terzi would point out that there was a small male readership too, and also most of their readership, regardless of gender, was incredibly transient. Right now, people only bought their titles when they had a wedding to plan themselves. But Laodice had wild ambitions to appeal to people who loved love, whether they were getting married, had already been married, never intended to be married, or, like her, had been dreaming of an as-yet unrealized marriage their whole life. She wanted a magazine for romantics.

And as editor, she might be able to make it happen.

"Thank you, that will be all," Hera said politely, and Laodice realized she'd been standing there, staring into space.

"Yes!" she said. "I'll make those cuts. Uh, thank you for your time, Hera."

"Enjoy your stay in the Hippocampus," Hera said, presumably in case Laodice didn't already think she knew way too much about everything. The Hippocampus retreat story was supposed to be a closely kept secret. Though evidently not from the Olympus CEO.

"Um, yep," Laodice said, and escaped into the outer office, where Hera's junior assistant looked at her with sympathy.

"Looks like you've been through Hurricane Hera," she observed.

"Diana, is she actually psychic?" Laodice asked. "You can tell me."

Hera's senior assistant, Cyd, snorted. "Psychic, no. Smart, attentive, and has Mark Hermes feeding her all the gossip in the building, yes."

"Oh," Laodice said. "You mean she cheats. I feel better about that, somehow. Have a good weekend."

"Drinks next Wednesday?" Diana asked. "We could all use a cocktail in this heat."

"I'm on holiday for a week."

"Oh, right! Enjoy your leave!"

In the elevator, Laodice wondered if Diana had been able to tell she was lying. Not that she was going to be away—that was true—but that it wasn't really leave. Probably not. Olympus was always hectically busy, but in late June, with no major fashion events and less in the news cycle, the pace slowed to merely breakneck. A lot of people scheduled holidays.

The CFO was on his honeymoon. No one was going to wonder if a Bridal senior writer disappeared for a week.

The Bridal department was on the sixth floor. Laodice waved at Stephanie, the receptionist, and breezed past her into the main workroom. This late on a Friday afternoon, almost no one was still in the department—Thalia, working on the layout for the Persephone and Hades story, Telfer, staring at one of his spreadsheets with his earbuds in, and Miriam, in her tiny pink-wallpapered office off the main workroom. Laodice knocked on the glass door and walked in.

"All's well?" Miriam asked, in her cut-glass upper crust British accent. Laodice happened to know she'd picked the accent up at Oxford, along with her first husband.

"I've been asked to make a few cuts, but nothing major."

Miriam exhaled. "Excellent. I mean, technically, it wasn't one of our bigger weddings, but one does want to put one's best foot forward for the CEO's family. Now, next things. Close the door, dear."

Laodice did, and sat down.

"Is everything set for the Halcyon retreat story?"

"I'm all packed, and meeting Eli at my place in half an hour."

"Fabulous." Miriam leaned back. "I do wish I could go myself. This could be quite the coup."

"Do you really think this kind of thing could become popular?" Laodice asked. "I mean, engagement parties are great, and most people like to do something right before the wedding, but this is sort of in-between."

Miriam smiled. "Which is exactly why I think it might be successful, especially with the wealthy. Between the engagement and the pre-wedding celebrations, there are often months where the excitement and attention lag. The Halcyon retreat is being pitched as a way to solidify your bond with your partner, a full week focusing on each other and mingling with others in the same boat. But the way they're selling it... It sounds something like a reality TV show without the cameras or the fear of a bad edit—luxury, exclusivity, and bragging rights."

"We're not even supposed to use our own cameras," Laodice said. She'd read the small print carefully. "Phones are confiscated."

"Yes, that might be a drawback for those who like to preen on social media," Miriam said thoughtfully. "But they could preen about their digital detox afterwards. You're taking a burner phone, of course?"

"You bet. And my laptop."

Miriam gave her an approving look. "Nevertheless, I think Halcyon might have spotted a potential goldmine. They certainly think so or they wouldn't have offered to host a reporter for their soft opening."

"But is it a coup for us? A cover story for *Goddess* is good, but..."

"An exclusive cover story," Miriam reminded her. "One with broad appeal, if our Telfer is correct, and that boy is usually right on the money. We'll get a lot of clicks, and perhaps some viral coverage, which is a wider audience and more revenue for us. Halcyon will burst onto the scene and book out, then probably raise their already extortionate prices. Their vendors will get a lot of interest from people who can afford to pay big. This may be one of those rare occasions where everyone profits."

"And the couples?" Laodice pressed.

"Will have a marvelous time, and probably not even notice how much they spent having it." Miriam folded her hands on her desk. "And all you have to do is enjoy yourself, my dear, and do your usual splendid work. Find the human interest, and bring out the romance."

"It's not an advertorial, right?"

Miriam shrugged, her smile undimmed. "No. If you have an awful time, you should report that too. Though of course, at that point it probably won't be a cover story."

Laodice grinned. "You don't think 'A Horrible Time in the Hippocampus' will move numbers?"

Miriam ignored that. "Now, in case I need to get in touch, your name at Halcyon is Elle Evagora, yes?"

"That's right."

"Lovely name. Where did it come from?"

"My sister calls me 'L' sometimes, like the letter, so I figured I'd respond to it. And Evagora was our maternal grandmother's surname."

"Ah, very nice." Miriam's expensively ageless face didn't move much in the forehead, but she somehow gave the impression of frowning thoughtfully. "You should have let Stephanie make that social media profile for you. For Elle, rather."

"No, thank you," Laodice said. "Elle takes her privacy seriously." She'd locked down her personal accounts years ago, when her sister Xena's social media stardom had taken off. Xena was fearless, mocking trolls or ignoring them, whichever worked best for her in the moment. Laodice, who'd at first delighted in spreading her sister's work, had been less able to deal with the attention that followed. Now her accounts were for family and friends only. Elle Evagora didn't even exist, but Laodice felt weirdly protective of her.

"Thank goodness I've resisted publishing photos of our staff," Miriam said. "Otherwise I wouldn't be able to send you at all. As it is, we're risking that a previous bride's sister or maid-of-honor will be getting married herself, and recognize your face."

"I try to sort of fade into the background at weddings. People aren't there to see me."

"Have you practiced the name with your Eli? Make sure he knows not to let it slip."

Laodice laughed. "We haven't practiced, but I'm sure it'll be fine. Eli will think he's wooing a whole new girl."

"Ah! Is there active wooing?"

"Well, we've been together for eight months, so..." Her longest relationship since college. Seventy percent of engagements happened after the couple had been together for two years. "Maybe the setting will be inspiring."

"Mm," Miriam said neutrally. "Is Eli your Mr. Right, then?"

Laodice had tried not to ask herself that question recently. "More like Mr. Right Now," she admitted. "I mean, I like him a lot. He's fun and affectionate, and he's really energetic—"

"You sound like you're describing a puppy, my dear, not a man."

"Miriam!"

"Take it from someone who's been divorced twice and widowed once, Laodice. You must admit I've the experience to judge." Her eyes twinkled. "And I'm not slowing down either. My advice is to take your Eli and show him a wonderful time, file the best story you've ever written, and...consider your options from there."

"I'll see you Monday after next," Laodice said, and escaped from the office, Miriam's unrepentant laughter ringing in her ears.

The only person left in the workroom was Telfer Terzi, steadily turning press releases and vendor email approaches into copy. It was important work, and it sold a hell of a lot of advertising pages. Telfer was good at it. Laodice could happily acknowledge his good qualities as long as he didn't open his mouth.

"You have to cut four inches from the Stormer wedding report," he said, without turning around.

"Excuse me?"

He swung his chair to face her, dark eyes unreadable. "We've got a new headpiece picture. The designer advertises with us, and it's a valuable relationship. Art and Design says they need the extra space for the close-up detail."

If any of her other colleagues had said it, Laodice would have sighed, maybe damned all advertisers to hell, and cut the paragraphs without argument. Of course, none of her other colleagues would have said it quite like that.

"Not my problem," she said, with some relish. "I am officially out of here. You'll have to make the cuts yourself."

He tilted his head back, so that even though he was sitting and she was standing, he could give the impression of looking down his long nose at her. "Fine," he said. "But you can't complain that I've butchered your deathless prose this time."

"Make sure you don't leave out any big society names," Laodice said, and smiled sweetly at him. She was much better at keeping up with who was who, and they both knew it. "Or you'll face the wrath of Miriam. Ciao! Don't miss me too much!"

"Not likely," Telfer muttered, and turned back to his screen.

Laodice mentally gave herself a point for winning that one, and swept out the door. A nice drive through the countryside, luxury pampering in a beautiful hotel, excellent sex with her hot boyfriend, and best of all, no Telfer Terzi for a whole week.

The Halcyon retreat promised to be the time of her life.

***

Laodice was very fond of her little studio apartment. The rent was barely affordable on her salary, but the eighth-floor walk-up was warm and bright, and the thrifted furniture made for a romantically eclectic mix. She'd long ago taken William Morris's famous advice to have nothing in her home that she didn't know to be useful or believe to be beautiful.

Of course, her collection of ceramic frogs on the pantry shelves and pastel mixing bowls might not be Morris's idea of beautiful, but they made her happy. She loved everything in her apartment.

With, right now, the notable exception of her boyfriend.

She took another deep breath, and focused on keeping her tone neutral. "What do you mean, you've changed your mind about going to Halcyon with me?"

"Um," Eli said. "Pretty much...that." He gave her a hangdog look, which would have looked more appealing if he hadn't been six foot four, lounging comfortably against her breakfast bar, and had also left his suitcase at home, because he'd decided not to come at the literal last hour.

"You said you thought it would be fun."

Eli's eyes shifted. "Yeah. I mean. I thought it would be. But it's a lot."

"What is?"

"It's a couples retreat. For engaged couples. And we're not engaged, right?"

Laodice tried to produce a light laugh, but it sounded strained. "I think we'd have noticed. No, we talked about this, remember? We're undercover, like those heist movies you like. I'm going as Elle Evagora."

Eli looked momentarily intrigued. "A secret identity?"

"That's right," Laodice said. "And you can have a different identity too, if you like." That wasn't what she'd prepared, but if it would sweeten the pot for him…"It'll be like we're spies. Seven days in a luxurious retreat, lots of fun activities, probably incredible food. Everyone else there is going to be a millionaire, minimum. We'll be pampered like nothing else."

"Couples activities," Eli said, his face falling again.

"We've been dating for eight months," Laodice reminded him. "We are a couple."

"Sure!" Eli said eagerly. "And I love being in a couple with you. But we're not an engaged couple."

"We're playing pretend, Eli," Laodice said, with what she hoped wasn't too much condescension. Eli wasn't stupid, people didn't let you play with stocks and bonds all day if you were actually stupid, so how could he not be grasping this? "Come on, rush hour's nearly over. We can swing past your place and pack a bag, then we'll be on the road." She caught the shift of his eyes and stopped. "Or is it something else?"

"Mm?"

"Eli. What's going on? What's the real reason?"

He expelled a breath. "Okay, well. I mentioned at work that I'd got all this time off, and Simon and Ian said they had private box invites for a Minotaurs game in Miami next Tuesday."

Laodice's head swam. "You want to blow me off so you can go and watch basketball?"

"Private box," Eli repeated, as if the words were a magical talisman. "And I was like, maybe I can leave the retreat for the game and come back, but then I remembered you'd said it was like a whole week away from the rest of the world, that was part of the package." He looked proud of himself for remembering what she'd said. "So I figured I shouldn't go at all."

Laodice took a deep breath and forced her voice to calm. "Eli. This is for my job. I can't show up at a couple's retreat by myself. It's going to completely blow my cover with the other guests."

"Maybe you can tell them your fiancé's sick or something?" he offered. "You don't really want me to be there if I don't want to be there, right?"

"No," Laodice said, through gritted teeth. No other answer was possible.

He nodded, handsome and self-assured and totally infuriating. "Yeah, that'd be bad for both of us. So you go and do your thing, and we can catch up next Saturday."

Laodice stared at him.

"What?" he said.

"You cannot possibly think we're staying together after this."

He looked genuinely taken aback.

"Eli! You committed to this weeks ago! It's a potentially huge deal for my career, at a time when I need big wins. And you're blowing me off at the last minute so that you can hang out with your stupid work buddies at a game!"

"But I don't want to break up," he said. "Hey, hey, you know, it's okay, I'll come with you and then I can pretend to be sick on Monday and be like, oh no, I have to go home, and then I can go to the game—"

"No!"

"Ugh, fine, I'll stay for the whole thing. Ian will be mad but—"

Laodice threw her hands into the air. "What are you not getting about this? You're unreliable. You've let me down. This is me breaking up with you."

Alarm sparked in his face. "I'm sorry," he said, and she couldn't help noticing it was the first time he'd actually apologized. "Honestly, Laodice, I didn't realize it was such a big deal. I can come, it's fine. We'll have a good time." He gave her a big, goofy smile, the one that had pulled her across a bar to him eight months ago, the one that had made her think *maybe this one*.

Laodice had never had the urge to attack a lover before, but through the red mist of ascending rage, she eyed her ceramic frogs and wondered if hurling one at his big, goofy smile would really be all that bad.

It would. It would definitely be bad. She clenched her fists tight in her skirt instead. "Eli, you are the last person I'd be willing to share a bed with right now. Give me my spare key and get out of my home."

"Hey," he said, starting to look annoyed. "Maybe this wouldn't be such a big deal if you weren't so clingy."

"Out!" Laodice shrieked. She'd get the spare key later.

"But I love—"

If he was refusing to leave, she could definitely throw a frog at him. She grabbed the biggest one and pivoted, gauging the distance.

Eli must have seen the absolute sincerity of the threat. He pushed away from the breakfast bar and backed towards the door. "Fine! I'm leaving!" He scrabbled at the door handle and got out, half closing the door between them. "I'll talk to you later, when you've calmed down."

"Never talk to me again," Laodice snarled.

"You don't need to be such a bitch—"

The rest of his sentence was lost in the crash of ceramic against wood. Laodice stood with her fists clenched, staring at the fresh scar in her front door and the shards of frog flung across her welcome mat, listening to the hasty footsteps scurrying away.

A broken relationship, a destroyed ornament, and the biggest story of her career was threatening to slip away from her like mist in a breeze.

Okay. Okay. Fine. Laodice could handle this. She could handle anything. She grabbed her suitcase, stepped over the debris, and left.

First stop, Olympus.

Chapter Two

Telfer Terzi was used to having Friday nights to himself.

Sometimes, one of his colleagues would be sweating over a last-minute deadline, or working later to secure a Monday off, but usually he was able to sit down and focus on getting work done, without considering the effect he sometimes had on his co-workers.

Or the effect one in particular had on him.

He could shut out most distractions when he really needed to focus, but Laodice Troiades was impossible to ignore. She took up so much space every time she entered a room, and not only with her impressive curves and sweeping skirts, but with her shimmering charisma. For most people, she was sunshine, a radiant beam of warmth and generosity. Time and again he'd seen people soften and glow when she directed her attention towards them. It was an excellent strategy—he'd learned to turn on the charm himself, when necessary—but it didn't seem to require any conscious effort on her part. She was genuinely interested in and predisposed to like most people, and they naturally responded to it.

For him, of course, she was a thunderstorm.

Laodice was his professional rival, his personal nemesis, and his grudgingly acknowledged private attraction. Whenever she was around, he was always a little aware of her, even if she wasn't directly interacting with him, arguing over his market projections or trying to get him to support one of her unworkable notions.

But on Friday nights, Laodice dated, in her continual quest for The One. Over the last eight months she'd dated Eli Kaon, who seemed to be in the running for the position. Telfer had met Eli and considered him the human equivalent of lukewarm toast, but if Laodice wanted to throw all her fire and ambition at a cardboard cutout of a man, that was naturally her prerogative.

Telfer didn't date. Friday nights were his.

But on this particular Friday night, even alone in the office, with his earbuds in and his screens aligned at the right angle, it was somehow still difficult to focus. He should be rejoicing—Laodice wasn't going to be there for an entire week, and his productivity should improve accordingly.

Unfortunately, he couldn't help thinking about her being off on that Halcyon retreat with her Ken doll of a boyfriend, getting the story *he'd* brought to Miriam.

Telfer had been there when the Halcyon venture was first ideated. He'd been the one offered the lead. Brandon had agreed to an embedded reporter for their soft opening, provided that the guests were suitably anonymized.

Miriam had praised him for the scoop, and then pointed out that the assignment really required a couple.

Telfer had had an answer for that. He'd suggested hiring a professional actor, or perhaps an escort. Miriam had considered it before assigning the story to Laodice instead.

Because Laodice was the better wedding writer—he was willing to admit that—but more importantly, because she had a partner and he didn't.

And he wouldn't have cared—he *wouldn't*—except that this gave Laodice a very good chance at securing the Bridal Editor position when Miriam left, and *he* wanted that job. He could lead Bridal to snap up more of the market share. He could leverage the digital opportunities and make *Goddess* and *Bliss* synonymous with weddings, until no bride (and a small but growing selection of grooms) would ever *dream* of getting married without buying a copy.

But if he wanted to be the editor in charge of Bridal, he needed a big win. And coming up with one on this Friday night was proving to be more of a challenge than he'd hoped.

Even through his earbuds, he caught the sound of the door opening behind him, and the exasperated huff that followed.

He turned, and Laodice Troiades was standing there, still in the flowing pink thing she'd worn to the office that day, her hair starting to fall out of its loose updo. Automatically, he checked the lines of her skirt. They were crumpled. She'd been twisting the fabric in her fists again, her sure tell of emotion poorly contained.

Interesting.

He met her eyes and then jumped to his feet.

"You're bleeding," he said.

"What?" Laodice said, and then touched the bright spot on her cheekbone, bringing away her hand to inspect the smear on her fingers. "Oh, hell. That's perfect. Where's Miriam?"

"Gone. Sit down, I'll get the first aid kit."

"I don't need—" Laodice started, but he was already heading to the reception area, where Stephanie kept their department kit in her lower desk drawer.

"Sit down," he repeated.

"I'll do it," she said impatiently, and held her hand out for the kit.

"Come on, you can't see your own face," he said, and was relieved when she sighed and slumped into her usual chair, her body language allowing him to approach. "What happened?"

"Ricochet, probably," she said, which made little sense, and then, "I really liked that frog," which made even less.

She hissed when he dabbed at the cut with the sterilizing wipe. The cut was an inch long, but shallow, and most of the blood had already dried. Telfer heroically didn't look down her top, but he couldn't help noticing how soft her skin was, tender and smooth as a rose petal.

"I don't think it needs stitches, but a couple of butterfly closures wouldn't hurt."

"Okay," she said. There was a hesitation, so brief he nearly missed it. "Thank you."

"You didn't feel this?" he asked, carefully peeling back and placing the tiny adhesives over the cut.

"I feel it now," she said, with the rueful good humor he'd seen before. Never directed at him, though.

"Okay," Telfer said, and sat back on the desk opposite. "Now. Why are you here, and not halfway to the Hippocampus?"

Laodice's spine straightened and her chin came up. Telfer found himself oddly relieved. "Eli is no longer coming with me to Halcyon. I need to get in touch with Miriam so we can discuss back-up plans."

Ah. Telfer felt his own spine straighten as he spotted the opportunity.

"Eli's not going?"

Laodice glowered at him. "That's what I said."

"Why?"

"Because he's a lying sack of *shit*," Laodice snarled, and then regained her control with obvious effort. "Look, it's fine. I'll find someone else."

"Who?"

"My sister," Laodice said, and for a moment Telfer envied the certainty with which she said it, her unshakable belief that if she asked for help with something this important, her family would support her.

But the problems were obvious.

"Which sister? The one who looks like you dressed up as a librarian, or the famous influencer who one of the other attendees is bound to know?"

Laodice frowned.

"And do you really want to be doing couple activities with your sister anyway?" he asked, pressing his advantage. "Obviously, nothing weird would actually be happening, but it would *feel* strange, wouldn't it?"

"You're saying this in your smug 'I already have a solution' voice," Laodice said suspiciously.

"I do," Telfer said. All right, he sounded a little smug. "It's me."

"No," Laodice said, with an immediate conviction that could have been disheartening if he wasn't already aware of how she felt about him.

"I'm the only real option," Telfer said, spreading his hands. "In fact, I'm a better option than Eli. You can rely on me to uphold a cover story *and* as your colleague, I can help gather background and pursue my own leads."

"It's a week! You don't have the leave."

"I do, actually," Telfer said, ignoring the way her eyes immediately narrowed. It wasn't *technically* a lie. He did have the leave *available*. He just hadn't asked for this week off. "I was planning to get a lot done in a time of fewer distractions," he added, and that was true. "Look, you know I wanted that story. It should have been mine anyway, but I'll settle for half of it. You do the human interest, and I'll chase the vendor connections."

"You seem to be missing the part where it's a *couples* retreat for engaged *couples,* and *we* can barely be civil in the office," Laodice said. Her cheeks were flushed, and her dark eyes were sparking. Any minute now, she'd start shooting verbal lightning.

Telfer shrugged. A small and petty part of himself liked pushing Laodice's buttons.

"That presents no real difficulty. Couples argue all the time."

"We'll be sharing a room," Laodice pointed out. "Sharing a bed."

"I won't get handsy if you don't."

Laodice's jaw dropped, her plush lips opening. "As if— I would *never—*"

"Then there's no problem." Telfer stood. "If you wouldn't mind giving me a ride to my place, I can grab my bag and we'll go." And he'd better compose a hasty email to Miriam, apologizing for the short notice and explaining that he'd be working remotely. Miriam had a soft spot for him. He tried not to exploit the advantage. But in this case, he'd make an exception.

Laodice didn't move.

Telfer eyed her. It was a perfectly logical proposition, but experience had taught him that Laodice didn't always respond to logic. For a moment, he was worried that she wouldn't see reason.

Then she deflated. "I suppose you're the *second* to last person I'd be willing to share a bed with right now."

Telfer felt triumph rush through him. "Rude," he said. "I'm not a murderer or a venture capitalist."

"There have got to be some decent murderers," Laodice said thoughtfully. "All right, Terzi. I can't believe I'm saying this, but you can be my fake fiancé."

"Let's not forget that I'm doing you a huge favor here," Telfer said. "You should be thanking me."

Laodice snorted. "You're doing this out of naked self-interest."

"So are you," Telfer pointed out, and then had an inconvenient and frustratingly fuzzy image of a naked Laodice flash through his head.

"True," Laodice said, and thrust her hand out. "So, since we're both getting something out of this, and neither of us can sabotage the other without ruining our own work, I propose a truce for the duration of the retreat."

Telfer raised an eyebrow. "And then we return to our cut-throat competition for Miriam's place?"

"Yes," Laodice said. "Agreed?"

"Agreed," Telfer said, and shook on it.

Laodice's palm was soft, but there was strength in her grip. Her hair chose that moment to tumble down completely, releasing a waft of sweet scent in his direction. She let go and stepped past him, grumbling as she tucked her hair up again.

Telfer stood still, wondering if he'd made a foolish mistake.

***

Laodice was utterly unsurprised when Telfer gave her directions to a multi-story apartment building downtown. He probably lived in an executive apartment with soulless corporate art, an expensive black leather couch, and a shiny chrome kitchen he had never sullied with cooking.

She was a little surprised he didn't comment on her car. It was a cherry red Alfa Romeo 1974 Spider Veloce that she'd bought for a song at a junkyard. Laodice had done most of the restoration in evenings and weekends during her junior and senior years of college, and the result was a classic convertible sports car that guys typically either coveted or pretended not to while not-so-secretly writhing with envy.

A few men had openly disbelieved that she'd fixed it up herself. Those guys didn't get a second ride. Or a second date.

Telfer just folded his long legs into the single passenger seat and gave her directions. Laodice spotted a parking spot and swooped in.

"I'll be back in a minute," Telfer said, and disappeared into the building before she could even respond.

All right, he wasn't going to invite her in. Laodice didn't want to see his apartment anyway. She touched her cheek, and then checked the wound in her rearview mirror. The cut didn't look too bad, and she could admit that Telfer had done a decent job of tending to it.

But what the hell had she been thinking? Working with the man for five days a week was bad enough. How was she going to survive seven nights in close proximity with him, *and* keep up the charade of a happy couple?

"And what were the alternatives?" she asked the mirror version of herself, who grimaced in response.

"Talking to yourself?" Telfer said. He was holding a single slim black suitcase. "That's a sign of insecurity, you know."

Laodice started. "Thirty to fifty percent of people have inner monologues," she retorted.

"And I'm one of them, but I keep that shit locked up. Is there room in the trunk or should I put this in…" He looked at the package shelf behind the seats. "The back seat?" he said doubtfully.

Aha. He hadn't praised her car because he didn't know the first thing about it. "There's room," Laodice said, and got out to open the trunk for him. His case sat neatly on top of hers in the deep hollow. "How did you pack so fast? That wasn't even five minutes."

"I keep a go-bag, and I added extra underwear and shirts. I assume Halcyon has laundering services, if necessary."

Laodice had meticulously planned her outfits to give the impression of wealth, but not of trying too hard. It had required hours, and several consultations with her younger sister Xena, who spent a lot of time with rich people and those who desperately wanted to become them.

Must be nice to be a guy.

"I thought maybe you had a packing list, like Joan Didion," she said.

"I don't think I'd look good in a leotard and skirt," Telfer said, and then frowned at her surprise. "What?"

"I'm shocked you can quote from that list."

Telfer looked down his nose at her, possibly his least attractive expression. "It gets trotted out in multiple stories every summer. Besides, I'm a journalist, of course I've read *The White Album*."

"Oh, are you a journalist?" Laodice asked, scooping her skirt under her butt as she slid back into the seat. "I hadn't noticed, what with all your focus on the bottom line."

"My finance background makes me *valuable*," Telfer said meaningfully. "Especially to people who understand that journalism is a business, like Hera. She was very happy with the results of my influencer initiative."

Laodice scowled. The influencer initiative was a sore spot, because Telfer had started it with a proposal to her sister. Xena was a businesswoman, and Laodice didn't exactly want her to miss out on opportunities, but had Xena really had to do *such* a good job on her promo and product placements for *Bliss*? Xena's numbers had shot up even higher, and Olympus had gotten real cut-through on markets that normally didn't have much interest in print. Telfer had ridden that wave of smug superiority for over a year.

But after a moment, Laodice relaxed. *She* was the one who'd written up the Persephone/Hades wedding. She was the one Miriam trusted to bring back an exclusive cover story on the Halcyon retreat. Telfer might have the edge when it came to figuring out new ways to make a buck, but editors needed to be writers, first and foremost, and there, she definitely came out on top.

The rush hour traffic had died down by the time they got out of the city. Telfer didn't say much, and Laodice kept her eyes on the road. Every now and then someone would buzz past them, but highway cruising on a gorgeous summer evening with the top down was still an idyllic way to pass the time.

Even if the company was less idyllic. Her second thoughts were getting a lot louder, now that her initial panic had died down.

Worse, Telfer's reference to packing had brought the contents of her own suitcase into her mind's eye, and while Laodice was confident in her daywear, her nightclothes were a different story. She'd packed in happy anticipation of excellent sex with Eli, who, despite his now-obvious flaws, was *fantastic* in the bedroom. She had some saucy lingerie, a silky shortie set with a low v-neck camisole top, and a brand-new diaphanous peignoir that went with a hot pink satin teddy. All wasted now; she definitely wasn't going to be wearing any of that around Telfer.

Well, she'd also packed exercise clothes. Maybe she'd see if she could sleep in her yoga pants.

Telfer was squirming a little, slouching in the seat and then folding his legs awkwardly and straightening again. Laodice glanced at him. She wouldn't hear a word said against the Spider, but she could privately admit the seats weren't quite as wide as she'd like. However, Telfer's skinny butt should fit just fine.

He reached up and smoothed down his hair, scowling, and she grinned as she diagnosed the problem. Laodice was maybe wider than the Alfa Romeo engineers had envisaged, but at five foot five she was the perfect height for the Spider. With the top down, she could look comfortably through the windshield without slouching or craning, and the slipstream passed cleanly over her head.

Telfer was taller, well over six feet, and the slipstream was hitting *him* right in the face. Even when he slouched a little, the wind went right through all that thick, dark hair. She'd never seen his hair out of place, but now it looked as if someone had been combing their fingers through it, deliberately trying their best to muss it up.

He looked like an annoyed cat, grimly submitting to the hairdryer after a bath.

He slouched again, and Laodice caught him wincing as he readjusted. Well, she didn't mind if Telfer suffered some discomfort, but causing him actual pain wasn't really in the spirit of their truce. She took the next exit and parked at a truck stop which had some fast-food options, a small convenience store and, all the fates be praised, an actual roadside diner.

"Why are we stopping?" Telfer said, getting out with her. "Aren't we already running late?"

"Check-in is any time this evening," Laodice said. Through her teeth. Why was it so hard to do this man favors? "And I don't know about you, but I haven't eaten, and we should put the top up before it gets dark. Because otherwise you'll be cold *and* your hair will look like that."

Telfer flattened his palms against his head and glared at her. "Well, we should get something to go."

"We are not *eating* in my vintage sports car! I spent far too much time restoring that interior for you to spill mustard all over it."

"I wouldn't spill—" Telfer said hotly, and then hesitated. "You restored this car?"

"Yes!" And if he said one disbelieving word, she was going to leave his ass here, Laodice decided. Screw the story. She wasn't going to spend a week with a man who'd belittle her.

"Oh," Telfer said, and gave the Spider a long look. "That's impressive."

Laodice's shoulders settled. "It is, isn't it? Let's eat."

Chapter Three

At first, Telfer wasn't sure why the revelation that Laodice had restored her own car had unnerved him. It wasn't only that it didn't mesh with the image of her he'd derived from her romantic ideals and swishy dresses. He'd like to think that he could allow for people to have layers, and interests that lay outside the stereotypes.

No, he realized. It was because after working with her for four years, she still *had* layers that had been hidden from him. He'd thought he'd known the woman, that he had her measure, and then she'd revealed this obviously important aspect of herself that he'd never suspected. He hadn't been paying enough attention, and *that* was unsettling.

He'd then pictured her in a denim jumpsuit open at the throat and her long hair piled up into a jaunty headscarf a la Rosie the Riveter. That was also mildly disconcerting.

Laodice had ordered a cheeseburger and curly fries at the diner bar, instead of heading to one of the booths. He'd taken the hint and eaten his own cobb salad at a table alone, before heading to the convenience store and replenishing his stock of protein bars. It had occurred to him that the food at the retreat was a relative unknown.

Travelling with the top up *was* less uncomfortable. If he sat up straight, his head did brush the ceiling, but at least wind and bugs weren't flying into his face. And he'd fixed his hair in the diner bathroom.

"We should go over our stories," he said, breaking what had been a relatively peaceful silence. "My contact knows we're going, but he hasn't let the manager or staff know."

"Are you sure?" Laodice asked. "It's not much of a story if we're marked out for special treatment from the start."

"I made a bet with him," Telfer said smugly. "He'd break a promise, but he'd never cheat on a bet. We just need to keep our covers intact." And if they were treated well anyway and got the story they wanted, he'd owe Brandon a bottle of good whiskey. Winners all around.

"Mm," Laodice said, sounding doubtful. "Well, I'm registered as Elle Evagora."

"Okay. I'll be... Telford Aydem."

"How did we meet?"

"We should probably stick to the truth as closely as possible," Telfer said. "So we met four years ago at work."

"Uh-huh. And instead of tearing down my ideas in your first editorial meeting, you were like, 'what a cool story, Elle,' and then we fell in love."

Telfer frowned. He couldn't remember many details of his first editorial meeting at Olympus. What stood out in memory was his heightened anxiety and the drive to make a good first impression, to demonstrate his value to Miriam and the senior writers. "We can work at Olympus, but not as journalists. I can work in Finance, and you could be..."

He trailed off. It was oddly impossible to think of Laodice outside of Bridal. She was such an excellent fit. If he became editor, he hoped that she'd stay. He didn't have any illusions about whether there'd be a place for him in *her* editorial team, but *he* was capable of logically assessing the value of an asset.

"I'll work in Wardrobe," Laodice decided. "I think I know enough about fashion to fake that, and there are plenty of girls from rich families in that department. I should fit in with the other Halcyon attendees."

"Penny Laconia hires nepo babies?" Telfer said. He'd thought better of the Head of Wardrobe.

"Penny Laconia recognizes the utility of accepting people who know people and are used to navigating complex social environments, while also having first-hand experience with luxe brands and trends," Laodice corrected. "Most of them are lovely people, and the ones that can't hack the pace or take instructions leave. The rest, she teaches. Do you know Diana? She used to be in Wardrobe, and now she's Hera's junior assistant."

Telfer had a vague memory of a pretty blonde behind a glass desk on the top floor. "Yes?"

"Her parents are huge in tech and her trust fund is massive. Her Olympus salary is basically pocket money. She doesn't need to work at all."

"So why does she?"

"Because she loves it." Laodice's voice was warm. Evidently, this Diana was a friend. "I won't say that everyone at Olympus is there on merit, but Diana earned her place years ago. I'll be Diana. Well, Elle. But Diana."

"All right. We met at work, we dated, and then we decided to get married."

"What's our proposal story?"

"I suppose I asked you over dinner. Unless you want to buck the trend of a male partner asking?"

"Over dinner?" Laodice said. "Fine. Okay."

"Is there something wrong with that?"

"Nope. Like you said, probably better to stick close to reality. That sounds like a realistic way for you to propose."

Telfer had the impression he'd just been insulted. "Did you want one of those big surprise proposals, then?"

"I can't believe you work in Bridal," Laodice muttered. Before he could respond she sighed. "No, that's not fair. You're good at your job."

"Thank you?"

"But yeah, Telfer, when I get engaged, I want a special proposal, whether it's me proposing or the guy. A party with all our friends, or a moonlit walk that turns into a grove lit up by lanterns, or while he's accepting his second Academy award."

"The last one's pretty specific."

"In that scenario, my future husband is Juan Lopez. He already has one Oscar."

"Ah," Telfer said. "I thought—you and Thalia were talking about that baseball game proposal last month."

"The one where the guy asked the girl in front of thirty thousand people and she said no?"

"Yeah. You said it wasn't fair for him to put that pressure on her. I agreed."

"Not out loud, you didn't. Were you eavesdropping?"

"It's a relatively small space, and you're loud."

"Hey!"

"That wasn't an insult. It was a statement of fact."

"Hm," Laodice said, and sped up to pass a delivery truck. It was full night now, and a huge orange moon was rising to the east, turning the ocean into glittering light. The hills of the Hippocampus were visible ahead, gentle folds around the bay. "All right, yes, I didn't like that one, and not because it had an unhappy ending. She was obviously taken completely off guard, with all those strangers staring at her. I feel that you only do a proposal like that if you've already agreed with your partner that you want to get married *and* you'd checked that a public proposal would be fun."

"So... Perhaps that was a discussion we might have had over dinner?"

"All right, fine. You brought up the topic, I agreed that I'd like to get married and *then,* a few weeks later you whisked me away to a log cabin and proposed formally."

"Great." He eyed her unadorned hands, sure on the steering wheel. "Didn't I get you a ring?"

"Shit! I had a ring ready, but I left it at home. Fucking Eli."

"It's fine."

"It's not fine! People are going to notice if I don't have a ring."

"It's my grandmother's ring, and we're having it resized," Telfer offered. "It's an emerald marquise with a prong setting, and some diamond accent stones. I'll send you a photo you can show people."

Laodice paused. "This is an actual ring you have pictures of?"

"Sure. I upload photos of all my valuables to the cloud, for insurance purposes." Nene Filiz would have approved of Laodice, he thought. His grandmother had been a spitfire, in her day.

"Oh. Yes. Okay." She was silent for a moment. "I don't know if this is going to work, Telfer. Couples have a shared history, shared stories and in-jokes. They know each other."

"The other couples will be far more interested in themselves than us. Besides, we know each other."

"Really. What're my favorite flowers?"

"Orchids," Telfer said readily.

"Huh," Laodice said. "Lucky guess."

***

Telfer used his phone to get the last directions to Halcyon, which, it turned out, wasn't in the Hippocampus proper. The retreat was nearly twenty minutes out of the main center, tucked away near the top of a hill, with an undulating, steep driveway. Laodice's car managed the turns easily, and he watched her shift in and out of gear with ease, mesmerized by the smooth motion of her hand.

"Nice driving, Elle," he said, trying the name out.

She smirked. "Thank you, Telford."

The car headlights showed glimpses of woodlands. A sign announced that they were on private property, but it was another few minutes before they were through the forested area and the building came into view.

Neither the brochure nor Brandon's gleeful description of the place had properly prepared Telfer for the sight. Laodice was laughing even before she took them through the open, elaborate gates. Above them, Halcyon loomed, built from buttery yellow stone. It was a confection of a fairy-tale castle, with a full complement of turrets, crenellations, and flags fluttering from the central tower, all of it lit up from within and without so that the entire place was a beacon. In that light, he caught a glimpse of formal gardens, with neat hedges and some manicured trees, a complete contrast to the unstifled woodland they'd just driven through. A marble fountain burbled on a smooth green circle of lawn, set in

34

the middle of a cobblestoned courtyard, with its own lights glimmering through the water.

It was, Telfer supposed, very romantic.

"I'm surprised there isn't a moat," he muttered, in an attempt to cover his own stunned reaction. Brandon had been smug about the real estate coup that had snagged him this place from the previous owners, and Telfer could understand why.

They parked in the courtyard. Telfer went to retrieve both of their suitcases from the trunk, which he figured was appropriately gallant. Laodice's case had vintage looking tan straps, but was far too pristine to be anything but new. It was also bright yellow. He looked at his slim black Samsonite and didn't comment on the contrast.

"Sunshiny," he said.

"A gift from my sisters," Laodice said, locking the trunk. "There's a hatbox that goes with it, but I didn't want to be gauche."

"Your sisters, right," Telfer said. "We should know a bit about each other's families. I've met Xena and Cassie. Let's pretend they think I'm fine. And you have a younger brother also, don't you?"

"Iulus. And you..." Laodice paused, and Telfer noted the moment where she realized she didn't know the first thing about his relations.

"I'm an only child," Telfer said. "My parents are no longer with us, but assume my uncle Burak adores you."

"Oh," Laodice said, and gave him a sympathetic look, presumably for his orphaned state.

Telfer pretended not to see it, and started towards the imposing oak doors. "Quick, your parents, what do they think of me?"

"They're reserving judgment."

"Come on."

"Well, you won points with my mother because of your romantic wood cabin proposal. But my dad doesn't like you nearly as much as Manny, Cassie's partner."

"Competing with the established son-in-law, got it." It was a still summer night. He could hear piano music drifting out of an open window above them. A few fireflies were hanging above the fountain.

And Laodice was tense as she walked beside him, her bared shoulders tight.

"Hey, Elle," he said, dropping his voice. "We've got this."

"Right," Laodice said. She stepped forward, and the door moved smoothly inward. A woman was standing in the doorway in an impeccable black suit and stiletto heels, her dark hair in a glossy bob. From her face, she might have been anywhere from her late 30s to early 50s. Behind her, he could see a hotel-style lobby, with a spiral staircase heading up to the right and doors heading back into the building. To the left was a bar, with a few couples gathered on couches.

"Hello!" the woman said, beaming at them. She was holding a tablet in one hand, but she didn't consult it. "I'm Sarah Tolna, your hostess, and you must be our last arrivals, Elle and Eli!"

"Oh, there must be some mix up," Laodice said. "I'm Elle, but there's no Eli."

Sarah's thin eyebrows rose. "Oh? What name do I put down for this handsome gentleman?"

"Hah, thank you," Telfer said. "I'm—"

"Telfer!" a hearty voice said, and Telfer turned with a sense of doom. He'd been in the place for thirty seconds, and his cover was *already* blown?

He didn't immediately recognize the guy making his way towards them from the bar, but something about the chestnut hair and stout build was familiar. The man was about his age, a little shorter, a lot broader...

"It is Telfer Terzi, right? Yeah, it's the Terz Man!"

"Carrick Balshaw," Telfer said, the name bursting into his brain. "Haven't seen you since—"

"Liam's wedding, right?"

"Right," Telfer said. Liam's wedding had been raucous. He had a vague memory of Carrick doing a keg stand in the latter part of the evening, right before he'd decided to leave. "Good to see you, man."

He felt more than saw Laodice relax behind him and start quietly going through the registration details with Sarah. Her cover was more important anyway, but he couldn't help being annoyed that Carrick had unmasked him immediately. What were the odds?

"How's it hanging?" he asked Carrick.

"Good, good!"

Sarah was handing Laodice two ornate iron keys, tied together with a red ribbon, and going over the benefits of their uniquely-decorated suite. No electronic keycards for Halcyon, apparently.

"Do you still work for, um, that magazine place?" Carrick continued.

"Yes, Olympus Inc. I'm in the Finance department."

"No, we'll unpack our own cases," Laodice was telling Sarah.

"Olympus, right!" Carrick said. "Yeah, you liking it?

Formalities completed, Sarah looked as if she were prepared to melt away and let them catch up, but she paused as the famous name caught her attention. Telfer groped for a way to distance himself.

"I'm actually looking for new opportunities at the moment," he said gruffly.

Which was true, although he was looking for new opportunities *at Olympus*. Laodice had come up to stand beside him. Without warning, she slipped her hand around his elbow. Telfer fought the urge to startle at the touch, and thought he'd probably succeeded. Wait, was he *bad* at this?

Carrick's eyes brightened. "Oh, really? Maybe this is my chance to be your guardian angel. Lots of moves afoot at Argive Holdings. You remember Dammond Argive? He graduated before us but he hung out sometimes."

"Yes," Telfer said briefly. For some reason, Laodice's hand had tightened at the name.

Carrick grinned. "I know, I know, easy break when you can go into the family business, right? But his grandfather's getting older, and Dammond's working on some big plans when it's his time to take over."

Telfer would have placed bets against Dammond Argive being able to organize a high school reunion, much less a multi-billion-dollar company. He supposed it was possible that the man had grown in the half-decade since Telfer had last seen him.

It was also possible that lightning would strike out of the clear sky and electrocute all of them, but it wasn't likely.

"I know for a fact he's seeking out men who can chase opportunities," Carrick was saying, obviously including himself in that group. "I can put in a good word." He smiled at Laodice. "Gotta give this lovely lady the honeymoon she deserves, right?"

"You're too kind," Laodice said, her voice smooth and a little smoky, as if she actually appreciated Carrick's clumsy attempt at flirtation. "I'm

Elle, by the way, since this one doesn't have the manners to introduce me."

"Maybe I don't want to share you yet," Telfer said, and Laodice gave him a mocking look, even as Carrick laughed loudly.

"Who could blame him?" he said, and nodded towards the lounging area where other couples were gathered. "I'm Carrick, and my fiancée Britt is over there. The redhead."

Carrick had always had a weakness for redheads. This Britt wasn't the slender, bouncy cheerleader type Carrick had gone for in college, however, but a medium-build woman in grey slacks and a white button up shirt. Her hair was in a loose bob, and she was listening calmly to the little brunette who was talking animatedly at her.

"She's lovely," Laodice said, and Telfer realized he'd been silent too long. But Laodice's obvious sincerity covered the gap. "I'm looking forward to meeting her. And everyone else, of course, since we can't all be lucky enough to know each other."

"Yeah, come join us!" Carrick said.

"We should—" Telfer said, but when he looked around for their bags they'd been spirited away.

Laodice tugged at his arm. "Come on, honey. Let's be social."

Telfer hoped that the clenching in his jaw wasn't too obvious. "Whatever you say, sweetheart."

***

Laodice had a naturally good memory for names and faces, and five years of wedding reporting had honed it to a fine edge. In addition to Britt and Carrick, there were four other couples on the retreat, making twelve guests in total. All but two of them were gathered in the lounge area, enjoying the drinks mixed by the attentive bartender.

Laodice had actually met two of the attendees before. Hazel Verney had been a bridesmaid at the Forrester wedding eighteen months ago, and Xavier Westlake's brother had married Simon Blair-Aiken about a year before that.

Fortunately, neither of them had looked alarmed when she introduced herself as Elle, and she was pretty sure they wouldn't have any inconvenient recollections. For most society weddings, she was merely an expected perk, like a designer gown or an elaborate cake. The guests would perhaps notice she was there, maybe give her a quote or two, and then immediately forget she existed.

Hazel's fiancé Jesse Heller "worked in Wall Street." Hazel had graduated from Midaeion in spring and was "exploring her options." Xavier was working at his father's law firm, and his fiancée, Yvette Long, was a junior partner at the same place. The "we met at work" story she and Telfer had hastily put together was obviously going to pass muster.

The other couple in the lounge were two men, Patrick Orwin and Samuel Donnelly. Patrick looked like a skinny-but-stylish IT nerd in white-framed glasses and a slim-fit cream polo shirt that showed off his dark skin to perfection. He turned out to be a landscape designer. It was big, burly, blond Samuel who was the software engineer. Telfer clearly recognized him, and after a few minutes of eavesdropping on their conversation, Laodice realized that Samuel wasn't merely an IT nerd. Well, he *was*, but he was also the inventor and owner of Liaison, one of the biggest dating apps of the last decade, and therefore easily a millionaire.

From what she could tell, with the exceptions of Patrick and Telfer, the attendees were all white, and in a fairly tight age range between mid-twenties to late-thirties. No retirees or later in life matches here, and she was willing to bet this was everyone's first marriage. People planning their second or third weddings, in her experience, tended to be less interested in other people's input on what they should be doing. She could do some sneaky search engine moves later, but for now she kept them talking, picking up background as they chatted.

Carrick, who kept interjecting comments into the conversation between Telfer and Samuel, had the popped collar and thinning hair of a former frat bro still caught up in his glory days. He worked for Argive Holdings, which Laodice would try not to hold against him. Laodice liked Britt, his fiancée—she was the oldest woman there by a good decade, definitely older than Carrick, and had an observant, amused quality that reminded Laodice of her sister Cassie.

"And what do you do?" she asked Britt. The couples had split into groups along gender lines, which Laodice hoped wasn't going to be a marker for the rest of their stay. She needed to talk to the men too.

"Oh, this and that," Britt said. "Did you say you were with Olympus Inc? The magazine publishing house?"

"Yeah, I work in the Wardrobe department?" Laodice said, trying to imitate Diana's occasional lapses into uptalk. "It's pretty cool, I guess?"

"It must be interesting to work for Hera Rheczack. I keep seeing profiles of her in various media."

"She's awesome. But I don't see her much, you know? I mostly help out the Head of Wardrobe with styling shoots and pulling pieces."

"That sounds, like, so amazing," Hazel said. Her cheeks were flushed, and Laodice wondered how much champagne she'd had. It was hard to tell; Kyle the bartender kept topping up their glasses. Laodice ran a self-diagnostic, and decided she'd better switch to water herself.

"I love your dress, Elle," Yvette put in. "Alaïa?"

Laodice smoothed the wrinkles in the raspberry pink poplin. She'd meant to change into one of her stealth wealth outfits, not rush into meeting the others in her work clothes. Still, it *was* a nice dress, made-to-measure by her mother, and the asymmetrical folds were kind of an Alaïa reference. Maybe she could get away with claiming it. Did Alaïa do plus sizes? Then she looked at Yvette's face. No. That was a test.

"Actually, it's a Penny Laconia original," she said enthusiastically. "The Head of Wardrobe? She's *so* cool. She makes something for every-one at the end of their first year with Wardrobe." This was actually true, although they tended to be fairly simple pieces. Diana had a gorgeous striped wrap skirt she still rotated through her outfit selections, and Xan-the, who was now editor of *Luxe*, had a black satin shrug on permanent display in her office.

Laodice watched Yvette assess the details on the dress and the close fit on Laodice's abundant bust, and then run a quick calculation on how much time a very busy, very important woman must have thought worth spending on a gift for Laodice.

Yvette's smile got several watts shinier, and she leaned in, adjusting her body language to match Laodice's. "It's *so* gorgeous. I wish I could wear that color."

"Is it hard to work in Wardrobe?" Hazel asked.

"Gosh, not nearly as hard as being a lawyer. What line of law are you in, Yvette?"

Yvette looked self-deprecating. "Properties and trusts, mostly."

Hazel hiccupped. "So not, like, criminals?"

"No, criminal law's a different field." Yvette took a healthy swig from her own glass, and held it out for a top-up as Kyle circled with another bottle and an inquiring expression. Laodice shook her head. Kyle winked at her, then set down another whiskey for Britt.

"I'd be scared, if I had to go into jails and talk to criminals," Hazel said.

Yvette considered her. "I don't have to do that."

Hazel looked mournful. "Jesse said he wanted to go to law school, but then he changed his mind."

"Why don't we get you a glass of water?" Yvette said, but Sarah Tolna bustled over to them, her tablet in hand, and stood in front of the bar. Even as she beamed at them, her forehead didn't move. Perhaps she patronized the same dermatologist as Miriam.

"Hello!" she said. "Hello, and welcome to all of you once again. We're waiting for the other couple to come down, and then we can officially get started!"

"Who're the other couple?" Laodice whispered to Britt, who shrugged.

Sarah touched her ear and murmured something to herself, and Laodice took note. Of the staff, she'd only seen Kyle and Sarah so far, but there was at least one other person running herd on the guests, and they were communicating via discreet earbud.

A young dark-haired woman in the same black skirt suit as Sarah, but wearing it with less aplomb, came out of the door behind the bar, holding a red box. At least three staff. Plus housekeeping and kitchens, presumably. She couldn't imagine Sarah sweating over a stove.

"Ah, here are Alma and Erik now," Sarah said, and something in her face made Laodice's spine tingle. She shifted, plastering a friendly smile in place, and felt it freeze on her face as the two latecomers came down the stairs.

Alma was a woman in her late twenties with reddish brown hair piled on top of her head. She was wearing a simple white slip dress and gold sneakers. Laodice noticed that with a tiny part of her mind, because the rest of her was gaping at the most beautiful man she'd ever seen.

Erik wasn't particularly tall or muscular—he was about the same height as his fiancée, in fact—but he moved with a sensual promise that made Laodice's mouth go dry. His finely molded jaw was lightly sprinkled with blond stubble, the same shade as his mop of sun-lightened curls. He was looking at them all with eyes the color of the ocean on a bright summer's day, his pink mouth quirking.

That *mouth*.

At that moment, Laodice couldn't think of anything but what those lips would feel like on hers.

Then her brain kicked back online and her instincts whirred into action. She'd always been observant, good at blending in, but standing apart. Her reaction didn't matter as much as observing the others.

Britt was smiling, but her hand had tightened around her glass, and Hazel's mouth had actually fallen open. She couldn't see Yvette's face, but she'd gone still. Of the men, Patrick and Samuel were staring, and Jesse was frowning at Hazel. Carrick looked at Erik, and then at Britt. Something moved in his eyes that Laodice couldn't quite catch. Telfer...was looking at her.

Right. He was also a journalist. He shifted his chin minutely to the side, and Laodice followed his eyes to Sarah.

Who was looking directly at the beautiful man walking towards them. Her smile looked sharp. Predatory.

Laodice stored all of it away to think about later. "Hello," she said, and stood up to make room for the new couple. "I'm Elle."

The tension broke in the flurry of introductions that followed, and then Sarah took over again, ordering more drinks and moving everyone around until they were all sitting with their partners, in a semi-circle around Sarah with her back to the bar. Laodice and Telfer had been placed by Alma and Erik, who were holding hands. She slipped her hand into Telfer's elbow and gave him a doting look.

He looked back at her, somber-eyed, which was irritating. Couldn't he even try?

"How's the cheek?" he asked, and Laodice's hand flew up.

"Ow," she said, as her fingers made contact with the wound, and then: "Honestly, until you reminded me, I forgot about it."

"I was going to ask you about that," Alma said. Her face was ordinary, without much definition or symmetry. Granted, anyone would look plain next to Erik's perfection. Her voice was beautiful though—a low and smoky contralto, so that even the simple phrase sounded like seduction. "I'm a nurse. Would you like me to take a look at it?"

"That would be great, if you wouldn't mind," Laodice said.

"Ahem," Sarah said, not particularly loudly, but she cut through the chatter that had risen again.

If she didn't want them to talk, she shouldn't have given them so much booze, Laodice thought indignantly. The thought was fuzzy around the edges, and she realized that she'd failed to stop Kyle from filling her glass again. Hazel was leaning against Jesse's arm, squinting to focus.

"Welcome to our happy couples!" Sarah said. "I'm so pleased to welcome you all to the inaugural Halcyon Retreat for Soon-To-Be-Weds!" She was definitely pronouncing the capital letters, laying emphasis on each word. "We'll start the program tomorrow," she went on. "But before you go upstairs for a good night's sleep—or other activities—"

"Woo!" Hazel cheered. Jesse shushed her.

"—I wanted to ensure that you all had the time and mental capacity to focus on the program, and on each other. Danielle, the box, please."

The younger woman handed her the red box, smiling anxiously, and Sarah set it on the low table in the middle of the group, ceremoniously flicking open the catches. Inside was a padded recess, with twelve narrow slots.

Sarah spread her hands. "Ladies and gentlemen, I will give you five minutes to set your out-of-office email responses. And then you must surrender your phones."

Telfer's arm went rigid under Laodice's hand. He evidently hadn't read the fine print. Yvette had, but wasn't happy about it, muttering something to Xavier when he took their phones forward. Most of the others gave them up with good grace, though Hazel begged permission to take one last selfie with her future hubby. Jesse smiled for the camera and then glared at his oblivious fiancée, who slid her phone into the box with glee.

Laodice added her own, thinking smugly of the burner phone nestled between the bras in her suitcase. Telfer handed his phone in with grim resignation. Alma gave her phone to Erik, and he moved forward, then hesitated.

"I have a laptop," he said, his voice soft.

Sarah laid a comforting hand on his shoulder, smiling kindly. "That's all right. There's no Wi-Fi available to guests, so you won't be able to get online with it. That's where most of the distractions are."

Erik looked over his shoulder at Alma. "No, I mean…can I give you my laptop, too? So I won't be distracted at all?"

"Oh, honey," Alma said, smiling tremulously.

"Of course," Sarah said, sweet as sugar. "I'll come up and get that later, shall I?" She closed the lid of the box with just as much ceremony, and handed it to Danielle. "Now, you're all welcome to stay down here and socialize as much as you like, but breakfast is at 6:30 sharp tomorrow." She wagged her finger at them, mock admonishing. "So don't stay up all night!" She sashayed through the door behind the bar, and Laodice hoped Sarah wasn't going to act like this all week. Being patronized was going to get old fast.

Telfer bent to speak into her ear. "I'll head upstairs now," he said, and Laodice blinked as his warm breath hit something tingly.

She turned to beam adoringly into his eyes. "I'm going to keep getting background," she murmured. "I won't be too long."

They were nose to nose. Laodice saw Telfer's eyes drop to her mouth. For a moment, she thought he was going to kiss her. Crap, they should have worked out some acceptable PDA rules.

He kissed her forehead instead, a warm brush of lips against skin, and then got to his feet. "Night, folks."

Laodice held out the keys. "We're in the Burlesque Fantasy suite," she said sweetly, and watched his eyes flicker as he took them from her hand. Yes, she'd thought he'd missed that part of Sarah's introductory spiel.

Hazel grabbed at Laodice's hand. "Noooo, stay!"

"I'm staying," Laodice assured her. Hazel looked perplexed, which might mean she was one of those "me and my partner do everything together" people. Or it might mean that Hazel was drunk, and everything was confusing her right now.

"So," Laodice said, sitting back in the seat, which had a little more room now that Telfer wasn't pressed against her side. "Xavier, tell me more about yourself. Where did you go to school?"

Chapter Four

Telfer put more thought than he needed into navigating the spiral staircase to the second floor, the better to forget the moment where he'd nearly kissed Laodice's parted lips. It had been a momentary impulse, brought on by the cover story and their proximity, but they should certainly speak about what gestures would be appropriate first. As it was, he could still feel her skin against his own lips, tingling from that brief contact with her brow.

The Burlesque Fantasy suite was at the end of the long second-floor hallway where the guests were housed. He passed a series of discreet brass plaques on doors—Nymph's Grotto, Evening Dream, Sleep Among The Stars—until he found their room and put the brass key in the lock.

His first impression was *red* with a touch of gold. His shoes sank noiselessly into the thick crimson carpet, and the walls were covered in a red and gold damask print. Fringed velvet drapes of deep scarlet descended from brass curtain rods. The dressing table was a faux-antique, with a gold-framed mirror outlined with lights; presumably a gesture towards a burlesque show backstage. The bed was covered in a silky red coverlet and an excessive number of feathery cushions, and was actually mounted on a little stage of its own. Here, it seemed to proclaim, with a wink and a grin, was where the *real* show was set.

Luckily, the bed was also enormous. He and Laodice would be able to keep to their own sides without disturbing the other.

After a moment's thought, he grabbed his laptop, kicked off his shoes and sat on the right side of the bed, tacitly claiming it. A gentleman would probably wait to ask Laodice which side she preferred, but she wasn't here and he wasn't a gentleman.

Fortunately, he made a practice of downloading work to his laptop, so he didn't need an internet connection yet. Half an hour later, he'd re-written three vendor press releases into actual stories, and was deep into the fourth when Laodice opened the door.

She stood in the middle of the doorway, and took in the room, her mouth slightly open and her eyes bright. "Wow," she said, and laughed. "This is a lot. I love it."

Telfer, with some effort, remembered he was annoyed with her. "You knew about the phone thing, I assume."

Her grin widened, and she pulled the door shut. "Didn't you read the brochure?"

He'd skimmed it, several months ago. "How do you propose to work without internet access?"

For answer, Laodice hoisted her suitcase onto the bed and threw it open, rummaging around the contents. Telfer caught a glimpse of hot pink ruffles and something silky and black. She plucked a phone from the pile of dainty things and brandished it at him. "Mobile data hotspot, at your service. Well, at *my* service." She shook her head. "I'm glad Sarah told me someone would unpack our bags for us. Gave me a chance to tell her not to."

Telfer grimaced. "Are you going to let me use it too?" He'd told Miriam he'd be working remotely this week. Without a hotspot, that would be impossible.

"Maybe. If you're nice to me." She looked pointedly at his laptop. "Besides, I thought you were on leave."

Telfer grunted. "Loose ends. Future project planning." Many deadlines for Wednesday. He could just tell Laodice that he planned to work remotely. He'd lied to make sure she'd bring him along, but she could hardly dump him now. On the other hand, he didn't want to let her know about a vulnerability. She already knew where most of his soft spots were.

"Not going to give up your laptop, like Erik?" She sat down on the bed and bounced experimentally. The dress ruffles fluttered over her breasts. "Good mattress."

"I should hope so, considering what everyone else is paying for this experience." Telfer considered her for a moment. She wasn't slurring her words, but her motions were more exuberant than usual. "Are you drunk?"

"Just fuzzy," she said. "Kyle kept refilling."

"I noticed."

"Yvette and I got some water into Hazel, but I think she's going to have a rough morning."

"Which one was Hazel?"

"The little brunette. Jesse's fiancée."

"So the tall brunette who tried to insult your dress is Yvette?"

Laodice yawned. "You caught that, huh?"

"I thought you handled it well. She certainly wants to be your friend now."

"Speaking of friends. That Carrick guy. Is he likely to be a problem?"

"I doubt it."

"Frat brother?"

"I wasn't in a fraternity." Telfer tapped out another line on the story—ideal baths for your wedding night, which reminded him he hadn't looked in the bathroom yet—and looked up when he realized that Laodice hadn't responded. She was staring at him. "What?"

"I don't know. I always assumed you were a frat guy."

"Well, I wasn't. Carrick and I met in an ECON 101 study group, who sometimes hung out socially. We were friendly, not close friends."

"Good thing he spotted you before you gave the wrong name. Still, what were the odds of someone you know being here?"

"You like statistics. What's the likelihood of being struck by lightning?"

"About 1 in 15000, over a lifetime," Laodice said.

Telfer blinked. "Really? I would have thought it would be much less likely than that."

"That's the average. Your personal odds change depending on where you live, how risk-averse you are, and so on." She grinned at him. "It's your bad luck you're so memorable. I've had actual conversations with Xavier and Hazel before, and there wasn't a flicker of recognition."

"You're memorable," Telfer said, without thinking.

Laodice batted her eyelashes at him. "Aw, Telfer, I didn't know you cared."

Telfer shifted irritably. "That's another statement of fact, not a compliment."

"So, factually, I am both loud and memorable." She thought about it for a second. "I'll take it. Passcode is 6511." She tossed him the phone and he caught it one-handed. "See what you get when you're nice to me?"

"I'll keep it in mind," Telfer said. His mouth was unaccountably dry.

There was a light tap on the door, and he slid the cellphone under a pillow. Laodice gave him a thumbs up, and then opened the door.

"Oh, hi, Alma. No, it's fine, come on in."

"I thought I could take a look at your cheek," Alma said. She was holding a small first-aid kit in one hand. She looked around the room. "Wow, they weren't kidding on the burlesque one, huh?"

"Yep! What's yours?"

"Evening Dream," Alma said. "Dark blue silk and gold stars on the ceiling. Sarah said we could have our pick, since we were first. Erik loves the night sky."

"Telfer loves burlesque," Laodice said, sliding him a sly look.

"I do," he said. "It's an intriguing art form, melding performance and desire."

Laodice blinked, but Alma smiled at him. "I think it's a lot of fun too." She sat Laodice down in an armchair. Telfer watched her for a moment, but she seemed steady and sober, and her manner was professional as she put on gloves, peeled back the butterfly strips and took a look at the wound.

"What did this?"

"Dropped a plate," Laodice said easily. "A shard must have hit me. I didn't even notice until Telfer took care of it."

"You did a good job," Alma told him, and carefully smeared a salve over the cut. "It's looking a little red, but this should take care of that." She cut new butterfly strips and stuck them on, then sat back.

"Thank you."

"You're welcome. Actually, I was glad of the excuse. Sarah came up to take Erik's laptop and 'check that everything was all right,' and I didn't really want to stick around and watch her flirt with my fiancé." She caught Telfer's look and shook her head. "It happens all the time. Sometimes I run interference for him, but he's trying to get better at handling it himself."

"That must be awkward," Laodice said, her voice warm.

Alma laughed. "I don't mind when people look. But if she keeps acting with intent, we're going to have a problem."

"Then I will continue to look," Laodice said cheerfully, and when Telfer coughed, she grinned at him. "What? I love you, but I have eyes."

Telfer felt his entire face go hot. "I, um," he said, grabbed his suitcase, and fled to the bathroom.

The bathroom was easily half the size of the bedroom, and possibly even more lavish. The dual sinks were carved out of smooth black stone, and the shower had a built-in bench and three showerheads, including a wide one that looked like a shelf, probably meant to imitate a waterfall. Red and black towels, check, huge mirror outlined with lights, check, and a commode that was almost disappointingly normal, although it was also red.

And then there was the spa tub, filled, hot and waiting for them. The rim was outlined in pink neon lights, flashing in a gentle rhythm, and an array of scents and lotions were lined up on a black tray table.

It was also the shape of a heart.

There were some oddly shaped handles in various places, and Telfer wondered why, and then processed that if Laodice was half-submerged *there* and he was bracing himself *there*, he'd be able to—

He clenched his fists, willing the blood rushing to his groin into his hands instead, but it was no use, he was imagining the water surging around and over her body, her skin glistening, a fierce look in her eyes as she urged him to join her—

Someone knocked twice on the bathroom door, and he literally jumped.

"She's gone," Laodice said. "Are you going to be long in there?"

"Ten minutes," Telfer said. His heart was thumping, but it was at least equal parts shock and lust now. He'd been right on the verge of indulging himself, and that was not an appropriate reaction to a woman who was his coworker, beside whom he was going to sleep that night. For seven nights.

She wasn't his to touch, not even in his imagination.

He took a quick shower, brushed his teeth, and contemplated his nightwear options. He saved his clothing budget for the clothes others saw. The pajama pants and old college shirt he'd packed had been washed so many times that they were butter soft and spectacularly comfortable, but they were also shabby and threadbare. The ribbed neck of the shirt had been pulled out of alignment and parts of it were almost transparent; the loose-fitting pants hung low on his hips.

Well, it was the best he could do. It wasn't as if he needed or wanted to impress Laodice anyway.

She was sitting on her side of the bed, but jumped to her feet when he came out. He saw her take in what he was wearing and pause, but then she went on: "Hey, sorry about saying I love you. I didn't mean to make you uncomfortable."

She was obviously sincere, which only increased his embarrassment. They were pretending to be engaged; of course he should have anticipated love talk.

"Don't worry about it," he said brusquely.

"We should set up some ground rules," she suggested. "But after I pee, because I'm dying."

"Unnecessary information," he said, but it was to the bathroom door, closing behind her. He heard her yelp, and then laugh.

"This bath!" she called.

"I know," he called back, and retrieved the burner phone. Setting up the mobile hot spot took no time. He added a description of their bath to the list under a heading of "The Weird and Wonderful," and left a square bracket note reminding himself to add mentions of various advertiser products. Then he uploaded everything to the Olympus servers, feeling better that the drafts were no longer just on his workstation.

After a moment, he pulled up his personal cloud drive, and went searching for a picture of their engagement ring.

Laodice came out in what looked like yoga pants and a loose T-shirt, the hotel robe wrapped securely around her. In keeping with the theme, it was deep red velvet with a wide collar of black feathers. It didn't really fit her frame, straining over her abundant curves, but at least the feathers did some work to disguise what he suspected was a lot of motion under that shirt.

"So, ground rules," she said, and he swung the laptop around.

"This is your ring," he said. "In case it comes up."

Laodice sat on the end of the bed and looked at the picture. "That's gorgeous. Is it really your grandmother's ring?"

"Yes. Her mother made her take it from the old country when she emigrated in the 60s."

"Where's the old country?"

"Türkiye. Her son was my dad, and she gave him the ring to propose to my mom."

"That's so romantic," Laodice said, and then glanced ruefully at her broad hands. "Well, no one will disbelieve the resizing story. Hey, uh, about your parents..."

"We should discuss those ground rules," Telfer said.

"Right. How much touching and cutesy stuff is okay? We need to make it look real, but I don't want to cross any boundaries." She considered him, her face unusually serious. "Plus, it doesn't look that realistic when you literally run away from me."

"What did you tell Alma?"

"That you're shy. So act shy."

"Right," Telfer said. "I'll do my best. I was taken aback because I didn't expect it. You can say that you love me again, now that I know it's on the table. I'll say it too. I think hand-holding, hugs, light touches—that sort of thing is all right. Was it okay that I kissed your forehead?"

"Yep."

"Okay, so let's say cheeks and so on are fair game."

"But not lips?"

Telfer's gaze dropped to her mouth. "I'd rather not."

To his relief, Laodice accepted that without further question. "Got it. I think all of that will be fine. Not every couple is super demonstrative in public."

Telfer nodded. "I find performative emotion off-putting."

"Of course you do," Laodice said, but without any real bite. "Okay. Anything else? I wouldn't mind an early night."

Telfer looked at her. "I don't recall much about the program. Are there any more unpleasant surprises, like the phones?"

"I'm not sure," Laodice said. "The program wasn't super explicit. We have group activities and couple activities. There's some stuff like cocktail mixing and dance lessons that I think they'll be bringing outside vendors in for."

"That's my part of the deal," Telfer said. "I want those contacts."

"There's also mindful meditation and soul connection therapy—new agey manifestation stuff. And some blocks on the draft I saw were TBC. I think we're basically just supposed to show up to everything, when we're told to." She yawned. "Breakfast is at 6:30. I guess we find out about the rest of the day then."

Telfer went to check the time on his phone, and realized he couldn't. "How are we supposed to wake up on time without alarms?"

"I didn't think of that," Laodice admitted, and scanned the room. "No alarm clock. I could set something on the burner, but maybe we should see what happens? I wonder if Halcyon didn't think of it either."

"A mystery," Telfer said. He wasn't sure if he liked it. He put his laptop away and gave Laodice back her phone, then slid between the sheets. *High* thread count, soft and smooth. He rolled onto his side and nestled his face into the most comfortable pillow he'd ever had, while Laodice completed her preparations for the night and turned out the lights.

He'd expected to have a period of awkward wakefulness, with the weight and warmth of her body beside his. But the mattress was perfect, and the darkness was complete, and he fell asleep so swiftly that he didn't notice the transition at all.

***

Laodice was in a long passage, and there was something at the end of it she really wanted, but the closer she got, the longer the passage became. Telfer was walking beside her in his scandalously thin pajamas, his face serious.

"Can't you go any faster?" he asked, and then the end of the passage glowed with soft yellow light and a melody of gentle chimes suffused the air, starting quiet and then becoming louder and louder.

"Is that the light at the end of the tunnel?" Laodice asked, curious, but unafraid. "Telfer, are we dying?"

"Good morning, lovebirds," Sarah's voice said sweetly, and Laodice groaned and rose out of the dream, groggily hugging her pillow. Sarah's voice wasn't any part of her idea of heaven. "It's 6 a.m. and it's time to rise and shine. Shake off that peaceful slumber and join us in the Main Gallery for breakfast."

Laodice cracked an eyelid open. Sarah wasn't in the room; only her voice, emanating from a hidden speaker somewhere. Laodice hadn't dreamed the lights, either. They were glowing around the room, increasing in intensity even as she squinted at them. Some kind of sunrise effect, probably designed to stimulate the transition from delta waves to theta waves, or some such crap.

Laodice had never claimed to be a morning person. She turned her face into the pillow, blocking out the light.

Telfer sat up. "Are you awake?"

"No," Laodice said, her voice muffled. Telfer had gone straight to sleep last night, almost before she'd turned out the lights. It was pretty cute, actually. She hadn't been so lucky; the dregs of champagne and adrenaline from the busy day had keep her exhausted, but awake. In the end she'd taken a sleeping pill and let that drag her under, but she was paying for it now.

"Come on," Telfer said, and when she didn't move or respond, he touched her shoulder tentatively. "I'll let you have first shot at the bathroom."

"Oh, fuck," Laodice said, and threw back the covers. "My *hair.*"

"I'm missing something," Telfer said, watching her race around the room with some bewilderment.

"I need to wash it and it takes *forever*," Laodice snarled. She reigned in her temper with some effort. It wasn't Telfer's fault she hadn't taken care of the matter last night. She should have set that alarm on the burner and warned him she was a demon hellbeast first thing in the morning. "Can you be fast with whatever you need to do?"

"Sure," he said, and went straight to the bathroom while she gathered her clothes and toiletries. A few minutes later, he emerged. "I showered last night, and I'll dress out here."

"*Thank* you," Laodice said, really meaning it, and dove for the shower.

There was no time to indulge herself with the more luxurious settings. She scrubbed down fast, wincing as she gingerly patted the cut on her cheek. Even moving as fast as she could, her hair demanded time. It was her best feature, long, shiny and healthy, with a natural bouncy wave she'd been styling since she was a teenager. At times like this, though, the temptation to imitate Cassie's sensible jaw-length bob was strong.

She'd have to skip the curlers. The retreat hairdryer was impressive, a top-of-the-line professional model with a powerful engine. Even so, she could feel the minutes slipping away as she worked the nozzle under her layers and finger-styled the waves.

"Can I get a time check?" she called through the door.

"Seven minutes to go."

Shit, and she was still naked. She scrambled into her underwear and bike shorts, and then shimmied into a light linen dress with bouncy off-the-shoulder bishop sleeves. Lipstick and mascara were all the make-up she had time for. A messy half-updo would work for the hair. She twisted and pinned big loops across the crown of her head, leaving the rest long and loose at the back. Some of the strands were still damp, but no longer dripping, and that would have to do. She plucked a few tendrils forward to frame her face, blew a kiss in the mirror, and left the bathroom.

Telfer was standing there with the burner in his hand, fully dressed in formal slacks and a white button up. At least he'd left the top buttons undone, and hadn't added a tie or jacket.

"You look nice," he said, which would have been fine, but he sounded surprised, which wasn't.

Laodice shot him a dark look and went looking for her sandals. They were top quality with an impressive name, sure to pass Yvette's label check. The semi-annual Wardrobe clear-outs didn't have many clothes in her size, so she always made a beeline for the accessories.

"I meant, with the time you had," Telfer said, and then he coughed. "I thought we should take the phone with us. In case Housekeeping finds it."

"You think?" Laodice said, sounding too sarcastic even to herself. She buckled her sandals and stood. "Sorry. I mean, good idea. I'm not great in the mornings. Can you hang onto the phone? There are no pockets in this dress."

She went for the door, and Telfer caught her wrist.

It was a light grip, his long fingers careful on her skin, and he released her the second she stopped.

"We should maybe be a few minutes late," he suggested. "If we keep perfect time, Sarah might wonder how."

"Right." Laodice shifted her weight. "So, uh, tell me about your hobbies. You know about me and the car. I also knit sometimes, and I collect ceramics."

"I play golf occasionally."

Of course he did. "Anything else?"

"I listen to podcasts."

Laodice gave herself a point for not rolling her eyes. Finance bros and their finance podcasts. Eli had been forever enthusing about the latest tip to maximize productivity and minimize risk. "Okay, so I'll make a girlfriendly complaint that sometimes you listen to your earbuds more than me."

"I wouldn't do that," Telfer said, sounding insulted.

"*Cover story*, Telfer," Laodice said, and decided they were now fashionably late enough. She opened the hallway door, just as Sarah's voice came through the speakers, informing the guests that now was the time to head down for breakfast.

Alma and Erik were coming out of the door across the hall, both dressed in jeans and T-shirts, and looking a little rumpled. Erik looked good rumpled. Laodice suspected that Erik would look good covered in mud and wearing an old potato sack.

"Good morning," Alma said, on a yawn she covered with one hand. The other was holding Erik's, because they were adorable.

Laodice reached for Telfer's hand, and he grabbed it with no hesitation, long fingers twining with hers. Laodice had held a lot of hands.

Telfer, she was prepared to admit, was decent at it—dry skin, firm grip. Loose wrist, not holding her clamped to his side. Top fifteen percent of hand-holders, definitely.

Did Telfer have a lot of hand-holding practice? Presumably he didn't have a partner right now, or he wouldn't have offered to accompany Laodice at the last minute, even in pursuit of a really good story. She couldn't recall him ever mentioning a partner at all, although it was becoming clear to her how little she'd engaged in more than necessary conversation with the guy.

She could have recited the romantic history of most of her co-workers from memory, but Telfer's was a complete blank. Maybe he didn't mix his work and personal life. Maybe he was asexual, or aromantic, or some combination along that spectrum. Carrick hadn't seemed to be surprised that he was here, engaged to a woman, but people didn't necessarily disclose their complete selves to their college study buddies.

"Sorry," she said, realizing that Alma had asked her a question. "I didn't hear that. I was deep in my own head."

"Elle prefers later mornings," Telfer said. He actually sounded affectionate. Maybe he was a better actor than she'd thought.

"Me too," Erik mumbled.

"I asked how you got so much volume in your hair," Alma said. "Obviously yours is thicker than mine, but it's so *bouncy*."

"Oh!" Laodice said, and was partway through a step-by-step explanation of her routine when Xavier and Yvette stepped out of the last door to the left on their corridor. The door opposite remained firmly closed, but Laodice could hear muffled voices from within.

Yvette was impeccable in an ice-blue sheath dress that cut off at mid-thigh. The dress exposed her sculpted arms, long, toned legs, and a pair of tan heeled brogues that Laodice immediately coveted. Her hair was straight and shiny, her subtle makeup was flawless, and she was absolutely scanning the other women to see if they looked better than her.

Apparently satisfied with the answer she came up with, she smiled brightly at Laodice. "Great dress. Sumeria, right?"

"Right," Laodice said. Sumeria was one of Xena's sponsors. On camera, she typically wore their athleisure wear lines, but they'd thrown the dress in as well, and Xena had donated it to the 'Make Laodice look rich' campaign.

"I love how they have an expanded size range. So inclusive!"

"Yep," Laodice said. "Well, you two look great, especially for this early."

"Normally I'd have been at the office an hour ago," Xavier said, looking at her with mild contempt. He was wearing pretty much what Telfer was, except his unbuttoned-at-the-throat shirt was the same pale blue as Yvette's dress. Had they matched on purpose?

"So you actually got to sleep in?" Telfer said heartily. "Great start to a vacation."

"This isn't a *vacation*," Yvette said. "We're honing our ability to connect and communicate and developing our relationship skills to maximize nuptial bliss."

Holy shit. It was a direct quote from the brochure, and Yvette's face was absolutely sincere. Maybe Miriam—and Telfer—were right. If Halcyon could convince people like Yvette that they'd *maximize bliss* with this thing, they'd be raking in the cash from ultra-competitive alpha girls.

In the silence that had greeted Yvette's pronouncement, the raised voice from behind the closed door became much louder.

"—embarrassing me!" a male voice shouted. "No, you know what, you're just *embarrassing*. Look at you!"

A softer voice, inaudible, then the shouting again, cutting over it. "I don't give a rat's ass! Stop being such a stupid bitch, get your shit together, and get down there." The voice got louder on the last words, and Laodice jerked back as she realized what that meant.

Jesse jerked the door open, his face a snarling mask of fury. He saw the inadvertent audience and hesitated, then bared his teeth in a wide grin. His eyes didn't change—flat and black and angry—and the rictus smile made things worse. Laodice felt the hairs rise on her arms and neck.

"Hazel's not coming down yet," he said, striving for jovial and sounding flat instead. "She's not feeling well."

"I could go and see her," Alma offered quietly.

"No, no, she needs a few minutes to let the painkillers kick in," Jesse said, and closed the door behind him with exaggerated care.

Yvette was looking at him with such loathing that Laodice was surprised he didn't spontaneously combust.

Jesse led them down the stairs, determinedly talking about the weather and pretending that they hadn't all heard what they'd heard. Erik responded politely, but Telfer was still and silent beside her, and Xavier and Yvette had dropped behind, talking quietly to each other.

Asshole, Laodice thought, and resolved to check on Hazel later.

Chapter Five

Telfer was not impressed by breakfast.

They'd been guided to a long table in the gallery room, apparently called that because there were a number of indifferent landscapes hung on the walls. Carrick and Britt had been seated already; Samuel and Patrick were sitting down when the rest of them arrived. Sarah came in, tinkled a small silver bell, and breakfast began.

Telfer had envisioned gourmet eating. And to be fair, the food was tasty. It was the portion size he took issue with.

Kyle, wearing kitchen whites, had presented each guest with a small square of rye toast, two soft-boiled quail eggs, a salad of microgreens, and half an orange. Telfer had eaten all of it, and waited for the next course, which apparently didn't exist.

What did exist were champagne flutes full of mimosas. Laodice drank half of hers, and then shook her head at the refill proffered by Danielle, who didn't really look old enough to be serving booze in the first place.

Telfer made eye contact with her before she could back away.

"Could I get a coffee, please?" he asked.

"Um," the girl said, looking at Sarah, who came over.

"We're preparing for morning meditation," she said, smiling prettily. "A light breaking of the fast, and no caffeine intake is essential if you're to receive the full benefits."

Telfer was tempted to ask for coffee anyway—and some more toast—but Laodice was watching, and getting the same experience normal guests did was important for her story. He asked for water instead. Sarah looked unhappy, but she could hardly object to that.

"Water for me too, please," Laodice said, and Britt signaled for the same.

Yvette watched them from across the table, obviously trying to figure out whether the winning move was to stick to the program, or follow the lead of others.

"Are you going to eat that?" Laodice asked, gesturing at Yvette's untouched plate.

"I never eat breakfast," Yvette said, and took a sip of her mimosa.

"I'll have it, then," Laodice said cheerfully, and Xavier looked sad he hadn't laid claim to the food first. His breakfast had disappeared as fast as Telfer's.

Yvette watched Laodice cut into the toast. "How far away is your wedding, Elle?" she asked. "Aren't you worried about fitting into your dress?"

"We haven't set a date yet," Laodice said. "And it will be the dress's job to fit *me*."

Telfer felt that was definitely a point for Laodice. "We're not setting a place at the high table for diet culture," he said. It was a direct quote from one of Laodice's stories, but he figured she wouldn't mind him borrowing it.

"Well said," Britt murmured.

Laodice grinned at him. "Thank you, honey. Do you want one of these eggs?"

"Yes," Telfer said, and accepted his tiny egg with a real sense of accomplishment.

"Here's our sleepy girl," Sarah caroled, as Hazel slunk in, dressed in a pink sundress and perfectly made up.

She looked a lot better than Telfer had thought she would, but he took in the slump of her shoulders and the quick, cautious glance she threw at Jesse, and wondered how much of it was for show.

Jesse jumped to his feet and pulled out the chair beside him.

"Here, darling," he said, a bit louder than he needed to. "I hope you're feeling better."

Hazel looked surprised, and then touched, as Jesse began cutting up her toast and cooing at her.

Don't fall for it, Telfer thought, and met Laodice's serious eyes. Yeah, they both knew there was something bad happening there. Laodice had never made a secret of her dislike for him, but he couldn't imagine her ever belittling him the way Jesse had Hazel, and Jesse was supposed to be in love with Hazel. Jesse was supposed to love Hazel so much that he wanted to spend the rest of his life with her.

Telfer thought that wouldn't be a great thing for Hazel.

Hazel ate her meager breakfast and Laodice finished her second half of an orange, while Sarah took them through the day's schedule. They had meditation, then a flower arranging workshop which was supposed to make them more aware of the love language of flowers, and would probably serve as paid product placement for the florist. Then they'd have lunch and "recreational siesta time," which made Yvette smirk and

Patrick and Samuel raise their eyebrows at each other meaningfully. Telfer mentally marked this as the ideal time to work on his deadlines.

The evening was reserved for something ominously called "The Great Couples Challenge." Telfer felt a flicker of doubt, but Laodice didn't look worried. Well, if she thought they could handle it, they probably could.

Some minutes later, sitting on a yoga mat cross-legged facing Laodice, he was less confident. The room they were in was dimly lit, and he was holding Laodice's hands, while irregular chimes rang out. Several pink salt lamps were softly glowing along one wall. Sarah's voice, smooth and sure, flowed over them, intoning the most ridiculous nonsense Telfer had ever heard.

"Gaze upon your beloved's face," she crooned. "Witness the universal love of the universe made flesh in your beloved. You are attuned to the fundamental harmony of life. You are resonating on the frequency of all souls. Within you, between you, light is born."

Laodice bit her lip hard, and Telfer closed his eyes, willing himself not to groan audibly.

"Look into the eyes of your beloved, within whom loving truth is bound in manifested divinity."

Telfer looked into Laodice's amused brown eyes, and tried to take apart the sentence. Was Sarah speaking in metaphor, alluding to something he didn't recognize, or was it all gibberish?

"Feel the soul-touch of your beloved lift you beyond the earthly plane into eighth-dimensional light."

Laodice's hands shook in his and she mouthed, "What the fuck?"

Telfer barked a laugh, which he made a cough, which became a real cough. He sputtered to a halt and wiped his streaming eyes. Sarah was staring at him in patent disapproval. Patrick was trying to stifle his own laughter. Britt looked serene and Carrick looked sympathetic.

Yvette was sitting ramrod straight, her eyes trained on Xavier's, a dreamy look plastered on her face, obviously determined to get a gold star in Being Great at Couples Meditation.

"Excuse me," Hazel said, and scrambled to her feet. Sarah turned to her, annoyed, but Hazel was already running out of the room, one hand clamped over her mouth. Even beneath the perfect makeup, she looked green.

"Excuse us," Jesse said, and stalked out after her.

Yvette momentarily dropped her attempt to earn Meditation Valedictorian to glare at Jesse's back, and Xavier tugged at her hands. She turned back to him, her face softening, and Telfer caught the motion of Xavier's thumbs across her wrists, a subtle caress that dropped some tension from her shoulders.

Alma and Erik were gazing at each other, too entranced to have noticed anyone else. Sarah looked at them for a moment, and seemed to be trying to work out if she was pleased or not. Erik was sitting in a beam of light coming in from a high window, and it was doing impressive things to his curls and cheekbones. Telfer had never been the slightest bit interested in guys, but Erik's beauty was almost unearthly. He had to appreciate it on an aesthetic level, if nothing else.

"Let's start again," Sarah said, her voice tight with frustration.

Telfer gazed over Laodice's shoulder this time, so they couldn't set each other off again, and tried to tune Sarah out. This wasn't a great omen for the rest of the retreat.

***

It was becoming clear to Laodice that Yvette didn't know where to place "Elle."

Elle worked in the Wardrobe at Olympus Inc, which could be a low-level opening position she'd worked her ass off for, or a favor called in from a rich relative. Elle Evagora wasn't a name that had appeared in the society pages or the rich lists, but she was wearing hard-to-get It Girl pieces. Elle was a fat woman, which was unusual among the yachts-and-lacrosse squad, and she wasn't apologetic or self-deprecating about her size, which was almost unheard of.

It would be easy to dismiss Yvette as a social climber or a mean girl, but Laodice wasn't so sure. It seemed more as if she needed to put people in their correct places so she knew where she stood—preferably on top, but if not, at least somewhere within an established hierarchy. Laodice's mixed signals were frustrating that desire for certainty.

She wasn't surprised when Yvette slipped in beside her as they left the meditation room.

"Wasn't that refreshing?" Yvette said. "I feel really rejuvenated."

"Meditation's never really been my thing," Laodice said. "I love yoga, so I've ended up doing a lot of it, but there's a reason savasana's my least favorite pose. And the guided part was a little...unusual."

Sarah's bonkers monologue had been much weirder than unusual. Guided meditation was common, and Laodice had at least heard of manifestation and energy work, even if she was dubious about the supposed effects. But Sarah sounded as if she'd grabbed a bunch of phrases from a thousand desperate MLM newsletters and thrown them together, either not caring or not understanding that she didn't even make internal sense.

She caught Telfer's glance, and realized that he'd filed her yoga practice away, another tidbit to pull out about "Elle," beloved fiancée.

Yvette made a face in agreement, then rallied. "It was a little out there, maybe, but I really felt us deepening our bond, right, Xavier?"

"Sure," Xavier said, looking at her fondly. Then he blinked twice and moved quickly, pressing towards the window overlooking the back courtyard. "Holy crap, that's a Spider Veloce!"

"She's mine," Laodice said.

"Elle restored it herself," Telfer put in. His voice was warm and proud. She had to give him credit: he was getting better at acting the loving fiancé.

"No shit? Is it all original, or did you do some mods?"

Laodice beamed at him. "Mostly original. Seats are reupholstered. I replaced the belts, and installed Koni shocks."

"Mind if I take a look under the hood?"

"Of course, I'd love to show—"

"Hurry up, slowpokes," Sarah sang out, her voice high and sweet. She was eyeballing them from the entrance to the gallery room where they'd had breakfast. "It's time to workshop our wedding florals!"

Xavier gave the Spider a longing look. "Rain check," he told Laodice, and he and Yvette hurried over.

"Last ones in are rotten eggs!" Sarah said merrily, as Laodice and Telfer slipped into the room.

The long dining table had been replaced by three smaller tables facing the far end of the room. They were laden with vases, paper wraps, ribbons, and other tools of the floristry trade, while to the side were buckets holding an abundant display of fresh flowers. At the front of the room was a smiling dark-skinned woman with natural curls and a light green apron that declared her the proprietor of Faith's Flowers.

Whatever Laodice might have thought about Sarah's meditation skills, Faith was clearly the real deal. She gave the couples a brief spiel on the history of her business and the traditional and modern role of flowers in wedding celebrations, then set about showing them how to choose blooms for a harmonious display.

Laodice lost herself in all that beauty for a while, hovering dreamily over the flowers on offer before she made her selections. She did notice when Jesse and Hazel came in. Hazel looked healthier, and Samuel and Patrick made room for them at their table without comment. Laodice and Telfer were with Britt and Carrick, who was making another run at persuading Telfer to quit his job and join Argive Holdings.

Dammond Argive wasn't a name Laodice had any fond feelings about. She stabbed a perfect chrysanthemum stalk into a foam base with too much vigor, and blinked when everyone turned to her.

"What do you think, honey?" Telfer said. It was unfair that the way he said honey sounded good. "Do you think I should throw in the towel at Olympus?"

Laodice made her eyes big and wide. "If you think it's best, sweetheart."

"But then we wouldn't see each other every day," Telfer said, bending over her. "Think about how sad we'd be."

"You guys don't live together?" Carrick asked, and Laodice came back to reality with a thump. She'd been enjoying the baiting, but Britt was looking curious too. Most couples *did* cohabitate before marriage.

"There's no room for me," Telfer said. "The ceramics collection takes up so much space."

"Hey," Laodice said, with more bite than she intended. He was trying to build on what he knew about her, she reminded herself. He didn't know that one of her favorite pieces was currently scattered across her kitchen floor, because the guy she'd considered asking to move in had turned out to be an unreliable liar.

Telfer's eyes flashed at her tone, and he backed off a bit. "We're looking for places to move into together," he said, his voice cooler. He'd actually been playful, Laodice registered. They'd been teasing each other, like real couples did.

"Rent's hard in the city," Britt said sympathetically, and Laodice almost agreed with her before she remembered that she was supposed to be rich. Rent wasn't a problem for Elle Evagora.

"I'm super picky, that's all," she said gaily. "We want to have the *right* place, with lots of light and a view."

"Argive could definitely help you out there," Carrick told Telfer.

"Give me the hard sell later," Telfer said. "I'm making my lady a bouquet."

Laodice glanced at what he was doing, and then stared. He really was. He'd laid a deep pink orchid stem in the middle, flanking it with two paler pink blooms, and then two creamy pale orchids on the side, the edges of the petals tinged with a subtle blush. Even as she watched, he included some sprigs of lavender for a hit of purple, added some greenery, and expertly wrapped the whole bundle in a delicate square of cream parchment. She watched his long, brown fingers knotting a dark pink ribbon around the whole thing, both shocked and intrigued.

"Nice work!" Faith said, coming over to check. "Where'd you learn how to do that?"

"My parents were florists," Telfer said. It had the ring of truth, and there was a dark flush in his cheeks. He held the bouquet out to Laodice. "Here," he said, too brusquely to fit the cover story, but she was far too stunned by the gesture to find any fault.

"They're *beautiful*," she said, taking the bouquet in both hands and breathing deeply. Lavender and vanilla rose around her, rich and sweet. "I could walk down the aisle with these." She meant it, and Telfer could apparently tell. He gave her a long look she couldn't interpret, and abruptly turned away.

"That's what we're aiming at!" Faith said. "Although since everybody in the bridal party has far too much to do on the day, we do recommend you get the experts in to create the bouquets you've designed. Let me get you our card."

"Actually, I had a few questions about your business model," Telfer said, apparently reminded of his mission. Laodice let him schmooze with the vendor uninhibited by her presence, while she put together a bouquet of her own. That was their deal; he'd take the vendors, and she'd handle the inside story of the retreat itself.

Right. She was on the job. She scanned the room in time to catch Sarah getting right into Erik's personal space with the excuse of plucking a stray leaf from his hair. Alma, who was by the flowers, didn't seem to have noticed.

Laodice couldn't see Erik's face, but his back was stiff. Sarah was smiling up at him, all shiny teeth and bedroom eyes.

It wasn't normally hard to write positive stories about people doing their level best to make sure couples could have a fantastic day, but it was beyond creepy for Sarah to be flirting with one of her guests. It was also terrible business.

Hazel had noticed Sarah hitting on Erik too. And Jesse had noticed her noticing. "Hey," he said sharply. "Remember me, your fiancé? The one you're making whatever *that* is for?" He gestured at Hazel's unstructured bouquet with contempt.

Laodice longed for Hazel to snap back at him, but she lowered her eyes, flushing, and muttered something about baby's breath.

None of this was great material.

Telfer appeared to be having better luck. He and Faith were deep in conversation about seasonal bouquets versus greenhouse offerings, and Patrick had been drawn into the discussion as well.

"It's a lovely posy," Britt said quietly beside her, and Laodice smiled at the older woman.

"Thank you," she said, and looked at what she'd managed to put together. She'd stuck to simple, placing an orange zinnia as the center, surrounded by a few fern strands. It was a little lopsided, and she hadn't wrapped the florist's tape very well, so it wasn't nearly as nice as Telfer's offering, but something about the careful geometry of the ferns and the precise placement of the zinnia petals reminded her of Telfer. Orange wasn't a color she'd ever seen him in, but it would look great with his dark hair and light brown skin.

When she scanned the room again, Sarah had moved on from Erik to praise Yvette's bouquet work. Jesse was talking to Hazel quietly, his gestures tightly controlled.

Maybe Sarah was having an off-day. Maybe she'd realize the inappropriateness of her behavior, give herself a strong talking to, and act like a pro for the rest of the week. Then Laodice could write the cover story she needed, impress Miriam and Hera, secure the editor's role, and mandate some kind of pumpkin-themed October staff event, so that she could see if her Telfer-in-orange theory was correct.

He was walking towards her, looking deeply satisfied with himself.

"This is for you," she said, and handed him the bouquet.

Her stomach chose that moment to gurgle. She reached automatically for her phone to check the time, but of course it wasn't on her. Telfer's hand went for his pocket, then stilled. No, he couldn't pull the burner out here.

"Does anyone have the time?" she asked.

"1:26," Britt said, extending her wrist. Unlike the smart watches that had also been confiscated, this was old school practical. A black leather strap, an analog face, with a few extra dials Laodice didn't immediately recognize.

"No wonder I'm starving," Laodice said. They'd been up since 6 a.m., running on the world's tiniest breakfast. Yvette hadn't eaten at all, and Hazel had presumably emptied her stomach. "Sarah! What time is lunch?"

"Oh, soon," Sarah said vaguely, and caught sight of Britt's watch. The scowl flickered across her face so swiftly that Laodice wasn't even positive it had been there, but she clapped her hands together. "All right, happy couples! In a few minutes we'll finish up here, and then it's time to eat."

Xavier looked almost as enthusiastic about that as he had about Laodice's car.

***

Lunch, to Telfer's relief, was more abundant than breakfast. He casually chatted with the others to check their reactions to Faith's workshop—universally positive—and ate an excellent pad thai accompanied by sparkling water and lime juice. Erik and Alma had dal instead.

"Vegan?" Patrick asked, chasing down a shrimp. "I was vegan for a while."

"Nut allergy," Alma said, and looked up as Danielle wheeled in the dessert trolley. "Oh, wow. Please tell me you have cheesecake?"

"Lychee cheesecake," Danielle said triumphantly, and Telfer applied himself to a giant slice.

Laodice had been uncharacteristically quiet throughout the meal. After lunch, when everybody returned to their rooms for "siesta," she occupied herself taking notes on the day.

Her energy and sense of presence had dimmed. Telfer should have been relieved about that. It should have been much easier to get his work done.

Instead, he found himself increasingly distracted. The last time he looked up, she was still seated at the ornate dressing table that served as a desk, with her laptop open, but she was gazing out the window, unmoving.

Telfer closed his laptop. "Are you okay?" he said gruffly.

Laodice turned to look at him and blinked slowly. "Are *you*?"

"Of course," Telfer said.

"You do realize that's the first time you've ever asked me that?"

"You're usually okay," Telfer said. He wasn't sure why this was a problem.

Laodice tilted her head. "We've worked together for *four years*, Telfer. There have definitely been days when I wasn't okay. You've never noticed before."

He'd *noticed*. He'd just never wanted to know the answer, in case he had to do anything about it. Besides, Laodice collected people around her like flowers collected bees, all of whom would be better at addressing emotional tumult than he was. It would have been pointless to add to the buzz. "You've never asked me, either."

"I know," Laodice said. "That might be my point, I think? I've been sitting here considering all the things I don't know about you. I didn't know your parents were florists. I didn't know that you'd lost them. I didn't know you liked pad thai and hated brownies."

"I don't hate brownies. I merely prefer cheesecake."

"But you know my favorite flowers are orchids."

"Your sisters give you orchids every year for your birthday," Telfer said. "They're delivered to the office. It wasn't a difficult conclusion to draw."

"What's your favorite flower? I bet it's not zinnia."

"Zinnias are fine."

"But what's your *favorite*?" She was looking at him steadily, her dark eyes taking in everything. It felt as if she were peering *through* him, peeling back layers, preparing to pin him to a board for dissection and categorization.

He swung his legs off the bed and stood up. "I don't have a favorite flower."

"Ice cream flavor, then. Movie. Tell me something about you."

"I don't see that it matters. Make up anything you like, and I'll confirm it."

"This isn't for the cover story," Laodice said, her eyes kindling. "You're sleeping beside me, for goodness sake. Would it kill you to share some *basic* personal information?"

Telfer's skin felt itchy. "I don't particularly feel the need to indulge you with small talk."

"*Unbelievable*," Laodice said. She jumped to her feet and yanked the robe from the back of the door. "Just when I was starting to think you might be a real person." She stormed past him and into the bathroom, and after a moment he heard the rush of water.

Telfer stood in the middle of the hotel room, distantly wondering why his heart was pounding so hard. His hands were shaking a little.

After a moment, he picked up his laptop and went back to work. Work demanded his skill with words, his ability to decipher and reinterpret information.

Work wanted what he could do, not who he was.

That was so much easier to satisfy.

***

It was hard to stay furious with someone when you were in the middle of the most luxurious bath of your life, but Laodice gave it her best shot.

She'd asked him the most *basic* questions, and he'd looked at her, all composed and certain of himself, and said he didn't want to *indulge* her.

The jet bubble stream pounding the middle of her back was really doing a number on the muscle knots where her bra band usually sat. She let it massage some of the tension out, still fuming. How could a man craft her a gorgeous bouquet—with her favorite flowers *and* her favorite colors—and then look so snooty when she asked about movies he liked? Most men *loved* talking about their favorite movie. She'd stopped bringing it up as a first date icebreaker, because they so often started monologuing.

He'd acted as if she'd been intrusive and nosy. Well, she *was* nosy, it was part of what made her a good journalist, but she wasn't *intrusive*.

What were the amenities in this thing like? She lunged for the shelf of lotions, splashing water over the floor, and selected a red glass bottle shaped like a curvaceous woman. It promised to smell like a wicked night backstage at a burlesque show. In Laodice's experience, backstage at any kind of show mostly smelled like sweat and hairspray, but she poured a generous glob into the bath and relaxed into the scent of gardenia and amber. Specks of light danced in the water, and she wasn't surprised to discover herself sprinkled with glitter when she climbed out. Her fingers and toes were pruny, and she'd no idea how long she'd spent in the tub, but her irritation had subsided.

It flared right back up when Sarah's voice came over the speakers again. "Listen up, lovebirds!" she declared. "I hope you've enjoyed your you time, because now it's us time! Meet in the lobby for the first Halcyon Couples Quiz!"

***

When Laodice emerged from the bathroom, smelling floral and glittering slightly, she didn't speak to Telfer. She barely looked at him.

This quiz was going to be a disaster.

The one good part of the whole miserable day thus far was the email Miriam had sent, approving Telfer working remotely, and even granting him official leave for three days, Wednesday to Friday. Provided he met his Tuesday midnight deadlines, that was one thing he didn't have to worry about.

"Great!" Sarah said, when he and Laodice appeared, the last couple downstairs. "Telfer, you go with the boys and Kyle, and Elle, you join the girls and me! And Patrick."

Patrick rolled his eyes.

Telfer glanced at Laodice, and she nodded, looking grim. Anyone operating in a modern wedding business ought to be considering same-gender couples, or people who didn't fit the binary gender mold. Sarah could have split the teams alphabetically, or via random number generator. Treating the gender binary as the norm, and, by that logic, deeming Patrick some kind of pseudo-woman, was another tally mark against Halcyon.

Telfer was disappointed. He'd been sure the retreat plan was a winner, and he'd recommended it to Miriam on that basis. An exclusive event for wealthy couples should have been a sure bet. Brandon had certainly thought so. He'd been enthusiastic about the project, and confident enough to invite a journalist to the soft opening.

Telfer felt bad for him. And also, for himself—he'd mispresented the quality of the retreat to Miriam, and that wasn't going to go unnoticed.

He even felt a little bad for Laodice.

***

"Okay," Kyle said, closing the door behind the men as they sat in the small conference room. "So, while we eat dinner, we're going to draw questions from this box and answer them. Then we're going up against the other group, to see who can answer the most questions right about their partner. There's a prize for the best couple, and also our pride as a team at stake. Don't let me down, boys." He winked.

Telfer tried to keep the panic off his face.

Danielle came in with several platters of charcuterie, which was apparently dinner, and Telfer grabbed a handful of olives while he thought. Maybe he could get a sudden headache or fake a food allergy, and ask Laodice to help him? It seemed like a desperate measure. Perhaps, if they were lucky, the questions would be things they did know. And if they weren't, well, often couples made assumptions or didn't know everything about each other.

"Jesse, why don't you go first," Kyle said.

"What are your favorite hobbies?" Jesse read. He snorted. "I know what Hazel should put for this one. Partying and spending my money." He looked around, obviously expecting a laugh.

He didn't get one. Even Kyle looked carefully blank.

"It was a joke," Jesse muttered.

"What's *your* hobby?" Samuel said.

"Lacrosse," Jesse said sulkily.

"I like watching old school mystery shows," Samuel said. "Anything where a little old lady or a British vicar stumbles into murder scenes. No computers."

"I play golf and listen to podcasts," Telfer said, glad that Laodice and he had at least exchanged that much information. He was cursing himself for shutting down her suggestion earlier. Why hadn't he been able to tell her a few of his favorite things? It was hardly privileged information, even if he did prefer to keep his personal life private.

Carrick claimed video gaming as his hobby, Erik quietly volunteered that he liked to read, and Xavier folded his arms. "Yvette and I don't have time for hobbies. We work. Unless you count the gym as a hobby."

"I think we all work, but the gym definitely counts," Samuel said mildly. "I've got...what's your mother's maiden name." He frowned slightly. "It's Dupree."

The questions went on, ranging from mundane details (what street had they grown up on? What where their favorite snacks?) to questions that were more intrusive (do you want children and if so, how many?) to the outright invasive. Telfer tried to give answers he thought Laodice might be able to guess, frantically searching his memory for what he could say about her in return. Samuel was looking more uncomfortable as they continued, and on the final round, he glanced at the card, and put it down.

"I'm not answering this one," he said.

"What does it say?" Telfer asked.

"What's your wedding budget," Samuel said flatly.

"It's meant to normalize budget setting," Kyle said, looking trapped.

"It's meant to incentivize competition and overspending," Samuel said, his voice measured. "I'm not interested in that kind of comparison."

Xavier looked a little disappointed, but Telfer got in before he could argue the point. "I agree," he said quickly. "Let's ignore that one. Kyle, can you go tell the others they don't have to do that one? Thank you."

"Um, Sarah might not—"

"Thank you, I appreciate it," Telfer said, putting a little steel into his voice.

Kyle went off, looking uncertain, and came back a few moments later, mumbling that it was time to meet back in the lobby lounge. He looked much more comfortable behind the bar, while Sarah harried everyone into position and put all the questions into "the Cauldron of Unity," which looked exactly like a round glass fishbowl to Telfer.

Laodice was looking subdued, and Telfer went towards her. If he could figure out how to phrase it, he should offer an apology for what had turned out to be a poor strategic choice on his part.

"Now, now," Sarah said, intercepting him before he could get there. "No collusion before the competition begins!"

Kyle was lining up shot glasses at the bar, swiftly pouring colored liqueurs into each. Telfer looked at the shots, then at the color-coded game board Danielle was wheeling into the center. "Is this a drinking game?" he asked.

"It is!" Sarah said triumphantly. "For every wrong answer, you do a shot!"

A murmur went round the group. Most people looked more en- thusiastic, and Telfer could imagine that the prospect of alcohol might improve the entertainment value of the event. But: "I don't drink," he said.

"Oh, right!" Carrick said. "I remember that."

Alma looked startled. "But last night Elle said you liked Lagavulin."

Telfer cursed internally. "I'll have a whiskey on special occasions," he said.

"Yes, that's right," Laodice said quickly. "Normally he's a sparkling water guy."

Telfer actually preferred still water, but he could handle some carbon- ation if it would smooth over this moment.

"Sparkling water it is," Sarah said, her smile wide and unmoving. "Add that to the shots, Kyle."

Some time later—impossible to tell how long without being able to glance at his phone—Telfer was wishing that he *did* drink. It didn't surprise him that Hazel knew much more about Jesse than vice versa, and Jesse grew more unpleasant with each question he got wrong, slamming back shots as if they'd personally wronged him. Patrick and Samuel were tied, with three wrong answers each, Alma and Erik had two and one wrong respectively, and Yvette and Xavier knew everything about each other, right down to, "We don't have any hobbies because we work too hard, unless you count the gym."

Carrick and Britt, surprisingly, were missing several answers. Britt got fewer right than Carrick and took her shots like a trooper.

And Telfer and "Elle" were a disaster. They got the hobbies right. She'd picked cheesecake for his favorite snack, and he'd chosen that in the hope that she'd remember they'd discussed it. He'd guessed correctly that she preferred dogs to cats. But many of the answers were impossible to figure out unless you actually *knew* your partner intimately.

The kids question was particularly bad. He'd guessed she wanted two children, and she'd guessed he wanted one. The real answer was none, for both of them, and Telfer felt the puzzled glances go around the room.

There were half the questions still to go, and Laodice was on her fourth wrong answer. Telfer handed her his "shot" instead of the poisonous green chartreuse Kyle had lined up for her. She flashed him a grateful look as she downed the water.

"That's cheating," Yvette said instantly.

"Yeah," Jesse said, squinting at them. He grabbed a shot from the bar and thrust it at Laodice. "Go on, get it down."

Telfer plucked it from his hand. "She doesn't have to drink if she doesn't want to."

"But that's the rule," Jesse said, his voice going high and whiny. "*I* did it."

"What are you going to do if I don't?" Laodice asked pleasantly. "Pin me to the floor and pour booze down my throat?"

For a moment, Jesse looked as if he were contemplating it. Telfer looked at his sulky face and felt an unexpected and unaccustomed impulse towards violence.

"We forfeit," Laodice said firmly. There was color in her cheeks, and her eyes were bright, but Telfer thought she was still mostly sober. She made eye contact and patted the seat beside her, and he sat down, absently enjoying the warm curve of hip and arm against his side.

Sarah put the unanswered questions back in the fishbowl, clearly giving up on the whole business. "All right then! That means the boys win!"

"Except for Patrick," Patrick mumbled. Samuel grinned and kissed his cheek.

"And our winning couple is Xavier and Yvette! Yay, Xavier and Yvette!"

Telfer clapped along with the rest, more out of relief than genuine good will. Yvette was looking particularly smug as Sarah gave them a gift card for a store in the Hippocampus, "to visit on your way home."

"This is crap," Jesse said. "The questions were dumb." Beside him, Hazel was very still.

"We all had the same questions, bro," Xavier said, but Yvette tapped his arm and he subsided.

"Whatever," Jesse said. "I'm going to take a leak." He walked behind the bar, heading for the door that led to the back.

"That's staff only," Sarah said. "Your guest room—"

"I'm paying forty grand to stay in this dump. I get to piss in your fucking toilet." The door banged behind him.

Kyle looked at Sarah with his eyebrows raised, and she shook her head. "Well, congratulations to our winners again," she said. "Now, feel free to hang out here, or go soak in the hot tub, but don't forget we're getting up early for more bonding meditation tomorrow!"

"What time is that going to be?" Britt asked, glancing at her watch.

"It's a surprise," Sarah said enthusiastically.

"Yay," Laodice muttered.

"Come on," Telfer said quietly, under cover of the others' chatting. "Let's go to bed."

***

"Not a great first day," Laodice said, climbing under the covers.

Telfer was typing rapidly at the desk, his hair still damp from his shower. "No."

"Thanks for the protein bar." Telfer had offered it to her from his stash when they'd gotten back to the room, and Laodice was hoping it would soak up the booze. She'd enjoyed the charcuterie, but she wasn't a big drinker, and that was now two nights in a row that she'd had to keep up with the rich kids.

"You're welcome," Telfer said.

"Well. Good night." She turned off the light on her side of the bed, and lay awake, while Telfer finished whatever he was working on, and climbed into bed himself, turning off the light a moment later.

There was a pause, humming with the tension of everything they weren't saying.

"My favorite flowers are water lotuses," Telfer said, his voice clear in the quiet air. "My favorite movie is *His Girl Friday*. I don't really have a preferred ice cream flavor because frozen desserts hurt my teeth, so I avoid them."

Laodice sat up and looked at him. In the near total darkness of their room, he was a vague shape on the other side of the bed, but she thought he was watching her too. "Is this your version of an apology?"

"If you want to take it that—" he started, and then hesitated. Laodice let the pause lengthen. "Yes," he said. Stiffly, but he said it. "I'm sorry. Obviously, you were right. We would have been much better off if we'd traded more information."

Laodice did like being told she was right. "Apology accepted."

"And it was rude of me to respond to your queries as if they were intrusive. I don't like small talk much, but I'm aware it's an important social courtesy, and you deserve courtesy."

Huh. That was... a pretty good apology, actually. "Well, thank you. I appreciate that." She lay back down. After a moment, she said, "My favorite movie is *When Harry Met Sally*."

"Harry's a jerk," Telfer said, sounding disgruntled. "Sally could do better."

"He improves," Laodice said. "He grows on her. By the end of the movie, he's all in. Plus, I bet the sex was amazing."

"It would have to be," Telfer agreed.

"I'm not saying I'd forgive Harry," she said, rolling onto her side and putting her back to him. "But Sally loves him, and I want Sally to get what she wants."

Telfer's voice floated to her in the dark, sounding puzzled. "I don't know how she could trust him. How could she be sure he wouldn't panic and run again? How could *he* be sure?"

"He says he wants to spend the rest of his life with her."

"And what if he's wrong?"

Laodice punched her pillow into submission and yawned. "You think Nora Ephron should have written a sequel? *When Harry Divorced Sally?*"

"Sure. I bet that'd pull in the crowds." She could hear the smile in Telfer's voice, and it pulled a smile from her too.

"You know what?" she said. "We've officially made it to the end of the first day without blowing our cover, *and* we've weathered our first inevitable fight. Maybe it wasn't such a bad day after all."

"Go to sleep," Telfer said, but he didn't sound annoyed.

Laodice decided that, against all the odds, that was good enough.

Chapter Six

Telfer jerked awake and sat up. His hand, flung out for balance, hit a warm, round mass, and he froze.

Then he carefully removed his palm from Laodice's spectacular ass—thankfully covered by bedclothes, but still a generous mound under the covers.

"—and shine, lovers!" Sarah's voice was saying, far too loudly. The glow around the room brightened. This time, he could hear electronic bird chirping in the background.

On the first night, he and Laodice had stayed on their own sides of the enormous bed. Last night, they seemed to have migrated towards the middle. Telfer was painfully aware of the unwelcome pressure in his groin.

Morning erections were a normal physiological response, he told himself. There was no need for him to feel awkward or embarrassed. Laodice might be impractical in some ways, but even if she noticed, she surely wouldn't hold an inadvertent bodily function against him.

Especially since she hadn't even moved yet. She was huddled under the covers, her back towards him, her face buried, the masses of dark chestnut hair spread over the pillows the only identifiable feature.

"—see you downstairs soon!" Sarah finished, and the room went momentarily silent.

Then the bird chirping was back.

"Fuck me, someone shoot those birds," Laodice moaned. She rolled over and flung the covers back so they lay across her thighs. She was still lying down, her eyes firmly shut. It seemed as if she proposed to get up in stages.

Telfer stopped breathing. Her skin was rosy and sleep-flushed, strands of that long, dark hair falling over her face. She was wearing her yoga pants and T-shirt, perfectly decent and covered up, but the soft cotton did nothing to conceal the fall of her heavy breasts or rounded stomach.

She looked eminently, deliciously *touchable*.

"I get first shower," Telfer said, and hurtled from the bed.

There was startled motion behind him, but he thought he'd moved fast enough that she might not have noticed the reason for his flight. He locked the bathroom door behind him and exhaled. Okay. He could hope the whole...situation would go away, or he could take it in hand, so to speak, and go into the day with desires satisfied, all the less likely to present him with inconvenient lust at an awkward moment.

When you thought about it that way, masturbating in the room next to your barely awake co-worker made perfect sense.

He started the shower, peeled out of his clothes, and stepped into the welcome rush of warm water. As he wrapped his hand around his erection and closed his eyes, Telfer fixed his mind firmly on a standard fantasy in his repertoire.

It was more or less a replay of an encounter from a year or two ago. His partner for the evening had been traveling on business, and he'd gone to her hotel room with the usual understanding that this would be a one time affair. She'd been stunningly beautiful, with long limbs and a wicked smile, smart and funny and a little sarcastic in a way that had made their bar room flirtation more interesting than the customary precursor to sex.

But the sex had been fantastic.

She'd nipped at his throat, mocking little love bites, as she'd slid her hand down his body and cupped his cock, and he'd thrust up into that grip, already slick from their foreplay.

Her long hair had brushed against his chest, then his belly, then his thighs, as she moved lower. In the fantasy, she teased the tip of his cock with her tongue, then slowly engulfed him, her eyes rolling up to watch his response.

She had Laodice's face, Laodice's eyes, Laodice's long dark hair pooling around his legs.

Laodice's mouth, wrapped around his aching cock.

Telfer thrust helplessly into his fist, two, three times, and came so hard that he nearly fell. He braced himself with his other hand against the shower wall and panted for breath while the water sluiced over his belly and thighs, washing the evidence away.

Hm.

This was going to be a problem.

When he emerged, Laodice didn't look as if she suspected what he'd been up to. She'd done something elaborate with her hair, adding a jeweled clip that caught the light. Telfer looked away before he could do something stupid like consider how the sparkle compared to the excited gleam in her eyes.

"I've decided that it's a new day, and I'm going to be positive," she told him. "Sarah was probably nervous yesterday and trying too hard to do everything right. The flower arranging class was great, so we know that Halcyon can definitely offer an experience I can write about."

Telfer opened his mouth to point out that the flower arranging class had been run by an outside vendor, and then closed it again. Laodice would certainly have considered that. If he verbalized the observation, it would imply he thought she was incompetent or lacked insight neither of which were true. "I think that's a sensible approach."

Laodice beamed at him.

Telfer basked in the warmth. Then Sarah's voice broke in again. Objectively, the woman had a nice voice. Subjectively, hearing it was beginning to feel like sandpaper scraping along his nerve endings.

"Hurry up, slow-pokes!"

"We aren't in kindergarten," Laodice muttered. "Oh, are you good to take the burner again today?"

"No problem." Telfer checked the time in an automatic gesture before he slid it into his pocket, and frowned. "It's 5:43 a.m."

Laodice scrunched her nose, then strode over to throw back the heavy red velvet drapes hanging over their window. The sky was pale blue, the sun a glimmer on the horizon.

"It's possible that Sarah's problem isn't nerves," she said grimly.

"Well," Telfer said. "Let's see."

Unfortunately, the morning didn't offer much to make them optimistic. Danielle brought in water for the table before it was requested, but the breakfast servings were still minuscule. There were tiny white bowls of hummus, pita bread cut into slim triangles, and chunks of fresh cucumber and tomato.

"Is this supposed to be a Turkish breakfast?" Carrick asked, in an undertone.

Telfer stared at the meager offerings. No cheese, no olives, no jam, and no soft, pillowy squares of pide bread. He could feel whole generations of Turkish matriarchs rolling in their graves. "I sincerely hope not. Kahvalti involves *food*."

Carrick stifled a guffaw.

"Meditation," Sarah announced, and they spent an interminable period being told about the guiding beings that existed to lift them to higher consciousness and also something implausible about soul bonding on the cellular level.

Telfer felt himself drifting off at one point, only to be wakened by Laodice's tug on his hands. She tilted her head towards Sarah, and after a moment Telfer realized that the "guided meditation" had shifted to an unmistakable sales pitch for Sarah's side hustle, which seemed to be a spiritual life coaching business, delivered remotely "so that you can access your true manifestation of Universal Light!"

Telfer scanned the room to see how the others were reacting. Alma and Erik were gazing at each other, apparently oblivious to the rest of the world. Hazel looked confused, and Jesse sullen. Yvette and Xavier were exchanging raised eyebrows. Patrick looked fed up, Samuel was clearly miles away, doing something else in his head, Britt was listening with apparent equanimity, and Carrick was asleep.

Even as Telfer noticed it, Carrick slumped and let out a sound that was a mix between a snort and a snore. He jerked awake, but the tension had broken as the rest of them laughed. He gave everyone a sheepish smile.

"Sorry," he said.

"That's all right, I think we were finishing," Patrick said. He got up, and Telfer shuffled to his feet too.

Sarah clearly didn't agree, but there wasn't much she could do with her guests pointedly preparing for departure. She announced there would be a short break before the next class started.

"Great," Alma said. "And could we get some snacks? Crudités or something?"

"No nuts," Erik said. His voice was soft, and Telfer realized how little he'd heard the man speak.

"You got it!" Sarah accompanied them out to the lounge space that had become their de facto group gathering spot, animatedly discussing snack options with Erik. At one point she touched his arm, then tossed her hair back and laughed.

"Subtle," Laodice observed. She'd followed Telfer out and was standing right next to him. Well, of course she was. That was their cover. But the scent of something sweet was rising from her hair. It was making him distracted. And hungry.

"Could I speak to you two for a moment?" Alma asked, and ushered them closer to the grand entrance, away from where the others were gathered.

"Sure!" Laodice said cheerfully, and lowered her voice. "Do you want us to run interference?"

Alma looked over her shoulder, where Erik was stoically eating crackers while Sarah talked at him. "Oh, that? No, don't worry about it."

"It doesn't bother you, that she keeps flirting with Erik?"

"Only when it bothers him," Alma said. "And it's pretty unprofessional behavior. I don't think much of her ethics. But no, I'm not jealous. I know Erik would never cheat on me. There was one bad moment in our relationship when I thought he was concealing things from me, and it almost drove me crazy. Have you heard of the advice columnist, Ask Cassandra?"

Laodice jumped. "Um, sure. It's an advice column in *Agora*, right?"

Alma's gaze sharpened. "Right, you both work at Olympus."

"I'm in the Wardrobe," Laodice said hastily. "We don't talk to the writers much. And she's anonymous anyway. I heard that she might even be a guy."

"I suppose," Alma said. "It doesn't really matter. But Erik was being shady about how he was spending his time, going away on trips frequently, and he seemed to have much more money than a freelance copywriter should be earning. Instead of talking with him about it, I made the mistake of bringing this up to my sisters, and they were like, he's married, he's got a rich wife, you're the side piece, do some snooping."

"Uh, wow," Laodice said. "That was supposed to be your *first* move? That's some bad advice."

"I seriously thought about it," Alma confessed. "I mean, I didn't *think* he could be such a monster. But if he was... I got as far as making an appointment with a private investigator. But the next day, Cassandra answered my email. She told me to talk to him *first*."

"I remember this!" Laodice said, and looked at the lounge space again. Samuel and Patrick had joined Erik, and Sarah was heading through a staff door, talking on her headset again. "Is this the one where the guy was secretly a bestselling romance author?"

Telfer was impressed. Writing longform was something he'd occasionally considered himself, but the dedication and craft required were intimidating. He looked at Erik with new respect. "And the trips were for writing purposes?"

Alma smiled. "Yes. They were writing retreats, where he'd lock himself away somewhere isolated so he could meet his deadlines."

"*Wow*," Laodice said. "What's his pen name?"

Alma's smile deepened. "He has several, and that's private." She paused. "I have his permission to tell you this, of course. Erik's working on being more open about what he does, but he's not ready for any kind of general announcement."

"Oh," Telfer said. "Well, that's kind of you. We're honored by your trust."

"What I'm saying is that all of this is off the record," Alma said firmly.

The journalistic jargon made Telfer straighten. Laodice was looking carefully neutral.

"I know who you are, Laodice," Alma said quietly. "I know you don't work in the Wardrobe department at Olympus. You reported on my dad's second wedding, nearly five years ago."

Laodice looked chagrined, and then puzzled. "I don't remember meeting you at all."

"We never spoke. But I saw you talking to people at the reception, and I enjoyed the piece. I remembered who'd written it."

Despite the disaster unfolding before him, Telfer couldn't help but feel vindicated. "See?" he told Laodice. "You *are* memorable."

"Not to Hazel or Xavier, and I actually interviewed them," Laodice said. She was eying Alma with wary respect. "Um, thank you? And also, wow, your memory is amazing."

"I assume you're here on assignment," Alma went on. "I'm letting you know that I know, because I don't want Erik's career in the piece. I don't want you snooping around to find his pen names."

"I was going to anonymize everyone," Laodice said. "And we do have permission from the Halcyon owners to be here."

"From Sarah?"

"Sarah doesn't know," Telfer put in. "She's the hostess, not the business manager."

"Ah. That was the one thing that didn't make sense. I thought she'd be sucking up to you a lot more if she knew you were reporters." She refocused. "I'm happy for you to keep doing your job. I don't mind us being background characters in your story. And I won't tell anyone else what's going on, so long as you can guarantee that Erik's job is *not* a story."

"This feels like blackmail," Laodice said, sounding more interested than offended.

Alma didn't even try to deny it. "Well?"

Laodice glanced at Telfer, who shrugged. Her decision.

"You've got a deal," Laodice said.

Alma's shoulders relaxed. "I hoped you'd be reasonable."

"Sure, but I want to be clear," Laodice said firmly. "I'm agreeing because I wouldn't be writing about Erik anyway. I wouldn't try blackmailing journalists as a general rule. We tend to get talkative about it. This was a risky move."

"I'd risk a lot to protect Erik," Alma said fiercely. Her lips were drawn back from her teeth, her eyes bright and hard. The friendly, caring nurse was gone. Telfer felt the hair on the back of his neck rise.

Then Alma relaxed, serene and positive again. "But I'm glad I don't have to. I like you guys. Maybe we could all meet up for dinner or something when we're back in the city?" She looked rueful. "My sister

Laura is always pushing us to double date with her and her husband, but I'd honestly rather do it with you two."

Laodice opened her mouth, probably to confess that their "relationship" was also a ruse, and Telfer broke in.

"Maybe after the story's out," he suggested. "And we can all trust each other a little more."

Alma nodded, accepting that. She seemed focused on making sure that Erik's secrets were safe, but there was a limit to how many lies you could expose to someone, and still hope for them to act normally around you. Their cover story was on shaky ground as it was. Frankly, he was surprised that Alma, perceptive as she was, hadn't suspected that too.

***

Britt's watch said it was nearly 10 a.m. by the time the next class was ready, and Laodice wondered how long Sarah had meant to lecture them about the benefits of signing up for her Enlightenment package. Did she really not know how the guests were responding to her? Samuel and Britt were too patient, and Hazel and Carrick too good-natured to object, but Laodice thought everyone else was annoyed with her to one degree or another.

It was a real pity she was their hostess, because once again, the class was fantastic. The guests had filed into the big gallery room, where a perky, dark-haired couple introduced themselves as Luala and Richie and promised to introduce them to the wide and wonderful world of wedding dances.

"Have you ever wanted to try the drama of a tango?" Richie asked. He and Luala moved into a close, angular grip, eye-fucking each other intently, until he spun Luala out.

"Perhaps you want to do a choreographed dance with your attendants," Luala suggested, moving in time with Richie as they did a step-step-and-clap move Laodice had seen on social media all summer.

"Or maybe you want to be the center of attention for a swing spectacular!" Richie said, and Luala jumped into his arms, was easily spun around his body, and then flipped over his back. She sank into an effortless split and then popped back up again.

"But whatever you want to try, we're here to help," Luala concluded, and Carrick whooped and started the applause, his broad face alive with pleasure.

Luala and Richie grinned at each other, and then cheerfully bullied everyone into the middle of the room to do some basic warmup stretches, which led into simple dance moves so smoothly that it took a moment for Laodice to catch on that she was doing a box step. Hazel was a fantastic dancer, smooth and fluid, and Patrick was nearly as good, adding flashy spins and head bobs as he moved. Carrick flailed along with great enthusiasm, and the rest of them gamely followed with various levels of skill.

Telfer was doing the bare minimum, she thought, but that was all right. He kept looking at her and hesitating as she bounced and twirled, probably confused by the increasing pace and number of steps as the warm-up routine got more complex. Out of all of them, he was definitely the most stiff.

The Laodice of three days ago would have cheerfully attributed that to the stick up his ass. The Laodice of today... Well, she didn't like Telfer, precisely, but it was a little harder to *dislike* him. He was helping her out, on his vacation time no less, and he'd apologized for dismissing her request for basic facts. She could have interpreted his stepping in over the shots last night as high-handed Telfer-know-best stuff, but it hadn't felt like that.

It had felt like he was on her side.

And that was an unexpectedly reassuring place for him to be.

She whirled, did another jump—she was *not* wearing the right bra for this—and grinned at him.

Wonder of wonders, he smiled back.

Something in her chest tightened, and a shivering warmth radiated from the spot, descending into her belly. Telfer was handsome, and she'd always known it, but she'd never *wanted* him before. Now he was in his shirtsleeves, collar loosened, and there was something in his eyes she didn't recognize.

Or maybe, did recognize, and didn't want to consider.

The warm-up routine came to a breathless halt before she could react, in a flurry of clapping and happy voices. Even Jesse seemed to be having a good time—he whirled Hazel into his arms and dipped her, and she came up laughing, her eyes shining with love.

"All right!" Richie said. "Great work! Let's group up and we'll practice the most common wedding dance. Anyone know what that is?"

"The waltz," Laodice said, a split-second before Yvette could.

"That's right! Now, just for fun, we're going to mix you up so you're with different partners! I'm giving you three seconds to get used to the idea, three, two, one, go, Luala, go!"

This, apparently, was the cue for Luala to cheerfully bully everyone into new couple configurations. The dancing teachers were as relentlessly perky as Sarah was, and Laodice wondered why they didn't grate on her nearly as much.

It was the sincerity, she decided. Luala and Richie were genuinely enthusiastic about dance and its place in a wedding, and Sarah, for all her polish, wasn't sincere at all. Her enthusiasm was surface deep, like a shiny layer of lacquer over rotten wood.

She started with Xavier, who asked if they could maybe check out her car after lunch.

"Absolutely," Laodice promised, and was rewarded with the sight of Xavier trying hard to please. It didn't seem to come naturally to him, but she appreciated the effort as he rotated her in careful circles. She could see him mentally counting the beat, and while it wasn't unpleasant, there was a definite improvement when he was swapped for Patrick.

"*One*, two, three, *one*, two, three," Luala chanted, as Patrick twirled Laodice under his arm. "Getting ahead of us, Patrick!"

Patrick's teeth flashed white in his dark face. "Is that against the rules?"

"No, not as long as your partner can follow your lead! Looking good, Laodice!"

Laodice caught a glimpse of Samuel and Telfer dancing on the other side of the room, which looked considerably more awkward.

"They're both trying to lead," Patrick chortled. "Silly boys, these men of ours. Want to try a dip?"

"If you're sure you can hold me," Laodice said gamely, and Patrick bent her back in a gentle lean.

"Perfect!" he said, and then Carrick replaced him, his ruddy cheeks even brighter than usual.

"This is fun," he declared, looking both delighted and surprised. He grinned at her. "It's nice to know there's maybe one thing I can do better than Telfer."

"You're doing great," Laodice assured him.

Erik was next, careful and soft-voiced, with most of his attention where Alma was dancing with Telfer. "Isn't she good?" he asked, and Laodice politely agreed. Actually, she thought Alma was losing the beat, but arguing with the hopelessly infatuated never went anywhere.

Honestly, it was nice to see a man so completely in love with his intended. She might find that much devotion a little off-putting herself, but she could see why Alma never worried that he'd cheat. Certainly, Erik would never decide that he wanted to blow off his girlfriend so he could watch a stupid basketball game with his buddies.

Reminded of Eli's douchery, she was scowling when they switched partners again. The prospect of dancing with Jesse didn't make her any happier, even though he was on his best behavior, the hand on her mid-back perfectly impersonal. She was relieved when he moved back to Hazel, and Telfer came to join her.

Relieved, and maybe a little bit glad.

She held her arms out to Telfer, resting one hand lightly on his shoulder and the other in his outstretched hand. His other arm came around her back, and she was suddenly very close to him, gazing up into dark eyes that looked as startled as she felt.

The attraction was obvious, electric, and undeniably mutual.

The music stopped before they could take their first steps, and they dropped the hold immediately, stepping away from each other and breaking eye contact.

"Okay!" Luala said. "Amazing work, everyone! For your first dance with your partner, we're going to step it up a notch. The wedding dance can be many things, but for most people, those things include *performance*, because you're in front of a crowd!"

"Although you may not even notice them," Richie put in. "And of course, these people will be your nearest and dearest, so they'll all be wishing you well. The most sympathetic audience of your life!"

Laodice wasn't so sure. One of the first things she'd noted for her own eventual wedding was that she was going to control the hell out of the guest list. No second cousins her mother wanted to be there because otherwise they'd feel left out, no one from work who wasn't also a personal friend, and definitely no estranged relations there for a last-ditch reconciliation effort. *Her* wedding was truly going to be for the people she loved, and who loved her best.

Laodice been planning her wedding since she was seven, bullying Xena into being her flower girl and begging Cassie to fill the celebrant's role. The groom had always been played by Mr. Bones, the full-sized anatomy school skeleton her father had once brought home from a garage sale. Mr. Bones had flexible, skinny fingers that were easy to slide a plastic ring onto, and he looked dapper in a bow tie.

It was a shame Mr. Bones wasn't available for the real-life position. True, he wasn't much of a conversationalist, but he was much more reliable than half the men she'd dated in search of true love and a happily-ever-after.

Richie and Luala had kept talking while Laodice reminisced, and she came back to herself with a start. She must have missed something; the couples had shuffled into a loose circle, looking expectantly at herself and Telfer.

Luala motioned at them encouragingly, beckoning them into the center.

"Oh!" Laodice said, realizing what was happening. Well, all right, a solo waltz for a few bars wasn't so bad, especially after they'd all seen each other be goofy and awkward anyway. Luala and Richie were *good*. They'd structured the class so that everyone had been relaxed, then pushed a little outside their comfort zone by dancing with others one-on-one. Now they were ready to trust their audience and perform under observation.

At least, she was ready. She took a few steps towards the center, and stopped. Telfer hadn't followed.

"Come on, Telfer," Luala cheered, and started a quick round of encouraging applause.

He came to her then, but the stance was wrong, his arms extended so that they were too far apart from each other. Laodice could feel his shoulder, rigid under her touch.

"Get a little closer," Richie said, and Laodice took a step in, expecting Telfer to meet her there.

Instead, he dropped his arms. "Sorry," he said, looking at a point somewhere over her shoulder. "I think I hurt my ankle in that last bit. I'm going to sit down for a second."

It was a damning and obvious lie. Laodice felt the blood rush to her cheeks and twisted her hands in her skirt, fighting to control the humiliation surging through her.

Even the effervescent dance teachers hesitated, as they watched Telfer limp to the side of the room and lean against the wall, leaving Laodice alone in the circle of watching people. Then Richie stepped forward.

"Lucky me, I get to cut in," he said lightly, and Luala started the music.

Laodice summoned her most blinding smile, and prepared to dance her ass off. How had she *ever* thought Telfer Terzi was hot?

Chapter Seven

Telfer usually either ignored or didn't notice disapproval from others, but there was no escaping the looks he was getting as they all left the dance class. Frankly, he deserved it. Laodice had danced with Richie—who was a far better match for her grace—and Telfer had spent the rest of the lesson castigating himself for being an idiot.

The problem wasn't that he hadn't wanted to dance with Laodice. The problem was that he'd wanted it *too much*. Laodice was fun to look at even when she was standing still, but her body in motion was all vibrant beauty. In the warm-ups, she'd bounced and whirled, her hair flying around her shoulders and that damn jeweled clip twinkling at him.

He'd been relieved when they had to dance with others, and a split-second later, he'd been consumed with envy for all the men who'd been able to hold her in that close embrace. He'd even been envious of Patrick. And then they'd come back together at last, and it was *his* turn to hold her.

He'd steeled himself. He'd reminded himself that she didn't like him, she certainly didn't want him... And then she'd looked at him. He'd seen her pupils dilate, felt her breathing pick up, and it had been like jumping off a cliff into a dark pool.

Telfer didn't know if the water would welcome him, or if there were rocks beneath the surface.

So he'd stepped back from the edge, unwilling to risk...he wasn't sure what. Something. Laodice's good opinion, perhaps, which was becoming oddly more valuable as the days progressed. And what a great job he'd done of that, embarrassing her in front of the others, with his stupid fake ankle injury and his ridiculous false limp.

He wasn't surprised when she left without even looking at him, chatting happily with Hazel and Alma. At least she had something good for her story—until his colossal error, the event had been a masterclass in excellent wedding preparation.

Telfer was supposed to schmooze with the vendors, setting up possible leads for later Olympus stories or advertising content, but he couldn't face that right now. He went back to their room instead, leaving Laodice to enjoy her lunch without him. He'd make a meal of protein bars. And shame.

***

"I know you said he was shy, but I didn't really see it until today," Alma said, passing Laodice the fruit bowl.

Laodice took a banana and shoved two apples into her sundress pockets for later, not really caring that they made unsightly lumps on either side of her hips. They weren't being fed enough, and she was in no mood to beg Telfer for snacks, even if he owed her.

"That's right," she said, remembering the lie she'd told Alma on their first evening. "The shyness doesn't come out often, but I think it was having to go first."

"Still kind of a jerk move, leaving you up there like that," Yvette observed from her other side, and Laodice frowned at her.

"It's not the sort of thing you can control," she said. Wait. *Had* Telfer been taken by a sudden bout of stage fright? She could have sworn that seconds before, he'd been more than happy at the prospect of dancing with her. But she hadn't imagined that sudden tension in his body. She'd just thought that it was disgust.

Yvette shrugged. "I suppose so," she said, and looked across the table. "Hazel, why don't we check out the hot tub before siesta? Laodice's going to show Xavier her car."

Laodice had completely forgotten, but Xavier brightened, and she didn't have the heart to refuse him.

"Sure!" Hazel said, and then turned to Jesse. "Do you want to hot tub, hon?"

From Yvette's face, she hadn't planned to include Jesse in the invitation.

Xavier was gratifyingly impressed by the Spider's restoration, enthusing over the Kamm tailer and rear bumper design. It turned out he'd been a gearhead since high school, and had a 1974 Volkswagen Karmann Ghia garaged in his home town, waiting until he had the time to restore it.

"You must be busy, if you're leaving a beauty like that untouched," Laodice said sympathetically.

"The work doesn't stop," Xavier said. "But Yvette's a machine. She doesn't get tired and she doesn't slow down. I've seen her go through briefs and contracts hour after hour. If I didn't remind her, she might not even take bathroom breaks."

"Telfer works hard too," Laodice said. She could give him credit for that, at least. "He's usually first into the office and last out. Even stays late on Friday nights."

Xavier gave her a confused look, and Laodice remembered that Elle and Telfer didn't work in the same office, only in the same building. "I have to go and drag him away whenever we have a date," she said quickly.

Xavier looked superior. "We're disciplined about that. Tuesday and Friday nights and Sunday mornings are our time. Maybe you and Telfer could work out something similar. Especially since you don't live together."

"It's a good idea," Laodice said, and put the bonnet down. "Well, we better get back inside for siesta."

They went in as Yvette was coming out, presumably to look for them. Laodice walked ahead, but their voices floated to her in the muggy summer air.

"Any luck?" Xavier asked.

"No," Yvette said, sounding both annoyed and miserable. "I think she knows what I'm going to say, and she doesn't want to hear it."

"You'll get her, sweetie," Xavier promised, and there was the soft sound of lips meeting. They were obnoxious, Laodice thought, but admittedly a cute couple.

Well, now what? Everyone else would be enjoying their siesta time, but Laodice didn't want to head upstairs yet. If Telfer really had had some sort of panic attack, she wanted to give him time to recover. And if he'd just been being a jerk, she didn't trust herself not to point that out. Loudly.

There were no other distractions in sight. It was weird that Halcyon's management hadn't considered that people without phones might like some board games, or something to read, or a pack of cards. There were no TVs, in either their rooms or the common areas, and there wasn't even a hotel gym on site, although there was an empty room by the hot tub that she thought had been meant for one.

It was a Sunday afternoon. What would she normally be doing? Recently, Sundays had been reserved for chores, followed by movies at Eli's place, or dinner with her parents. But previous to Eli, Sunday afternoon had been a great time to log into the dating apps and start screening some possibilities. Laodice had taken full advantage of the dating scene. Sure, it often ended in rejection. She'd more than once been told she was coming on too strong, or expecting too much, right before she was dumped, again.

But she *did* feel deeply, quickly. She *was* a lot. And one day, she'd find someone who wanted all of her.

She'd thought—well, all right, she'd hoped—that that person could be Eli. He did share her energetic approach to life. And it had been a long time since she'd dated someone for more than a couple of months.

But she'd left him three days ago, and she didn't miss him at *all*.

As she floundered with this realization, still standing in the lobby, Kyle emerged from the door behind the bar. He looked surprised when he saw her, then nodded a greeting.

Laodice walked over to meet him. He could be a great source of background for the story. And if not, he could be a distraction.

"Can I get you something?" he asked.

"It's…well, I'm not sure what time it is, but it's too early for me." She eased up onto one of the plush bar stools. "A tonic water would be great, though."

"You like it with lime, right?"

"I do. How did you remember that?"

He shrugged, and poured her drink, topping it with two lime wedges he pulled from a small fridge under the bar. "I used to work in a cocktail bar in the city. Remembering someone's usual was a good way to get a better tip."

Laodice sipped her water, and put the glass down. "Actually, can I ask you about that? Sarah said we shouldn't tip, but I wanted to check that was all right with you."

He grinned, flicking a blond strand out of his eyes. "Nah, we're being taken care of. Don't worry about that."

"How many staff are there? I've seen you, Danielle, and Sarah."

Something flickered in Kyle's eyes, and Laodice knew she was about to be lied to. She'd seen that look on too many bridesmaids lying about how much they *loved* their dress, too many parents pretending they approved of their child's new spouse. "Nah, there's lots of staff," he said. "There's the kitchen workers, and housekeeping, and the groundskeepers…a lot of people. But they're all supposed to stay out of sight. Part of the whole Halcyon deal is giving you privacy."

It was completely plausible, and it wasn't true. Laodice sipped her drink, giving herself time to think of an angle, and caught Kyle's eyes snagging on her mouth. Aha.

"Or the illusion of privacy," she said, sighing. "Did you hear about how my fiancé abandoned me in the middle of the dance floor? That was kind of public."

"I might have heard something," Kyle said, and moved a little closer to her. "Tell you what, if I had a girl like you, I wouldn't let her dance alone."

Laodice cast her eyes down and then looked up at him through the lashes. "No?"

"Absolutely not."

"I was really *loving* the class up until then, too. Who's organizing those?"

"Oh, that's all Sarah. She's really great at that."

Well, having poor social skills didn't prevent someone from being a dynamite facilitator, Laodice supposed. "Do we have meditation every day?"

Kyle's teeth gleamed. "Yep. Opening your mind to the cosmic adventure."

"I bet you know what else is coming up in the schedule," she said, and leaned forward. Kyle responded to the flattery and repositioning both, shuffling even closer. "Care to give me a hint?"

"Tonight is cocktail mixing with me. Tomorrow's all about the music," Kyle said, smiling at her with intent.

"Oh? Are you going to serenade us?"

He grinned. "I could. But it's more about setting the scene at your ceremony and reception."

"Aw," Laodice said. "And Tuesday?"

"How to preserve the memories of your day. Photos, pressing the flowers from your bouquet, that kind of thing."

"Do we get to go on any field trips? I feel pretty cooped up in here. Kind of shut off from the world."

"I think it's cozy," Kyle said. "Who needs the world?"

Laodice laughed, and also tossed her hair back, one of her go-to flirt moves. "I don't need the whole world. But I'm dying for a cheeseburger."

Kyle's eyes flickered. "I'll see what I can do."

"You've got pull with the chef?"

He smirked, enjoying some kind of private joke. "You better believe it, babe."

Interesting, Laodice thought, and put that in her mental file. "A cheeseburger and curly fries," she said, and sighed, a motion that she knew made her breasts heave and jiggle.

Kyle looked around the space theatrically, but the only people around were Carrick and Jesse, heading towards the spiral staircase, out of easy earshot. "I know a great diner in the Hippocampus. We could sneak out tonight. Maybe talk a little more." The emphasis he put on *talk* indicated that a nice chat wasn't really what he was after.

Laodice paused, disconcerted by his willingness to proposition someone in a relationship. Well, this wasn't like Sarah hitting on Erik, who had never reciprocated her interest—Laodice was definitely and deliberately putting out signals. Perhaps Kyle assumed she and Telfer were polyamorous. Or perhaps he didn't care.

Either way, she needed a way to retreat that would still leave him open to feeding her information later. She was casting around for one when Telfer's voice sliced through the atmosphere, cool as a night breeze.

"Mind if I cut in?" he asked.

***

Telfer sent his last piece to Miriam, closed down the mobile data hot spot, and shut his laptop. Despite Halcyon's distractions, he'd completed his assigned work with even more than his usual productivity. He could log in tomorrow or Tuesday to go over Miriam's comments and make adjustments, and then he was done.

But it wasn't nearly as satisfying as it should have been. Four years ago, he would have obsessed over those pieces, spending hours over the wording on each to make sure it best positioned the vendors with the various brand identities embodied by each title. *Bliss* was fun, casual and aimed at the younger and less moneyed market. *Goddess* was more traditional, more luxe, and more likely to involve names people would recognize. He'd written those keywords on post-it notes and stuck them all over his apartment, so that he'd internalize the messaging.

Even more crucially, aware that he had a significant experience gap, he'd studied bridal writing. He'd gone through the Olympus archives, reading every back issue of the major two titles, and a generous sampling of their smaller offerings and digital content. Laodice had only been in Bridal for a year before him, but she was clearly the best wedding reporter on staff, so he'd read and re-read her work, highlighting phrases he thought were interesting and original, noting elements of structure and style, and admiring the way she managed to cram so many quotes and names in without making it seem forced.

The long hours and constant grind had *worked*. He'd gone from being a business specialist with a minor in communications to being a real writer. And now he was inches away from an editorial position which would give him stability, security and a chance to innovate in a sometimes stagnant environment, and it somehow felt...flat.

He'd never told Laodice that he'd studied her work and taken it as a model. It would have felt like giving her a point in their intense, unspoken competition. Now he was wondering if he'd misjudged her. Perhaps if he had shared his admiration, she'd have responded with generosity instead of triumph.

It didn't matter.

It shouldn't matter.

He checked the time again, and frowned. Laodice would be wanting to get her notes on the dance class organized and uploaded. He'd been hoping that she'd come upstairs of her own accord, but perhaps the collegial thing to do would be to find her and suggest that she could have exclusive use of the room. He wouldn't blame her for not wanting him in close proximity—he could at least give her until the next couples gathering before she had to reconcile to his presence again. He could listen to a podcast in the—no, wait, he couldn't, not without his phone. Well, he could find something to do.

Halfway down the stairs, he heard voices.

"—fucking owe me," Jesse said. He wasn't speaking particularly loudly, but the venom in his voice caught Telfer's attention.

"Keep your voice down," Carrick said, his voice quieter, but still perfectly audible as it floated upwards. The stairwell shaft must be acting as a kind of amplification chamber.

Eavesdropping was an ethical gray area, but Telfer had never let that stop him. He eased back to the center spine of the curving staircase, so he could be less easily spotted from the ground, and listened.

"You've got a nice life," Jesse said. "A nice fiancée. A bit too ball-busting for my tastes, but I guess you like that in a woman. She seems like a straight shooter to me. How would she feel about some of the things I could tell her?"

"We're not discussing that here."

"I want a job at Argive, Carrick," Jesse said, his voice getting louder. "You keep offering to smooth things over for your old college buddy, so you can fucking make it happen for me."

"That's not a good idea," Carrick said urgently, and Telfer realized that the rise in volume was because they were getting closer. He silently retreated a few steps, and then deliberately scuffed his feet and coughed as he made his way down.

Both men stopped talking.

"So put in a good word for me!" Jesse said, as Telfer came into view, looking his blandest. Jesse smacked Carrick on the shoulder, with what was probably meant to be friendly force, and grinned at Telfer. "Coming to grovel?"

"Something like that," Telfer said.

Carrick muttered something and brushed past him, heading quickly up the stairs. He looked harried and sweaty, though the air conditioning was still pumping out frigid air.

Jesse loitered, apparently happy to have a new target. "You're going to have to put in some work, man. Elle looked *pissed*." He gestured generally towards the bar, out of sight. "She's trying to get her revenge by flirting with the barman. Women, huh?"

"Thanks for the tip," Telfer said, and something in his voice must have revealed his distaste, because Jesse gave him a narrow-eyed look.

"My advice? Stay on top of that shit. They pretend it's all just friendly, but—"

"I didn't ask for advice," Telfer said flatly, and walked right past him.

Laodice *was* talking to Kyle the barman. Telfer couldn't tell for sure if she was flirting, since she'd never flirted with him, but she did seem to be doing some unnecessary hair tossing, and her voice was low and sultry. Kyle was looking at her with interest, which spoke well for his taste, if not his morals. In fact, he was so intent on Laodice that he didn't even notice Telfer's approach.

"Mind if I cut in?" he asked pleasantly.

Kyle jumped. "I'll, ah," he said, and fled through the door behind the bar.

Laodice straightened on her bar stool, a queen on her throne. "Way to scare off my lead," she said, but she didn't actually sound angry. "If you wanted to cut in, you should have kept dancing."

"I'm sorry about that," Telfer said. "I felt suddenly self-conscious." Actually, he'd been all too conscious of *her*, but he knew better than to say so.

"That's okay." Laodice finished her drink and slid off the bar stool. "You saved me from having to come up with a graceful way to cut and run, so you're provisionally forgiven."

Telfer fell into step with her automatically as she headed towards the stairs. "I thought you might need the room."

"I do. I have some thoughts and questions I want to get down." She sounded abstracted, her eyes distant with thought.

"Do you need a sounding board?" he offered. He was pathetic. He'd been all noble intentions, prepared to give her space and privacy, but the instant she seemed as if she might not outright reject his company, he was finding reasons to be close to her.

"Sure, might be good," Laodice said, and his stupid heart actually skipped a beat. She started to say something else, but they were at the foot of the stairs by then, and he pointed up, making a shushing gesture.

She rolled her eyes, but stayed quiet until they were back in the room, where she made a beeline for the end of the bed and sat down, shucking off her sandals with an ecstatic sigh of relief.

Telfer thought of other occasions that she might make that sound, and wandered over to the window to get his mind back on track. Sounding board. Right. "So, why were you flirting with Kyle?" he said, without turning around.

There was a rustling noise, presumably Laodice working her way up the bed to sit cross-legged, her back braced against the pillows. He'd noticed she liked that position.

"I wanted some background," she said. "Have you never flirted for a story?"

Telfer looked at her. Sure enough, she was cross-legged, bare feet tucked up under her thighs, reclining against the pillows. "I don't really flirt much," he said.

Laodice gestured at him. "I mean, you probably don't have to."

Telfer wasn't quite sure how to take that, and his confusion must have shown, because she went on hurriedly, her cheeks staining pink. "Anyway, I got some of the schedule. Tonight is cocktail mixing. Mocktails for you, I guess."

"Oh good, grenadine," Telfer said dryly.

"Tomorrow is something to do with music, and the day after is photography and something else." She frowned. "Telfer, is this retreat what you expected?"

Telfer considered the question. "I wasn't sure what to expect," he said finally. "It seems off, somehow, but I don't know if that's my skewed perspective."

"I wondered that too, whether not being here as a couple is making us see things differently. But the whole experience feels a lot less luxe than I expected. They're really not feeding us right, for one thing."

"I noticed that," Telfer admitted. "I ate the last of the protein bars, sorry."

Laodice waved that away. "They were your bars in the first place. Thank you for sharing."

"I thought that the tiny portions might be a wealthy people thing."

"Maybe. But I've attended a lot of society pre-wedding events. Even if nobody *eats* the food, it's there, and there's lots of it."

Telfer frowned. "Are you planning to canvass the couples?"

"Yes, but there might be a perception problem there, too."

"How so?"

"Because they're probably having a lot of sex," Laodice said. "No electronics, no distractions, nothing to do between the scheduled activities... I wouldn't be surprised if people come out of this experience feeling really positive about it because of that. All those happy post-orgasmic hormones."

Telfer's brain was screaming warnings at him, but he couldn't stop the words from spilling out of his mouth. "You could be having sex, if you wanted."

Laodice laughed. "With Kyle? No, thank you."

"No," he said, because he'd done it now, and there was no way out but through. "I meant with me."

Chapter Eight

Telfer had made the offer in such a matter-of-fact tone that it took a moment before the words sank in.

When they did, Laodice sat up bolt upright in her pillow nest. "You can't be serious."

Telfer shrugged. "Like you said, there's not much else to do." He was standing by the window, the sunset light spilling blue highlights over his dark hair and limning his bared forearms in gold.

"But..." Laodice said, and found she couldn't go on. It was so clearly a bad suggestion that she couldn't, for a moment, voice the many obvious reasons why having sex with Telfer would be a terrible idea. "I thought you were repulsed by me," she found herself saying instead. "And that's why you didn't want to dance."

Telfer looked genuinely flabbergasted. "Completely the opposite. I think you're very attractive. I've thought that since the moment I met you."

Laodice stared at him. He stared back.

"I'm not assuming you reciprocate my interest," he said. "Just thought I'd make the offer."

"Wow, romantic," Laodice said, but it was a little more breathless, a little less sharp than she would have liked. She appreciated, in a numbed-with-shock kind of way, that he hadn't gotten into her personal space, or made any actual moves. It was a verbal offer, easy to refuse. Why wasn't she refusing?

"Romance is not on the table," Telfer said firmly. "Sex only. Unless you're not interested in one-night stands?"

"I've had plenty of one-night stands," Laodice said, and managed to clamp down on the impulse to say *though I was wondering if you might be asexual.* Clearly, he wasn't. Instead, what came out was, "But we don't *like* each other!"

Telfer eyed her speculatively. "That could make it better," he suggested. "Hate sex can be incredible, if you do it right."

Laodice tried to look stern. "Well, I don't have sex with people I hate. Not that I actually hate you," she added. "But we work together and we fight all the time, and it seems like sex would be, um..." *An unnecessary complication. A potential HR disaster.*

Probably really hot.

"Got it," Telfer said, looking totally unmoved. "I won't bring it up again."

Laodice sought frantically for a subject change, and was almost grateful when Sarah's voice rang through the room. "It's time for couples cocktails mixing, lovebirds! Come and join our very special mixologist, and concoct the perfect concoction for your reception!"

Laodice looked at her laptop. Telfer's proposition had driven the mystery of Halcyon from her head for a moment, and she was oddly relieved to feel her curiosity flooding back. "Crap, I really need to do these notes. You go, though, and report back."

"We shouldn't do these things alone," Telfer said. "It looks weird."

He probably didn't mean to sound patronizing, but Laodice bridled anyway. "I'm aware of that," she snapped.

"I'm not saying you aren't *aware*, I'm saying you're not *participating*."

"Don't you dare lecture me about participation! You made me look like an idiot this afternoon."

"That was because I like you too much!" Telfer said, and then blew on before she even had time to react. "Besides, I was still *there*. I wasn't holed up in the suite like a hermit."

"Get out!" Laodice said, and as Telfer huffed and left, she found herself almost grateful for the argument. Like a thunderstorm relieving pressure, it had cleared some strange tension from the air, getting them back to normal.

Like she'd ever have sex with Telfer.

Ridiculous.

He banged back into the room, eyes blazing and cheeks flushed. "There's a bag of cashews in my satchel if you get hungry," he snarled.

"Thank you," Laodice snapped. "I *appreciate* your *concern!*"

The problem was, she kind of did.

***

Telfer didn't bother calling himself names this time. He'd made the offer, it had been refused, and now that was that. He'd put it out of his mind and move forward.

He was moving perhaps too fast, though, as he realized when he nearly charged into Hazel in the hallway.

She squeaked, one hand on the door she'd walked through, as he pulled himself to a stop right before the collision.

"Sorry," he said. "I was thinking about something else."

"I'm glad your ankle's better," Hazel said gamely.

"Right, yes," Telfer said. He should probably have been limping. Well, too late now, and he was pretty sure no one had believed him anyway. "I think it was a cramp. How are you? Did you enjoy the dancing?"

"Oh, yes! I love dance. I used to do ballet."

"Used to?"

Hazel's eyes strayed back to her door. "It takes up a lot of time, the classes and everything."

And Jesse had complained about that, Telfer deduced.

"Is Laodice coming?"

"She's not feeling well."

"Oh," Hazel said, and gave him a sympathetic look. "Jesse isn't coming either. He's, um, he has a headache."

And she was an even worse liar than Telfer, but he fell in step with her as they walked towards the stairs. "Do you want to be my partner for this, then?" he asked.

Hazel looked pleased, then alarmed, and he remembered Jesse giving him "advice" on how to deal with Laodice's flirtation with Kyle. What were the odds that Jesse considered talking to another man an inevitable prelude to cheating?

"Or not, it's okay," he said.

"Um, let's see," Hazel said, but the moment it was evident that they were both partnerless, Sarah paired them up.

"You can at least have the *experience*," she said, and then shot a look at Alma which indicated Sarah would have preferred it if Alma were the one with a headache.

Alma ignored her, which Telfer was beginning to think was best practice.

The "special mixologist" was Kyle, who had laid out a huge variety of spirits and liqueurs, and a smaller but surprisingly pretty good variety of non-alcoholic mixers, including something that was supposed to taste like gin. He talked them through some principles of mixology, had them taste tiny portions (Telfer declined the grenadine) and then set them to crafting cocktails for their partners, apparently to be available at their reception.

"Will you even have alcohol at the reception?" Hazel asked doubtfully.

"Sure. Laodice drinks, and so do a lot of our friends and family. Why don't you make me a mocktini? I've always wanted to be Cary Grant."

"Okay!" Hazel said, and while she made him a dirty mocktini, heavy on the olive juice, he tried to draw her out on what she thought of Halcyon. It was difficult. She didn't exactly lack personality, but her own thoughts and desires were buried under a heavy layer of "Jesse likes" and "Jesse thinks." It wasn't until Telfer made a chance remark about Halcyon's attempts to imitate a medieval castle that Hazel got animated on her own behalf.

"It's definitely much more of a historicist castle, like Neuschwanstein," she said. "Castle romanticism was huge in the 1800s, and those are what we think of when we picture the typical fairy-tale castles, but they're really not medieval at all."

"No?"

"No, real medieval castles were designed to hold off besieging armies. Most of them were square stone keeps, not pretty at all. Unless we're talking about the motte-and-bailey style, of course, where the keep might be wood. People used to think that they switched to stone because it was better militarily, but now we think it might have been more about prestige. Stone looked more impressive, it was more expensive, and it lasted longer."

"Really," Telfer said. "Do you want some of this hibiscus syrup?"

"Sure!"

"Tell me more about motte-and-bailey," he said, and Hazel happily embarked on a detailed and enthusiastic description of English castle warfare in the civil war between King Stephen and Empress Matilda, while Telfer listened and made her a floral concoction. He had no idea what it tasted like, but it smelled good, and Hazel's thanks seemed sincere. His own mocktini was nice; gin without alcohol tasted dry and herbal, and it went well with the briny olive juice. It was a bit like drinking mezze in a glass.

Samuel was apparently also a history buff, and he joined the conversation to talk about the post-Anarchy rebuilding phase, and that started a round of historical-places-we-have-been. Telfer made his own unexciting contribution (Colonial Williamsburg) and Yvette got passionate about Angkor Wat and the royal palace at Phnom Penh.

Telfer barely noticed Patrick slipping away, but he saw him return quarter of an hour later, looking unsettled. He pulled Samuel away from the discussion and they exchanged a few words before bidding the others good night and heading upstairs together.

"Another round?" Kyle said. "You want to give your guests options."

"Sure!" Hazel said immediately, and Telfer couldn't bring himself to disappoint her, making a game of seeing how many garnishes he could fit on Hazel's next drink.

He couldn't help wishing that Laodice was there.

***

Laodice had really meant to follow the strictures of the retreat as closely as she could. She'd needed internet to upload her notes and observations, and she wasn't quite willing to lose complete track of the outside world. But so far she'd used the burner phone strictly for work and for figuring out the time. She hadn't loaded any apps on it before she came, not even her ebook reader.

It wouldn't be in the spirit of the retreat for her to violate those rules any further.

She finished the last of the cashews from Telfer's satchel and decided that she was totally going to do it anyway.

It took a moment to work out how to log into her group chat from her laptop, and a much longer moment to get through password verification—her own phone, which she'd normally use to confirm the approach, was tucked in that box downstairs. Laodice persevered through the security questions instead, and was even more relieved than she expected when she found her sisters already talking in the chat about a trip Xena was planning to take to the boutique vineyard Cassie's partner ran.

[Cassie] The carriage house is booked out, but Manny says you're family, so you get to stay in the main house.

[Xena] can I film in the main house?

[Cassie] Nice try.

[Xena] pleeeeeease?

[Laodice is active in chat]

[Xena] shes alive!

[Cassie] How's the retreat going?

[Laodice] It's interesting. Not what I expected

[Cassie] Oh?

[Laodice] Let me think about it a bit more. I think my story's going to be different from the one I thought I'd write

[Cassie] What does Eli think of it?

Laodice sat back against the pillows, momentarily surprised. But of course her sisters didn't know she'd broken up with Eli. She hadn't spoken to them since it had happened.

[Laodice] He's not here. Long story short, he tried to get out of the trip at the last minute so he could hang out with his fucking boys

[Cassie] He what

[Xena] dump him

[Laodice] I did.

[Xena] GOOD

[Xena] he was a dick

[Xena] and he looked like he'd be bad in bed

Laodice cackled, the sound obnoxiously loud to her own ears in the silent room.

[Laodice] Unfortunately, he was pretty good at that

[Xena] sounds fake but okay

[Cassie] Are you okay?

[Laodice] Actually yes

[Laodice] Maybe it's because this place is surreal, but I don't miss him at all

[Laodice] Is that weird? Am I heartless? I loved him, and now I just don't

[Cassie] Do you want advice?

Laodice hesitated. She loved her sister, but Cassie was a professional advice-giver and she didn't mince words, even for family. Laodice should only say yes if she was willing to listen.

[Laodice] Go ahead

[Cassie] I think you didn't love Eli any more.

[Cassie] I think you fell for him fast, and fell out of love slowly, over the last couple of months. The last time I came into the city you barely mentioned him. You were way more interested in talking about whether you should apply for Miriam's job and if Telfer Terzi might beat you to it. Eli didn't come up until you talked about the retreat.

[Cassie] And that's super normal. Lots of people fall for someone, and then it doesn't work out. They drift apart or they pretend they're going to be friends or whatever. But I think that because you go so hard and feel so much, maybe you needed a big dramatic moment to realize it was over.

[Xena] cassie you are the worst when you're right

[Xena] the absolute worst

[Cassie] L? Are you there?

[Laodice] I'm thinking.

[Laodice] I don't think you're *completely* right. I was already starting to realize he wasn't my forever guy.

[Laodice] I mayyyyyy have been thinking that the retreat might have nailed things down one way or the other

[Laodice] but yeah. Throwing a frog at him was a good clarifying moment

[Cassie] Real frog or ceramic?

[Xena] pls say real

[Laodice] Ceramic, sorry

[Xena] boo

[Xena] wait, who are you there with then?

[Laodice] a co-worker

[Xena] who?

Laodice bit her lip. She had, over the years, said some things that recent revelations might have shown her in a different light. But Xena was like a terrier. She didn't let go once she'd grabbed something. She had no sense of shame and not a lot of regard for other people's feelings.

[Laodice] Telfer Terzi

[Cassie] Seriously? I thought he was your nemesis.

[Xena] is he the fatphobic one?

[Laodice] He's not fatphobic

[Xena] you said he stared at you in a disapproving way when you wore crop tops

[Laodice] Turns out I might have been mistaking something else for disapproval.

[Cassie] HAH

[Cassie] He likes you. I *knew* it.

[Laodice] you did not!!

[Cassie] I watched you two interact for maybe three minutes total and there were definitely sparks

[Laodice] sparks of rage!

[Xena] i love this

[Xena] are you smashing the nemesis

There was a light knock on the door, and Laodice shoved the phone under a pillow. "Hello?" she called.

There was no reply.

Housekeeping, probably. Wait, she should seize a chance to talk to one of the alleged many staff who were allegedly staying out of sight. Laodice hopped off the bed, her knees protesting at their sudden unfolding. When she opened the door and scanned the corridor, it was empty. Not even a handcart filled with toiletries and cleaning supplies.

Strange. But she wouldn't be surprised if Sarah was behind it. She was fully capable of making housekeeping hide if there was the smallest possibility of a guest having to acknowledge their existence.

She went back to the conversation, which had continued in her momentary absence.

[Xena] you have to tell us if you're smashing the nemesis

[Xena] it's the rules of feminism

[Xena] hellooooo???

[Laodice] We came as *co-workers*. We're *pretending* to be a couple.

[Laodice] Howeverrrr this afternoon a sexy times offer was made, and also rejected

[Cassie] To whom?

[Xena] fuck I love you cassie. "Whom." amazing.

[Laodice] He made the offer. Quote: "I think you're very attractive. I've thought that since the moment I met you."

[Xena] holy shit

[Xena] love confession

[Laodice] No, he was clear that romance was off the table. Sex only.

[Xena] SINCE THE MOMENT I MET YOU is love language

[Laodice] I think he's just precise

[Xena] do it.

[Xena] hot nemesis sex

[Xena] working HARD late nights in the office

[Xena] meet me at the photocopier in 2 mins

[Xena] (so you can bend me over it)

[Cassie] I don't think that's a good idea.

[Xena] BOOOOO don't listen to her

[Xena] listen to me, the fun one

[Cassie] You work literally five feet from each other in the same office.

[Laodice] okay wait a second

[Laodice] YOU banged your BOSS while you were LIVING on his PROPERTY

[Cassie] That was a short term contract with a definite end date.

[Laodice] And now you LIVE TOGETHER

[Cassie] Fine, I'm a hypocrite, but you're talking about a relationship where one of you is soon going to directly report to the other, *indefinitely*. If Olympus's HR policy doesn't ban that, they damn well should. It's actually pretty bad that he even proposed it.

[Laodice] I'm not talking about a relationship!

[Laodice] And he *proposed* a one night stand, *explicitly*. He's not trying to start an inappropriate longterm thing with his future boss!

[Xena] you're defending him

[Xena] that's cute

[Xena] also I like that you're assuming you're going to be the editor, very girlboss of you

Laodice rubbed the sore spot between her eyes. She could *feel* Cassie marshaling sensible objections from her beautiful office in the historic home she shared with her partner. What right did Cassie have to give Laodice advice on this particular point, anyway? When Cassie had baulked at her growing attraction to Manny, Laodice had told her to go for it, and that had worked out *incredibly* well.

Besides, there seemed to be an important detail both of her sisters had missed.

[Laodice] You can both stop talking about this. I said no, remember? He said, that's cool. He won't bring it up again. End of topic.

[Cassie] I'm sorry.

[Xena] i'm not

[Laodice] ANYWAY what's going in YOUR love lives?

[Cassie] Manny and I continue to live happily in sin and our mothers continue to press us for wedding dates

[Xena] i might take some of the mom pressure off you soon

[Laodice] how?

[Xena] shh it's a surprise

[Xena] watch my channel Wednesday

[Laodice] I might not be able to.

[Xena] you have to

[Xena] im gonna break the internet

[Cassie] What are you planning?

[Xena] it's a surprise!!!

[Cassie] Are you and Zac adopting a pet or something?

[Xena] S.U.R.P.R.I.S.E.

[Cassie] I'm just saying, puppies are cute and Mom will absolutely lose her mind, but you both travel a lot

[Xena] CASSANDRA APOLLINE TROIADES DO YOU KNOW WHAT SURPRISE MEANS

[Xena] anyway I have to go byeeee!!!!

[Xena is inactive in the chat]

[Laodice] I have to go too

She logged out, still annoyed with Cassie. It was unlike her sister to miss the salient facts, such as the part that she'd turned Telfer down, and he'd said he wouldn't bring it up again, so if she *did* want to take him up on it, *she'd* have to make a move, and she obviously wasn't going to.

It was nice that he thought she was attractive. It had been kind of fun, working with him on this story, bouncing ideas off him and talking out Halcyon's oddities. They might even become casual work acquaintances. Friendly colleagues.

Anything more than that was impossible. Cassie was right. Xena was wrong.

Whatever Xena was planning was sure to be spectacular, though. She'd have to remember to get online on Wednesday.

Laodice rolled off the bed, filled with a restless energy she couldn't contain. She tried to pour it into some flow yoga, and when that didn't work, attempted to soothe herself with another luxurious bath.

And if her fingers slipped beneath the water and through her intimate folds while she had some hazy thoughts about being bent over a photocopier by a dark-haired man whose face she determinedly did not picture...

Well. There were some things she *didn't* tell her sisters.

Clean and warm and finally relaxed, Laodice crawled into bed already half-asleep, and barely registered the soft sounds of someone moving around the room later that evening.

She did jerk partly awake when there was a crash and a loud curse.

"Telfer?"

"Yes?"

"Are you trying to get ready for bed without turning the light on?" She felt heavy and slow, as if sleep was dragging her back under.

"I didn't want to wake you," Telfer said. "It seemed like a logical choice a few minutes ago."

Laodice burrowed deeper into the covers. "Lots of things seem like that," she said drowsily. "And then you think, oops, maybe I was wrong. Like you and me."

There was a pause.

"Laodice?"

"Mm?"

"What do you mean?"

"I don't know," she mumbled. "Come to bed."

Another pause, so long that she was nearly asleep before any response came. "Okay," Telfer said, his voice softer than she'd ever heard. "Good night."

Chapter Nine

Telfer woke up flat on his back with a dead arm and tried to make sense of where he was and why he was so hot.

He was definitely on his side of the bed, having firmly fixed in his mind before he went to sleep that he wasn't going to wander. There had been no migration to the middle for him this time.

Laodice, on the other hand, had apparently breached the invisible boundary with no thought at all for the sanctity of borders. Fully half of her body was sprawled on his, which was the reason for his dead arm, his high temperature, and his rampant erection.

Her head was lying on his chest, her hair spilling over his threadbare t-shirt. He could feel her warm breath puff out with every exhale. One of her arms was flung across his stomach. His t-shirt had ridden up there, and the soft flesh of her inner arm was pressing against his bare skin. Her open hand had fallen so that the pads of her fingers brushed his side every time he breathed. One of her thighs lay heavily over his, inches from his throbbing cock.

Telfer held his breath until his vision started to go fuzzy. That was obviously a short-term solution, but maybe he could make himself pass out. Then she might wake up and remove herself and he could pretend he'd never noticed.

Laodice snuggled closer, her hand tightening possessively on his waist. Or not.

"Hey," he said, exhaling.

She mumbled something and pressed her face into his chest. He felt the light touch of her lips. The sensation sent a lightning bolt straight to his cock, and he nearly levitated straight off the bed.

"Wake up," he said urgently, no longer worried about saving face for either of them.

"Mm?" Laodice said, and turned to look up at him, still resting on his chest. Her sleepy smile as she blinked herself awake clutched at his heart.

Then her eyes widened as consciousness struck like a hammer blow.

"Argh!" she said, and scrambled backwards to the edge of the bed and then off it. "I'm sorry! I'm so sorry!"

Telfer sat up, making sure his groin was covered in rumpled bed clothes. "It's okay," he said, gingerly testing his numb arm. It prickled in a way that promised to be even more unpleasant in a moment.

Laodice's face and throat were deep pink, and she seemed to be having trouble making eye contact. "I really am sorry."

"It really is okay. Tonight we can—" He hesitated, trying to come up with a solution that would keep them apart in their sleep. This was difficult, because what he really wanted to do was tumble her back into bed and see how far down that blush went.

"We can build a pillow barrier! Xena and I used to do that when we stayed in motels with our parents, because otherwise she kicked me, and Cassie always got the foldout bed because she was the oldest and—" She took a deep breath. Her breasts bounced under that damn t-shirt. "Pillow barrier. It'll work."

It probably would. What a shame.

"You can have the bathroom first," he said, because he wasn't getting up until the blood had a chance to return to his brain, and Laodice sputtered agreement and got moving. After the door had closed, Telfer realized he'd missed his shot to take matters in hand. Touching himself in the shower was only barely acceptable. He certainly couldn't jerk off in the bed they shared.

He imagined that for a second—moving his hand up and down, giving his wrist that twist he really liked—with the exciting addition of Laodice watching, eyes narrowed in concentration, as if she were taking notes for later use. Then he clenched his eyes and hands and got up. Not everything went away if you ignored it, but erections would.

As he dressed, he realized what he should have noticed earlier. He'd woken up of his own accord, with no Sarah-alarm. And he'd been able to see Laodice perfectly well in the light that was coming into the room through the drapes. He pulled them back and stared out the window. Bright daylight, and a well-risen sun.

It took some searching, but he found the burner phone on the dressing table, between a bottle of lotion and a tangle of earrings.

It was nearly 9 a.m.

Laodice emerged from the bathroom, still a little pink. She was wearing loose linen slacks and a tight peach crop top with big puffy sleeves, and Telfer was seized by the momentary urge to lick her bared stomach.

"Sarah didn't wake us," she said. "Did we miss it? What time is it?"

"I was thinking the same thing," Telfer said, and tossed her the phone.

She checked the time, her eyebrows popping, then dropped the phone in her pocket. "That's weird. Let's snoop."

There were no sounds of anyone else stirring as they walked down the corridor. Telfer wasn't surprised. The cocktail class had become a bar hang once Patrick and Samuel had gone, and it had been after midnight when he'd got back to the room. People were probably making up for lost sleep from the previous early mornings.

He'd deliberately started a round of reminiscence about the old days with Carrick, hoping to find some insight into Jesse's blackmail attempt. Carrick had been reasonable casual company in college, but Telfer, with some surprise, had discovered that he actually liked this older version. They even listened to some of the same podcasts. At one point during the night, Telfer had noticed Britt's indulgent expression, and realized that he and Carrick had been gossiping about the behind-the-scenes dramas of one of their favorite shows for nearly thirty minutes straight.

So it was Carrick and Britt's door he stopped outside, rapping lightly on the wood.

After a few moments, Britt poked her head out, her red hair sleep-rumpled. She was wearing thick glasses, through which she squinted at him suspiciously.

"What's up?"

"It's late," Telfer said. "We were wondering if maybe we missed the call for breakfast and meditation."

Britt frowned, more thoughtful than annoyed. "I didn't hear any-thing."

"Well, see you down there," Laodice said cheerfully.

Telfer followed her lead, and stepped carefully going down the stairs. He could hear muffled voices, but no one seemed to be in the magical amplification spot that would carry the noise to them clearly.

Then he heard Kyle, briefly clear. "—cancel on us, we're fucked."

Sarah's voice, dismissive: "It's not a problem. These people are—" and then it was inaudible again.

The contempt in Sarah's voice had been palpable, and Telfer had a strong suspicion who she'd been referring to as "these people."

Laodice kept moving, her wary expression smoothing out into something blandly happy, and Telfer did his best to emulate her. "Good morning!" she caroled, as they approached the little lounge.

Sarah and Kyle both startled. They were carrying wide, flat boxes emblazoned with the logo of a Hippocampus patisserie that had gone viral a few years back, and Kyle grabbed for his as it began to tip. Sarah recovered faster, turning her corporate smile on like a flashlight.

"Good morning, love doves!" she cried. "Hope you enjoyed your lie-in!"

"It was great," Laodice said. "Wow, is that breakfast?"

"Brunch! We thought we'd give you a little treat."

"No meditation this morning?"

"Nope." She gave Telfer a playful look, as artificial as the flowers on the reception desk. "You can even have coffee, Mister Caffeine Fiend. I'll go call the others now." She ruthlessly dumped her box on top of Kyle's and bustled off.

In the gallery dining room, Danielle was laying out plates and cutlery. Laodice offered to help Kyle with the boxes, shooting Telfer a look. More flirting, he figured, and wandered over to help Danielle instead.

"You don't have to," she said, but she looked grateful.

"I can handle napkins," he said. "What's with the late start?"

"I don't know," she confessed. "I thought I'd overslept, but Sarah said it was fine. Normally she makes sure I'm up on time."

"You sleep on-site? You don't have a phone alarm or anything?"

Danielle shook her head. "We can't have phones. Sarah says the guests might find them distracting."

She sounded uncertain about it, and Telfer was once again aware of how young she was—about nineteen or twenty, he thought. Cutting employees off from phone access in their non-working hours seemed like a huge overreach to him, but maybe to someone in her first job it felt like the way things were.

"Good morning, love doves!" Sarah's voice boomed over the speakers. She'd evidently decided that a good cutesy couple title was worth repeating. "Join us in the gallery room for a scrumptious brunch!"

"Would you mind finishing this?" Danielle asked. "I have to go get the drinks."

"Go for it," Telfer said, and finished setting the table. Laodice was smiling and tossing her hair as she and Kyle laid out a selection of fruit and pastries, but it was taking him a while to warm up to her. Kyle was an idiot, Telfer decided. If Laodice was looking at him that way, he'd warm up immediately.

He took his normal seat, just as Sarah came in and saw Laodice helping.

"Oh, you don't have to do that!' she said, sounding genuinely appalled. "You're a guest!"

"I wanted first pick of the treats," Laodice said, and picked up a plate to prove it.

Danielle came back in, carefully balancing a huge coffee pot, and Telfer made a straight line for it. His was black, and Laodice liked milk, no sugar. He carried both mugs over to the table.

Laodice sat down beside him, and slid a blueberry Danish onto his plate. "Have you seen any other staff?" she asked quietly.

Telfer shook his head, and took a bite. Tart blueberries and sweet, smooth custard took all his attention for a moment. Flakes of buttery pastry drifted down to land on his shirt, and he brushed them away. A futile gesture, because he immediately took another bite. He was *starving*.

Laodice was staring at his mouth.

"Is something wrong?" he asked.

She started. "No, you're fine."

"With the staff," he clarified.

"Right. There aren't any." She shot Kyle a cautious look. "I think Kyle's been doubling as the chef, and Danielle isn't just Sarah's assistant. I think she's doing housekeeping as well."

"Danielle lives on site," Telfer contributed, his voice equally low. "And she isn't allowed to have a phone."

Laodice's jaw tightened, but she stopped talking as Danielle poured more coffee and Britt and Carrick joined them at the table. The others drifted in shortly afterwards, except for Jesse and Hazel.

Hazel appeared alone as the meal was wrapping up, slipping into the room with her head bowed. There was no trace of the animated young woman who'd discussed siege warfare so avidly the night before.

"Is Jesse's headache still bad?" Patrick asked meaningfully.

"Yes," Hazel said.

Patrick exchanged a look with Samuel. "Because I'd really like to continue a discussion we started yesterday."

Hazel looked blank. "Well, he's asleep," she said, and reached for a muffin. She'd barely taken a bite when Sarah took her place at the head of the table.

"All right!" she said. "As you've probably guessed, things are a little different this morning! We haven't scheduled a class, and the weather is glorious. This is a wonderful time for you to wander around the Halcyon gardens. Features include the enclosed herb and vegetable garden, the rose walk and the hedge pleasaunce. and I encourage you to pair off and go your own way, delighting in each other and the joys of nature."

This wasn't the schedule Kyle had given Laodice, but Telfer kept his mouth shut and clapped politely with the others. If nothing else, wandering the gardens would give him and Laodice a real chance to talk.

***

"Okay, so Halcyon's a scam," Laodice said, the second they were alone. She'd deliberately taken Telfer away from the others, and they were wandering around the herb garden, enclosed by a low woven wood fence. The little plots held a number of plants she could identify—rosemary, purple sage, several kinds of thyme—and more she couldn't.

In case anyone came around the corner, she was holding his hand.

"Absolutely a scam," Telfer agreed. "Wage-skimming?"

Say what she would about Telfer, it was a real pleasure to have someone along who could keep up with her. Eli would have needed everything explained from first principles before he'd take her seriously.

"That's my read too," she said. "Sarah's put a lot of imaginary employees on the books, and she's skimming their salaries. The others get a cut to stay quiet. They probably don't see anything wrong with it, if the work gets done. But of course, the work isn't getting done. A place like this needs a real staff." She pointed. "Look at those weeds. If someone was doing the maintenance before, they're not now."

"I think Kyle and Sarah are the real culprits. Danielle seems like a nice girl with a bad job."

"Oh sure, the cute girl with the big eyes is the innocent one."

"Does she strike you as a criminal mastermind?" Telfer asked, looking down his nose.

"Well, neither do Sarah and Kyle," Laodice pointed out. "Criminals, yes, but masterminds, no. They're being pretty obvious about it. I'm ninety-nine percent certain Kyle's bringing in most of the food from outside. Almost everything we've eaten is platters or stuff that could be reheated. I think that if we hadn't seen those pastry boxes this morning, no one would have mentioned where they came from."

Telfer looked frustrated. "It's so short-sighted. They can't possibly keep it up long-term. And this place could make real money if it were run well."

"Would it make money for them, though?" Laodice asked. "Hospitality employees aren't hotel owners. Maybe they figure they'll get a big payday and get out before they get caught."

"With the bonus of Sarah trying to get us to sign up for her enlightenment program?"

Laodice shrugged. "Like I said, not a criminal mastermind. Maybe she's multi-tasking. But you're the one who got the lead on this project. Is there any possibility it goes further up?"

"Halcyon is technically run by a shell company to reduce the liability. I got the lead from a contact in the business that's actually funding the venture. The project's his baby." He thought about it for a second. "He's not the most honest guy in the world, but I don't think he'd go for a penny-ante wage-skimming scheme."

"Right. And if he did, would he be dumb enough to tip off his friend, the journalist?"

Telfer snorted, which Laodice took as answer enough. "So where did the money for Halcyon come from?" she asked.

Telfer looked at her sidelong. "You're not going to like it."

"Okay. Tell me anyway."

"Argive Holdings."

Laodice tried to maintain her expression, but Telfer nodded. "I've noticed you tense up whenever Argive is mentioned. I don't know the specifics of your distaste, but it's a big company with a lot of divisions. Real estate, construction, hotels. Not a lot of specific wedding stuff, but Bran— my source works in Events, and that department's expanded fast over the last couple of years, under a new Vice President. They're being encouraged to throw money at the wall and see what sticks. My guy found the house and land going for a song and talked his boss into setting up Halcyon." He paused. "Actually, I think he did it based on a conversation the two of us had about gaps in the luxe wedding industry. I thought he was paying more attention than usual."

Laodice stopped. "This retreat was your idea? He took your concept and didn't give you any credit?"

"I wouldn't go that far," Telfer said, though he looked pleased. "I hadn't gotten much further than considering if there might be a market. He's the one who made it happen, with Argive's resources behind him. But I suppose he felt beholden enough to offer me the lead."

Laodice was still indignant on Telfer's behalf. "Which would benefit him too, if he's under pressure to get good press."

"Oh, he definitely thinks a feature in *Goddess* will make his mark. I'm certain he didn't even tell his boss he was sending a journalist. He's the kind of person who loves a dramatic reveal."

"And if it's a story about rich couples getting ripped off?"

Telfer shrugged. "He'll probably disavow any knowledge of the naughty journalists sneaking into his special project and do his best to cover his tracks. The problem with high risk, high reward is that people always underestimate the risks. But you're right. I don't think he'd commit crimes, and then invite me to discover them."

"Who's his boss? The VP, I mean."

"Dammond Argive," Telfer said, and raised a finger when she twitched again. "There it goes."

"Your source isn't Carrick, right?"

"No, Carrick works in Finance. Bookkeeping and compliance, mostly."

"Are you going to join him if you don't get Miriam's job?"

"I doubt it," Telfer said. "Although it might be worth considering, if you get the job and fire me."

Laodice laughed. "I wouldn't fire you!"

"You wouldn't?"

"You're very good at your job," Laodice said. "Why would I start an editorial position by getting rid of my best asset? I assumed you'd stop working for Bridal, because you wouldn't agree with my direction for the department. But you could transfer to any other Olympus title instead of going to Argive. They'd all be clamoring for you."

Telfer looked startled. "Huh. That's useful information."

"Well, okay. Are you going to tell your friend we think he's getting ripped off?" She held her breath. It was probably the right thing to do, but her journalistic instinct was ringing like a chime.

There was a pause. "Not...yet," Telfer said.

Laodice beamed at him. "Awesome. Why not?"

"At this stage we only have suspicions." He gave her a sidelong glance. "And you want the story. Whatever the story turns out to be."

"I sure do," Laodice said, and tossed her hair back.

Telfer hesitated. "You realize that a scam reveal won't be published in *Goddess*, right?"

"I don't see why it couldn't be." She smiled at him. "As you keep saying, weddings are big business. We don't have to be all hearts and flowers."

"Miriam will spike it," Telfer predicted. "But you might be able to pitch the story to *New Argus* or *Vanguard*."

"That's a really good idea," Laodice said, and turned up the wattage on her smile.

"You don't need to flirt with me," Telfer said sharply. "I already said I won't tell."

Laodice opened her mouth to protest when she realized two things. One, she had definitely been flirting, and after she'd woken up sprawled all over him, to boot. Two, Telfer was squeezing her hand urgently, tilting his head as if he heard something.

Their wandering had brought them past the herb garden, and to some paved pathways, lined with high hedges set at right angles. Telfer was right to shut her up; anyone could be behind those hedges, listening.

It seemed that Yvette had finally got Hazel alone to talk. Their voices were a little muffled from behind the hedges, but from the tone of their conversation, they hadn't heard Telfer and Laodice approaching.

Laodice stepped off the gravel and onto the grass verge, sneaking a few steps closer. Telfer was right behind her, apparently of the same mind.

"It's not all the time," Hazel was saying, her voice small. "I wish you could see what he's like normally. He's so wonderful."

Yvette's voice was calm. "I bet he is. Especially after he's yelled or frozen you out or broken something that belongs to you, right?"

There was a pause. "He would never hit me," Hazel said. She sounded caught between defiance and trembling hope. "I'm sure he'd never hit me."

If you've had to calculate the odds on that, it's already gone too far, Laodice thought, feeling sick. She glanced at Telfer, who was looking grim.

"I kept saying that too," Yvette said steadily. "Right up until he hit me."

Hazel gasped.

"And then I said, it was only once, and he's really sorry. Twice and he's really sorry, but I made him so mad. And then he kept hitting, and he eventually stopped apologizing, and then it was always my fault, no matter what I did."

Laodice concentrated on breathing without making a sound. Sometimes eavesdropping was journalistic curiosity, and sometimes it was a violation of trust. Maybe Yvette wouldn't mind them knowing. But maybe she very much would.

"Is it Xavier?" Hazel said. She sounded affronted on Yvette's behalf, so maybe there was hope.

"No," Yvette said, her voice sure and strong. "This was someone a few years ago. I left him."

"Good," Hazel said. "But Jesse doesn't—"

Yvette's voice ran over hers. "I left him several times, but I made the last time stick. It took a while, and it was hard work, and I would never have made it without help, so I am telling you, Hazel, if you think there's no one who will help you, *think again*. Because if I can let you skip even a month or two of what I went through getting away from him, I'll do it. If you need a place to stay, or money, or a lawyer, I swear I've got your back."

Go, Yvette, Laodice thought.

"I—" Hazel said, and her voice cracked.

Yvette's voice gained intensity. "You don't have to say anything right now. I know you're probably not in the place where you can ask for help. You're probably still hoping that it will work out, that when he promises to change that he means it. But you can ask me tomorrow, or eight years from now, and I'll do it. I will do *anything* to help you. And I want you to remember this, the *first* time he hits you." There was a rustling sound, presumably Yvette getting to her feet.

Hazel was making muffled, soft noises.

"Also, my official legal advice is that you don't marry him," Yvette added, sounding more clinical and less impassioned. "Divorce is an administrative nightmare, even if you do get half."

Hazel mumbled something, and Yvette said "*What?*" and sat down again with an audible thump.

"I said we're already married," Hazel said, snuffling, and Telfer grabbed Laodice's arm and hustled her away.

"Hey," she muttered in protest, but then she heard what he had, the voices of Samuel and Patrick floating through the garden towards them. They rounded the corner and saw Patrick animatedly explaining to Samuel why the roses weren't going to make it.

"Poor soil condition and bad transplant technique," he was saying, waving at a bush covered in healthy-looking pink blooms. "This bed wasn't designed for roses at all. I'd say they ripped out whatever was there and put these bushes in a week or two before we arrived. Absolutely *no* forward planning, and they're going to die without some serious care. Which they're obviously not getting."

Samuel looked at him fondly. "Well, don't volunteer, sweetheart. We're guests, remember?"

"I'd rather fertilize this garden than spend another minute in a meditation session," Patrick said, snorting. "At least you can zone out and mentally go through lines of code. I'm just sitting there while my ass goes numb and I think about all the mean things anyone's ever said about me."

"How's it going?" Telfer called as they drew closer, pitching his voice louder than it needed to be. Laodice squeezed his hand in appreciation.

"Good," Patrick said. "Well, not entirely good, Samuel is experiencing symptoms of serious internet withdrawal, but other than that."

"You should have let me keep my laptop," Samuel said, his voice mock mournful. "I could have broken into the staff Wi-Fi in no time."

Patrick pouted dramatically. "No, no, we are focusing on each *other*, not our screens."

"We're enjoying the focus time too," Laodice said. Out of the corner of her eye she spotted Yvette, striding towards the front of the hotel, looking like a woman on a mission.

"Yes," Telfer said. "I feel like we're getting to learn so much more about each other."

Which... Okay, yes, that was actually true. She now knew Telfer's favorite movie, his favorite dessert, and that dancing in public made him self-conscious.

Also, that he thinks you're hot.

"We're learning about our fellow guests, too," she said. "You guys are great, and it's been nice for Telfer to catch up with Carrick again and meet Britt."

"Do you know what Britt does?" Samuel asked. "I figured she was independently wealthy, but Patrick thinks—"

"—she's a cop," Patrick said, folding his arms.

Laodice blinked at him. "Really?"

"Believe me, Elle, if you'd been to as many protests as I have, you'd know it too. Even when they wear the right shoes and take off the body armor, there's still that ineffable cop aura. She's got it." He looked at Samuel. "Sammy thinks I'm being paranoid."

"I didn't say that. I said that police officers probably don't earn enough for this kind of thing."

"Then Carrick's the one paying," Patrick said impatiently. "I mean, you're paying for me. Elle's paying for Telfer, right?"

"Um," Telfer said.

"Patrick," Samuel said, a note of warning in his voice.

"Oh, come on. Money's this huge and powerful thing that exerts an incredible force on every aspect of our life, and we're not supposed to talk about it who has it and who doesn't?" Patrick spread his hands. "That gives it *more* power!"

Laodice pretty much agreed with him, but she wasn't sure that Elle would. "The trip was a gift from my dad." Telfer's hand tightened on hers, and she hoped that she hadn't contradicted something he'd already said. Well, he could always claim that he'd been embarrassed to admit it.

Patrick looked triumphant. "So your *dad* has money."

"He says he's 'comfortable,'" Laodice said, and nodded when Patrick's eyes lit up. "Which is, yes, code for rich." She flapped at her face, wishing she'd thought to pack a hat. "I don't suppose either of you has any sunscreen?"

"Here, honey," Patrick said, and handed her a tube. "They say black don't crack, but I'm not letting that UV in."

"You must spend a lot of time outside, too," Laodice said, smearing the goop on with relief.

Patrick sighed. "Not as much as I used to. I do a lot of my work in the office, these days."

"Too successful for his own good," Samuel said, and poked him. "Speaking of people with money."

"What do you think of these gardens?" Telfer asked.

Patrick took the change of subject with grace and embarked on a lengthy explanation of exactly how badly Halcyon's landscaper had screwed up. Laodice listened with half an ear, noting the moment when Hazel reemerged from her hiding place and went back to the castle, her head down.

"Hello, lovers!" Sarah's voice said, stridently cutting through the warm air.

"There are speakers outside?" Telfer asked, eyeing their surroundings.

Samuel pointed at a lamp post near the pagoda. "There. Speakers everywhere. But no cameras, weirdly enough."

Sarah had continued, oblivious to the byplay, inviting them in to lunch.

"Time to go inside, children, playtime's over," Samuel murmured. "It feels like we just had breakfast."

Patrick nudged him. "Come on, Jesse might be there."

"Why do you guys want to talk to Jesse?" Laodice asked.

Samuel and Patrick exchanged glances. "We better," Patrick said. "What if he tried it on them too?"

"Tried what?" Telfer said.

"He snuck into our room," Patrick said.

"What? When?"

"During the cocktail thing last night, when he supposedly had a headache. I went upstairs to grab a sweater, because of that damn air conditioning, and he was there. He tried to pretend like he'd mixed up the doors and come in accidentally, but I had to walk halfway down the hall, and I'd have seen him go in if he'd made a mistake. As it was, he had plenty of time to recognize he was in the wrong place."

"And afterwards, I found this stuck under the coffee table." Samuel fished in the front pocket of his jeans and withdrew a small round object, about half an inch across. It looked like a little silver coin, but Telfer inhaled sharply.

"Is that a bug?" he said.

"Yeah." Samuel looked at the object with contempt. "A cheap one. Battery-operated, transmitting to something close by. I'd check your room for them too."

"I was in the room all night," Laodice said, remembering that soft scratch on the door with a chill. What if that had been Jesse, testing to see if anyone was in there? "He couldn't have planted anything."

"Oh, that's right," Samuel said.

"But why would he bug your room?" Laodice asked.

"Blackmail," Telfer said.

Samuel looked puzzled. "I was thinking more like corporate espionage," he said. "I've got some fairly big deals coming up, and confidentiality is key. But I always get an exception in NDAs to talk to Patrick."

Patrick looked at him fondly. "Even though I don't understand a word."

"You're my rubber duck," Samuel said, and kissed him.

"Have you told anyone else?" Telfer asked. "Told Sarah?"

Patrick shook his head. "We probably should," he admitted. "But we want to talk to Jesse first. Maybe he's got a better explanation."

"And we don't want the backlash to fall on Hazel," Samuel said softly, and all four of them were silent for a moment.

"There's probably not much you can do to avoid that," Laodice said. "I get the feeling that no matter what happens—"

"I know," Patrick said. "I hate this. I feel like I'm watching a car crash in slow motion. Can't we do something?"

"She's got to want to leave," Samuel said, his eyes dark with some memory of his own. "It would be good if she can get out before the wedding, but an engagement is a lot of pressure."

Telfer squeezed Laodice's hand. She didn't need the warning. Telling them that Hazel and Jesse were already married would raise more questions they couldn't answer.

Patrick sighed. "So, in the meantime..." He brought his hands together. "Smash."

***

Lunch was several platters of pre-prepared sandwiches and salads, and Jesse didn't attend that either. Hazel was also absent. Patrick and Samuel exchanged glances.

"Could I have a tray or something?" Laodice asked suddenly. "I'll take some lunch up to Hazel and Jesse."

"Danielle can do that," Sarah said.

Laodice was already putting a plate together. "No, it's fine,"

"I'll go with you," Telfer said. That was what fiancés did, right? Even if it wasn't, he wasn't going to leave Laodice walking into a room with a potentially violent blackmailer by herself.

He braced himself for argument on the way upstairs, but Laodice was silent, focused on the platter in her hands. He probably should have offered to carry that for her, Telfer realized belatedly. He knocked on the door.

Hazel yanked it open. Her face fell immediately, going from joy to disappointment so quickly Telfer nearly missed the change.

"I thought we'd bring you up some lunch," Laodice said brightly.

Hazel twisted a strand of hair around her finger. "Oh. Thank you." She took the platter without much enthusiasm, then rallied. "That was nice of you."

"Is Jesse here?" Telfer asked.

"Um," Hazel said. "He's...in the bathroom?"

Laodice looked at her. "Is he?" she asked, her voice gentle.

Hazel burst into tears.

"Maybe we should go," Telfer said. He took a step backward, and found his wrist encased in a vise-like grip as Laodice tugged him inside instead. He closed the door behind them and discovered that in the two seconds it had taken to do that, Laodice had divested Hazel of the platter and got her sitting on the bed with one arm around her shoulders.

"Jesse's not here," Hazel said. She wasn't sobbing, but enormous tears kept welling up in her eyes and pouring down her cheeks. Telfer shifted from foot to foot. "He wasn't here when I came up last night."

"Does he do that sometimes?" Laodice asked. "Leave for no reason?"

"Oh no, there's always a reason," Hazel said. "Like I've embarrassed him, or accidentally flirted with one of his friends. He goes away to cool off."

Telfer felt sick.

"Or he's doing it to punish you," Laodice said, and when Hazel jerked, she added, "We overheard you and Yvette talking this morning."

"It's not like that," Hazel said automatically, though Telfer thought there was a hint of doubt in her voice. "I mean, people have a right to stay away if they can't stand to be around you, right?"

It had the cadence of a direct quote, and Telfer's hands clenched involuntarily. He looked around the room for something to do, some kind of action to take.

Jesse and Hazel had been assigned a room with a view of the garden, and that was echoed in their room, which was decorated in spring green, with a giant mural of three scantily clad women dancing in a garden while pudgy children with wings flew overhead.

He spotted the box of tissues on the nightstand and offered them to Hazel, feeling more useless than he could remember feeling in a long time.

"Thank you," she said, giving him a wavering smile.

"Does Jesse often tell you that he can't stand to be around you?" Laodice asked. Telfer could tell she was fighting to keep her voice even.

"Not that often." Hazel wiped her eyes. "And he hardly ever stays away overnight. I'm really worried about him, but I can't even call him! I don't have my phone!"

Laodice grimaced over her head at Telfer, and he grimaced back. Hazel worrying about him was probably precisely what Jesse was aiming for. Or perhaps he'd decided to get out before Patrick and Samuel told Sarah about his snooping, and scaring his wife was an added bonus.

"Do you know his number?" he asked. "Halcyon must have a landline available."

"I think so? But he doesn't have his phone, either."

"Right. I forgot."

"He took his laptop, so if I had my phone I could at least email him."

Laodice's hand went towards her pocket, and then halted. "You could ask Sarah for your phone back," she suggested.

"But then I'd have to tell her why." Hazel bit her lip. "I will. If he's not back by dinner."

"Okay," Laodice said. "I think that's a good plan. And Hazel... I don't want to pressure you, not when you're already under a lot of stress. But I agree with Yvette. What Jesse is doing to you is not okay."

"We do need to talk a few things over," Hazel said, that note of doubt in her voice again.

Laodice closed her eyes briefly, but Telfer thought that was probably as good as it was going to get right now.

"We also heard that you and Jesse are already married?" he said.

Hazel sighed. "We eloped a few months ago. It was very romantic but then we realized we wanted a proper wedding. And we hadn't told anyone, so we're only *legally* married. As far as our families know, the wedding we have will be the real ceremony." She smiled, a dimple popping up in her cheek. "And of course, we wouldn't have been able to come to Halcyon as an old married couple."

The legality was the point Yvette had worried about, not the romance of the "real" wedding. Telfer had some suspicions about who might have pressed for a secret marriage.

Hazel was looking worried. "You won't tell, will you? That we're married, not just engaged."

"No, of course not."

"Thank you for lunch," Hazel said, and hugged Laodice tightly. "Really. I appreciate it."

Laodice hugged her back. "Everything seems worse when you're hungry."

"If you need anything, we're right down the hall," Telfer added.

There was no one watching as they left, but he reached for Laodice's hand, needing a moment of warmth and human connection.

She took it without hesitation.

Chapter Ten

Telfer was quiet after they went back to their room. Laodice was grateful. She was still trying to process what she felt, what the best way to help Hazel would be. If Hazel had written to Ask Cassandra, she knew exactly what Cassie would say: get a safety plan, get a lawyer, get gone.

But the people who wrote those emails had already made a choice to seek some sort of help, even if they weren't admitting that to themselves or thought they weren't worthy of it. Hazel was getting *offers* of help, but she hadn't asked for it yet. The furthest she was willing to go was a tentative agreement that Jesse's behavior wasn't always exemplary.

And they were all working with limited information. What they'd seen of Jesse's abuse was only what they'd overheard and what he'd let slip in public. What was happening out of earshot, behind closed doors, was probably much worse.

For what it was worth, she thought Hazel was telling the truth that Jesse hadn't hit her.

Yet.

"Thank you for not being performative," she said.

Telfer was fiddling with one of the lamps on the nightstand. "What do you mean?"

"You know, being all I hate men like that, I'll punch him right in the face, I'll protect you little lady, he-man stuff." Laodice made a fist and puffed up her chest.

"I do hate men like that, and I do want to punch him in the face," Telfer said calmly. "But I didn't think it would be helpful to say so."

"Right, exactly." Laodice watched him for a minute. "What are you doing?"

"Checking." The lamp came apart in his hands, and he picked over the pieces. A shock of dark hair flopped into his face, and he shoved it back impatiently.

"Checking for—oh. But I was here."

"You were here *last* night," Telfer said. "Who's to say that Jesse didn't sneak in before that?"

"Good point." Laodice rolled off the bed and started looking under tables and in dressers.

An hour or so later, they had to admit defeat. If there were bugs in the room, they couldn't find them.

"I always lock the door," Laodice said suddenly. "Do you?"

"Of course."

"So, what, you were assuming I didn't?"

"No. I was assuming that he'd stolen a master key. Remember when he went into the staff area during that couples quiz thing?"

"Huh." Laodice sat back on her heels and regarded him. "Smart thinking, Mr. Terzi."

"Thank you, Ms...." he hesitated. "Evagora."

"We've already talked about the story a lot in here. I think you can use my real name."

"Laodice," he said, his mouth carefully shaping the syllables.

Laodice's skin tingled. She coughed, stood up, and rolled her shoulders back. "Do you feel kind of cooped up? Going into the gardens was nice, but I don't like all this sitting around while we wait for Sarah to yell at us to start the next thing. Would you mind if I did some yoga?"

"Not at all. But if I may offer another suggestion?"

"Go for it."

"Come with me on a real walk."

Laodice bent in half and touched the carpet then rolled up, feeling her spine settle back into place. "Around the grounds?"

"I was thinking a little further afield," Telfer said. "Out of the range of any speakers, or potential listeners. A nice long walk, where maybe we lose track of the time."

"Telfer Terzi, are you suggesting we break the rules?"

He wasn't precisely smiling, but there was a glint in his eyes, and the corner of his mouth was tilting upwards. "Can't be yelled at if we can't hear the yelling, right?"

Laodice felt temptation tug at her. "I should really attend whatever this evening's thing is. I already missed the cocktail mixing yesterday."

"You already know that's not the story you're writing," Telfer said. "Besides, what are the odds that we'd be doing something weird and borderline intrusive and possibly a grift of some kind?"

"High," Laodice said. "Well over fifty percent. If I want to write *that* story, I should be there for it."

Telfer spread his hands. "Or, counterpoint, we stay away and give Sarah a chance to stew about it. Maybe it gives you a better chance to shake something loose from her."

"You're too good at arguing," Laodice said. "This is how you get Miriam to turn down all my best ideas."

"I don't oppose—" Telfer stopped and leveled a look at her. "Walk, yes or no?"

"Yes," Laodice said, and rummaged through her case to find her walking shoes. Telfer apparently meant to go walking in brogues, but if he was that desperate to escape whatever was planned for the evening, she wasn't going to point it out.

After a quick debate about whether they'd alarm anyone if they disappeared, they left a brief note on the reception desk, which was, of course, unmanned. How many imaginary employees was Sarah drawing wages for? And how long did she think she could keep it up?

***

In Laodice's opinion, the strongest indication that Sarah was criminally incompetent was that she was holding all the classes indoors. At this time of year the city was a sweaty nightmare for anyone but the hardy or overly enthusiastic, too much heat shining from glass and metal skyscrapers, reflecting back from the streets. Sensible city dwellers spent their time scurrying between airconditioned buildings.

But at the top of this hill, with the seabreeze coming up from the bay to rustle through her curls, and the grass diligently soaking up the sun, Laodice was able to relax into the summer. She'd never been a nature girl. Cassie had settled into small town bucolism with shocking ease, and Xena was always off doing her hair-raising physical stunts in gorgeous locales, but Laodice was the city sister. She liked engines and bars and dancing. She'd loved clubbing, before her mid-twenties caught up with her and she couldn't easily shake off a morning hangover anymore. But other than an occasional yoga class in Ida Park, she wasn't into the great outdoors.

Birds she couldn't identify were chirping. An occasional bumblebee buzzed drunkenly over to investigate her top, apparently fooled by the color and voluminous sleeves into thinking she might be a giant flower.

And Telfer walked beside her, in a silence that for once she wasn't reading as irritated or judgmental.

She hadn't been completely wrong about him. He could *be* irritated and judgmental. But she was beginning to think she'd defaulted to that reading too often. Sometimes, he was just quiet.

Without discussing it, they'd wandered out of sight of the main building, tracking through the gardens and following a small trail that led into the wooded area further down the hill. Well, Laodice thought it was a trail, maybe. She wasn't sure how far the Halcyon grounds actually went, but as long as they didn't climb over any fences or go through any gates, she figured they could at least claim plausible ignorance.

The air under the trees was *delicious*. She'd never contemplated whether air could *taste* good before.

Something rustled in the bushes. An animal, maybe. Squirrel? Snakes? Bears?

Probably not bears. But weren't people supposed to make noise when they hiked through the woods, so the animals knew to get out of their way?

"Tell me something about yourself," she said.

"All right," Telfer said, after a barely noticeable hesitation. "My favorite podcast is called Dicing with Danger."

"That doesn't sound financey."

"It's not. It's a long-running table-top role-playing game podcast by four friends."

"What's a...any of that?"

Telfer looked patient. "Like Dungeons and Dragons."

"Do you *play* Dungeons and Dragons?" Laodice asked, her voice rising with incredulity.

"No. I like listening to other people play it. Well, not actually D&D so much, although that's really cornered the audio market. Lately I've been more into Powered by the Apocalypse games, which have an interesting mixed success mechanic and lend themselves more to narrative-focused games. What is it?"

"Shut up," Laodice said. "Shut *up*, you're a secret nerd!"

Telfer looked offended.

"No, for real, this makes you way more interesting." She stared at him, fascinated. "Tell me more things about you. What's your family like?"

"Depends how you think of it," Telfer said. "In terms of blood relations, it's basically me and my uncle. You'd like him; he's a lot like you. He didn't exactly know what to do with me when my parents died, but he basically got everyone he knew to help him out. So I grew up with a lot of honorary uncles and aunts and cousins."

"When—I mean, if you don't mind telling me—"

"I was nine. It was a car crash, very fast, both of them together. Uncle Burak was 24. He probably wasn't ready for a kid, especially not a nine-year-old who didn't really talk for a year, but he stepped up."

He said it so calmly. Laodice couldn't detect even a tremor of pain in his voice. But he wasn't looking at her when he said it, and she could feel a chasm opening beneath her feet.

She side-stepped. "What do you mean, he's a lot like me?"

"He's friendly, and he's sincere about it. I mean, he really likes people. When he's around, they feel good."

"Oh," Laodice said, not sure how she felt about that. Did Telfer mean that he *didn't* like people? Maybe that made his liking someone more valuable. Then her brain caught up to the compliment he'd just paid her. "And thank you. But I'm not sure I could step up like he did. That honestly sounds heroic."

"It was," Telfer said, and then he looked at her directly. Four days ago, she would have thought he was looking down his impressive nose, measuring her against some rigid rubric of success and finding her wanting. Now it seemed like he was paying attention. "And you could definitely do it. You've known Hazel for five minutes, and you're offering to help her."

"That's a special case. I mean, abuse is not special. There are a lot of abusers. But I'm seeing Jesse do it, and I can't *not* do something."

"Yes," Telfer said. "That's precisely my point."

Laodice stopped, and braced her hands on her hips, breathing deeply. The woods had thickened, with more shade overhead. She could hear water gurgling somewhere. The trail did seem to be a real trail, and she didn't think they'd get lost on the way back, but they'd been walking mostly downhill, which meant a mostly uphill return journey. "Let's rest a minute," she suggested, and perched her butt on a big rock that was jutting out of the ground.

It wasn't nearly as comfortable as the furniture at a five star hotel, but it felt better in a different way. She hadn't quite realized, until they'd gotten out of there, how confined and...corrupted Halcyon had begun to feel.

Telfer elected to stand, idly shifting from one foot to another. She'd *known* the brogues weren't the best idea.

He was looking at her again and made his making-a-decision expression, which was a degree off his paying-attention expression. Laodice wasn't sure what it meant that she could now distinguish them. Maybe she'd only had to start paying better attention, herself.

"I think Jesse's blackmailing Carrick," he said.

Jesse being a blackmailer made perfect sense, but affable, rather sweet Carrick didn't seem the type to have blackmailable secrets. "What about?"

"I have no idea. But I overheard them talking in the stairwell yesterday."

Laodice felt her eyebrows pop, remembering the way he'd nudged her to silence. "Jesse was trying to blackmail Carrick in a public place? Where anyone could hear them?"

"I don't think Jesse is the brightest bulb in the hardware store. Carrick was trying to get him to shut up and he kept going until they heard me coming."

"Jesse's a busy boy," Laodice said sardonically. "Bugging Patrick and Samuel, blackmailing Carrick, being an absolute turd to Hazel...what's he going to do to Erik and Alma?" She stopped. "Shit. You don't think he knows about Erik's romance author thing, do you? Maybe he bugged them too?"

"It's a possibility."

"Hm. I'll warn Alma.

"See? Stepping up. Even though she's blackmailing *you*."

"That's different. She's trying to protect Erik. Did Jesse sound like he wanted to protect someone?"

Telfer snorted. "No. He wants a job at Argive, and he thinks Carrick can get him one."

"Carrick does keep trying to sell you on a job there," Laodice said. She'd hinted, but... "I don't think you should do it. Dammond Argive is a shitty person."

"I know that," Telfer said. "I've met him. How do you know that?"

"Um, rumors," she said, but when he gave her a stern look she said, "He tried to get my sister fired when she accidentally revealed that he'd treated people in his life badly. When his grandfather dies and he takes over the company, who knows what things are going to be like over there? He's *not* a good guy, and I can't think he'd be a good boss."

Telfer stopped shuffling his feet and went dead still. "Your sister is Ask Cassandra," he said.

It had the flat tone of certainty, but Laodice tried a look of innocent surprise anyway. From Telfer's expression, it didn't succeed.

"I didn't say that," she said weakly.

"Of *course* she is. Dammond tried to get Ask Cassandra exposed and fired after she wrote that advice column for his ex- fiancée. Hera told him to go to hell, and *everyone* was talking about it. People speculated about who Cassandra was for weeks. *You* speculated! But it was your *sister*."

"Okay, but you can't tell anyone."

Telfer's eyes narrowed as he processed the information. "I should have worked this out much earlier. Hell, she came into the office last year to use your archive access. She told me she was a freelancer."

"Well, she is," Laodice said. "She's done some work for us and the Travel titles. She did that really cute story on wine country elopements this year."

"But she's *also* the anonymous author of Olympus's most widely read advice column."

"It's the most widely read?"

"By a huge margin," Telfer said. "Wasn't she involved in that attempted murder case shortly afterwards?"

"That makes it sound like she was attempting murder," Laodice said tartly. "She was the *victim*. Her boyfriend's uncle tried to kill her and Manny. He'd murdered his own brothers, decades apart, and he was trying to cover it all up."

"Right, I remember. You took three days off with no notice and I had to pick up all your deadlines."

Laodice stared at him. "Are you seriously carrying a grudge because I went to be with my sister after she *faced down a murderer*?"

Telfer looked taken aback. "Of course not. I'm saying that's how I remember."

"You don't remember it because your co-worker's sister was nearly *murdered?* You remember it because you were inconvenienced?"

"I remember the time period," Telfer said. "I'm not dismissing your sister's trauma."

"It sure *sounds* like you are," Laodice said. She jumped off the rock. "I don't get you, Terzi, I really don't! Every time I think you're like, smart and reliable and maybe even good to be around, you go and do something stupid like abandon me in the middle of a dance class or tell me the time my sister was nearly *burned alive* was a real bummer for your workload!"

"That's an ungenerous interpretation." He was starting to get mad, but she was plenty mad herself.

"The problem is not me," she snapped, angry that she'd ever thought it could be. "Go back to the hotel. I don't want to be with you right now." She started walking further down the trail, her anger giving her speed. Cassie had nearly *died*. They'd nearly *lost* her, and Telfer had been annoyed about deadlines?

"Wait," he was saying behind her, and she didn't listen, going faster until she heard hurried footsteps, racing to catch up with her. "Don't walk in the woods alone, Laodice, that's dumb."

She whirled to glare at him, wishing she could shoot laser beams out of her eyes. "I'm not dumb, you arrogant son of a bitch. I can't get lost. I have the phone. But if you stalk me one step further--"

"*Fine.* Fates forbid you ever listen to reason or give me the benefit of the doubt."

"Fuck you," Laodice said, really meaning it, and gave him the finger with both hands, putting a lot of force into the motion. She turned to keep going.

She had too much momentum. Her anger, and her pace, and the huge gesture of her swinging arms had pulled her off balance, and she realized it only when her foot skidded out from under her. She was at a place where the trail curved, and she fell right through the bushes that hugged the pathway. The greenery had seemed like an impenetrable wall, but was really more like a very penetrable curtain that snagged and cut her on her way down the short, steep bank. She tried to catch herself, to halt her fall, and thumped onto her butt, then her side, as she rolled twice and crashed into something at the bottom of the ditch.

She'd discovered where the water sound was coming from. There was a little stream down there, so she wasn't just shocked and sore, but wet through. She braced herself against the object she'd crashed into, and it gave awkwardly under her hand. She fell again, this time right on top of it.

It wasn't a log or rock. She felt cold, weirdly plastic skin and wet cloth, and was scrambling backwards, already screaming before her mind could even make sense of what she'd hit.

It was Jesse.

He was dead.

***

Telfer had never moved so fast in his life.

Laodice's scream rasped across his senses, a high note of pure terror that pushed him into motion before he could think. One moment he was standing at the edge of the ditch, cursing her name and preparing to climb down after her, and the next moment he was beside her, fists clenched, as she scrambled away from a huddled shape in the middle of the small creek.

"Are you hurt?" he demanded, and when he got no response he pulled her up, swinging her behind him, and pivoted back to meet the threat.

"It's Jesse," she said, and gulped for air. "I landed right on top of him. He's—I think he's dead."

Telfer steeled himself. The limp and unmoving body was a bad sign, but he knew the right thing to do. "Stay here," he said, and yet was unsurprised when Laodice swallowed hard and followed closely behind.

Jesse's skin was waxy and pale, and the eyelids were loosely closed. There was blood on the side of his head, matting his hair and smearing his face. Telfer was already certain, even before he touched the chill skin

171

of the throat, that there would be no pulse. He kept his fingers there by an effort of will alone, counting to fifteen in his head, before he drew his hand back and convulsively wiped it on his pants leg.

"Is he...?"

"Yes."

Laodice let out a shuddering breath. "For how long?" There was a touch of fear in her voice.

Telfer tried to remember what he knew about dead bodies. He was pretty sure that they didn't lose all their warmth right away. And even if he was wrong, there was something in the crumpled posture that suggested whatever spirit had animated Jesse had long departed. "You didn't hurt him. He was dead well before we got here."

Laodice made a nauseated face. For a moment, Telfer thought she was going to cry. He found himself moving towards her, for any comfort he might be able to offer, and then she took a deep breath and pulled her burner phone from the pocket of her slacks.

"Poor Hazel," she said, and dialed 911.

Telfer thought Hazel was, frankly, better off, but perhaps she wouldn't think so in the short term. He looked Laodice over while she was distracted. That tumble through the bushes could have been nasty, but she seemed to have escaped with some cuts and scrapes.

His own chest was tight with tension. The adrenaline of their fight had turned into the adrenaline of panicked action, and he realized that he'd also damaged himself, coming after her. His shoes would certainly never be the same.

Jesse was lying mostly on his side, legs and arms at awkward angles. He was wearing, as far as Telfer could remember, what he'd been wearing yesterday. Dark slacks and a polo shirt with a logo on it. Brown loafers.

Well, loafer. One foot was bare, a hairy ankle sticking out of his pants hem, mottled patterns on the exposed skin.

"Yes," Laodice was saying. "Yes, I'm here with a friend. No, we won't. Well, we did touch him—it—already. I fell onto him, and Telfer had to check his pulse. But we won't anymore." She pulled the phone away from her ear and checked something on the screen. "Seventeen percent left. Okay, yes. Yes, that's the number. Thank you. Bye, Jane." She lowered the phone and turned to him. "We have to stay here, and not touch anything. She wanted us to stay on the line, but I don't have enough battery, so she'll call back when police are closer."

She sounded small and scared, and he hated it.

"Jane?" he said.

"That's the emergency lady's name."

And in the middle of her own horror and shock, Laodice had remembered that.

"You're really something," he said, and Laodice blinked at him.

"Thank you?" she said, and then they both remembered they'd been fighting ten minutes earlier and broke eye contact.

There wasn't much to look at. Trees, rocks, water, and a dead man neither of them had liked.

"I missed my uncle's 50th birthday party," Telfer said. "When you went to be with Cassie, after the attempted murder. I had to take your stories, and one of them was a wedding out of town. I couldn't get back in time. That's why I remember. It wasn't because I was, um. Inconvenienced."

"Oh," Laodice said, and her cheeks flamed red. "I am such an asshole."

"No. You—I don't always come across the way I'd like to. I said the wrong thing."

"And then I interpreted it ungenerously," Laodice said, and Telfer wished that she had a worse memory for phrases. But she wouldn't be who she was if she did. "And picked a fight. Again."

"Sometimes I put the fight there to be picked," Telfer admitted. "Sometimes arguing with you makes everything, uh, more colorful."

"Well," Laodice said, staring at the ground. Her face was still scarlet. "Anger can be invigorating."

They both inadvertently looked towards Jesse, who was definitely lacking vigor.

The initial shock was wearing off. Telfer could almost feel Laodice's mind clicking into gear at the same time as his did.

"He's not exactly dressed for a walk in the woods," she said.

Telfer looked at his own shoes and decided to play Devil's Advocate. "Neither am I."

"Brogues are probably still better than loafers. He's lost one. Do you see it anywhere?"

"No. But there's lots of bushes around."

"Mm. When Hazel said he'd left, I assumed she meant he'd taken their car."

"Maybe she assumed that too, and didn't check."

"I'd check," Laodice said. "I'd want to know how I was going to get home, if he didn't come back."

Telfer had only seen Hazel show that kind of initiative about architectural criticism, but he knew he didn't need to point that out. "What's the timeline?" he asked instead. "The last time I saw Jesse was on the stairs, when he was trying to blackmail Carrick."

"I saw him right before that, in the foyer."

"He didn't go to the cocktail thing because of his 'headache.' After the first round of drinks, Patrick went up to get his cardigan, and then he found Jesse in his and Samuel's room."

"Patrick *said* he found Jesse there," Telfer corrected. If they were going where he thought they were going, it was going to be important to separate fact from hearsay. And Laodice nodded, so he knew she was thinking along the same lines.

"So Patrick said he saw Jesse then. They argued, and he didn't really accept Jesse's apology or explanation, but Jesse left before they could get into it further. Patrick went and got Samuel, Samuel found the bug, and then they planned to confront Jesse this morning."

"But Jesse wasn't at breakfast, or lunch."

"And Hazel said she hadn't seen him at all last night." Laodice blew out a breath, and he knew she was thinking the same thing he was. The thing they weren't saying out loud. If it *was* that thing, then the most likely suspect would be Jesse's nearest and dearest. And that was Hazel, publicly his fiancée and secretly his wife.

"So if everyone's timeline is correct"—and if they were all telling the truth—"then sometime after the confrontation with Patrick, Jesse went for a walk in the woods." Telfer paused. "It was dark by then. At least, it was dark when Patrick went upstairs to get his cardigan."

"So, sometime after 7? 7:30?"

"We could look up a sunrise-sunset chart. But what I mean is, did he have a flashlight?"

Laodice scanned the creek, and the brush she'd fallen through. "I don't see one."

"Or the missing shoe."

"Or his laptop!" Laodice said suddenly. "Remember? Hazel said he'd taken his laptop. That's why she thought she could email him."

Jesse could have stumbled into the woods along the same trail they'd followed, stupid enough to not bring a flashlight, and angry enough not to look where he was going. He could have fallen down the same bank Laodice had, or gotten lost somewhere else and wandered up or downstream. Perhaps the laptop and shoe had been discarded somewhere in the night. If he'd hit his head he might have had a brain injury. Then he'd stumbled into the creek and stayed there, while shock and hypothermia did their deadly work, only half an hour from the safety of Halcyon.

But if he'd lost a shoe and been walking barefoot, there should be physical evidence. Telfer walked a little closer to Jesse—to the body—and crouched down.

The waxy skin was mottled, with patches of red and purple forming a pattern he couldn't interpret.

Telfer stood up, abruptly nauseated. What the fuck was he doing? Playing detective over a dead man as if it were some sort of game or puzzle. Jesse was dead, and the fact that Telfer hadn't liked him wasn't relevant, because other people presumably *had*.

His wife. His parents. People had *loved* Jesse, and those people would be devastated by his loss. Whether it was an accident or the other thing. And Telfer was constructing a story in his head because it was a bigger distraction from the genuine tragedy of the death.

He stepped back, too fast, and stumbled into Laodice.

"Hey," she said, coming up beside him and putting her arm around his waist. "Hey, it's okay. I'm here."

He leaned into her side, glad of her solidity and strength, and forced himself to breathe. "He's really dead."

"Yeah," Laodice said, and leaned back, laying her head against his shoulder. Telfer's own arm went around her, more or less voluntarily, and they held each other for a moment in the cooling evening air.

"I need to tell you something," he said, without the *least idea* of what that would be, and then Laodice's phone shattered the moment.

She answered it at once, without any visible response to what he'd said, and Telfer let go and fell back a couple of steps. Had he even said it out loud? Or was his brain playing evil tricks on him in the presence of death?

"Sure," Laodice said. "Yes. We can do that. *No.*" Her voice went firm on the last word. "I'm sure it is. But no." She listened again. "All right. Thank you." She hung up and turned to him. "The police and ambulance crew are here. Well, they're at Halcyon. They want us to hike out, then bring them back to—to this spot."

"What did you say *no* to?"

"They wanted one of us to stay here."

"Oh, fuck no," Telfer said. Being alone with the dead man while the night crept in? Absolutely not.

"That's what I thought. I didn't want to do it, and I figured if I didn't, you wouldn't, so I said no." She eyed the steep bank with no favor. "Okay. Let's go."

Telfer went up the slope behind her, in case she stumbled, but they both scrambled their way to the top with no further injury, and set off back towards Halcyon in silence.

The parking lot had been taken over by an ambulance and two police cars. Sarah was there, looking tense as she talked to one of the police officers. There were a cluster of people in the doorway to the foyer—no one else approaching the intruders yet, but the news that *something* had happened had evidently spread.

One of the EMTs spotted Telfer and Laodice first, and there was a confused moment where police and EMTs were pulling rank on each other about whether the injured people or the reported dead body took priority.

"I'm fine," Telfer said, because he mostly was, so he was the one who got to meet Detective Bernard while Laodice sat in the back of an ambulance with a foil blanket over her wet clothes and had her scrapes cleaned and bandaged.

"Did you get *lost?*" Sarah said, her smile striving for understanding, and looking psychotic. Obviously, the police hadn't told her anything about why they were there.

"If you could return to the building, ma'am," Detective Bernard said politely. He was a sturdy looking older man with close-cropped salt-and-pepper hair and tan skin. Telfer watched Sarah retreat with some satisfaction.

Then Bernard turned back to Telfer, man-to-man and all business, and Telfer felt his spine straighten automatically. His uncle had been very clear on how to handle the police. Be polite, be respectful, give them plenty of warning when you were reaching into your pockets or putting your hands out of sight, don't tell them anything they don't ask for, and never, ever forget that they weren't on your side.

"Please show me to the body, sir," Bernard said, handing Telfer a flashlight, and Telfer walked with him and a couple of uniformed officers back down the path. They were moving quickly, and he was really regretting his shoe choices. It was close to true twilight when they arrived back at the right spot, but the broken bushes were a clear marker.

Had the bushes been broken *before* Laodice went through them? As they would have been if Jesse had stumbled in the same place?

Telfer didn't think so, but he couldn't be sure. Everything in his brain was flattening out as the adrenaline finally drained away.

"Thank you, sir," Bernard said, as a couple of his people gingerly picked their way down the slope with their equipment. "Now, a few questions, if you don't mind. You knew the deceased? You can positively identify him?"

"We were staying at the same place," Telfer said, rousing himself back to alertness with an effort. "I wouldn't say I knew him well, but enough to recognize him. Unless he has a twin who's also gone missing, that's Jesse Heller."

"Thank you."

"His... Hazel is back there. Will someone be with her?"

"We have procedures for notifying people of these unfortunate incidents. When you say Mr. Heller was missing, what do you mean by that?"

Telfer privately cursed himself for stupidity. Hadn't he just been reminding himself not to volunteer information? "I don't mean that he was officially a missing person. But he wasn't at breakfast or dinner, and Hazel hadn't seen him since yesterday."

"And no one thought that was alarming?"

"I only heard about it a few hours ago, but no. He was apparently in the habit of abruptly leaving from time to time. Hazel was worried about him, though."

"And you?"

"I thought he'd left to make Hazel worry about him," Telfer said bluntly. "I'm sorry, but I'm—" *dead on my feet* "—exhausted. Now that you know where he is, can I head back?"

"A few more questions," Bernard said. "When it became obvious that he was gone, why didn't anyone try to contact Mr. Heller?"

"Halcyon is a retreat for couples who are supposed to be focusing on each other. We all gave up our phones at the start of the retreat and there's no Wi-Fi available to guests."

Bernard's shaggy eyebrows popped. "But your girlfriend called us."

"She had a spare phone." Telfer didn't bother to clarify the *girlfriend* part, or explain why. The whole cover story was probably going to be blown up soon, but he'd let enough slip today. And he couldn't remember what name Laodice had given the emergency responder. He hoped it was her real one. "Elle Evagora" was all right for undercover journalism, but the police probably wouldn't get the joke. "Even if she had Jesse's number, it wouldn't have done any good, because he didn't have *his* phone. Though he left with his laptop. If he hadn't come back tonight, Hazel planned to ask the hotel manager for internet access so that she could email him."

"I see," Bernard said. He wandered over to the edge of the bank and looked down. Telfer craned over his shoulder. The officers at the bottom hadn't touched the body yet—they were conferring in low voices. One of them looked up and made a gesture Telfer couldn't interpret, but Bernard turned quickly and his voice sharpened on his next question.

"When was the last time you saw Jesse?"

"About...four or five p.m., yesterday."

"Can you be more specific?"

"No," Telfer said, and then decided that alone was verging on impolite, which was against Burak's Rules for Cops. "Halcyon doesn't have clocks either. Britt, one of the guests, she has a watch. She might be able to give you a better idea."

"Okay," Bernard said. He didn't have a notebook out, but Telfer recognized the look of someone filing away everything he said. "Any idea how Jesse might have gotten out here? Or why?"

"No," Telfer said.

"Did you or Ms. Troiades touch or move the body?"

So Laodice *had* used her real name. "Yes, we both did. She fell down the slope and landed on him. I checked for a pulse." He held up the two fingers that he'd used, in a gesture that felt stupid as soon as he'd done it. Of course Bernard knew how he'd have checked a pulse.

"She fell down the slope," Bernard repeated, and scanned the bushes. "How did she do that?"

"She turned before that bend to say something to me, turned back, tripped, and went down." Telfer looked at the body and swallowed hard. "Then she screamed. I thought she was hurt. I, uh, don't really remember getting down to her. She was already moving away from him by then."

"I see," Bernard said. It might have been a trick of the flashlight, but it looked as if his eyes had softened for a moment. "But you didn't see her land on the body? You don't know if she might have shoved him away or rolled him over?"

"No. You'd have to ask her."

"We will." Bernard surveyed him for a long moment. It was the kind of silence that invited the other person to fill it. Telfer was familiar with that kind of silence. He said nothing.

This might have been the wrong move, because Bernard's eyes sharpened again. "And what do you do for a living, Mr. Terzi?"

"I'm a journalist. With the Bridal department at Olympus Inc."

"Ah. You're media," Detective Bernard said, in much the same tone that someone might have said, "ah, a dead rat." "Well, I think you can head back now. I understand that you're staying until Saturday?"

"That was the original plan, but maybe now—"

"Please do stay," Bernard said gently. "In case we have further questions." He gestured down the path, a polite, but obvious dismissal. "Thank you, Mr. Terzi."

Telfer nodded back, but the other man was already turning away, preparing to climb down the slope after his officers.

It took longer than it should have for Telfer to make his way back to Halcyon.

To Laodice.

***

Laodice watched the police officers speaking urgently to each other and then into their microphones, feeling sore and sad and totally useless. She shouldn't have let Telfer go with them alone. Her hands stung under their bandaids, and her left forearm really hurt, but—

A small, slender figure broke from the doorway and raced towards the ambulance. Even in her panic, Hazel was graceful, her brown hair dancing behind her like a banner.

"Elle," she said urgently, and Laodice froze.

"Is it Jesse?" Hazel demanded. "I knew something was wrong! Is he hurt?"

"I—" Laodice said, and looked towards the nice blond EMT for guidance. The nice blond EMT had stayed with her while the police asked their questions, hovering in a way that indicated they'd happily step in if she needed them to.

"Ma'am, please go back inside for now," the EMT said. "The police will tell us more when they can."

"I have a *right* to *know*," Hazel said. "Elle! Elle, tell me, what *happened?*"

There was no denying that plea. "I'm so sorry," Laodice said helplessly.

Hazel reared back. "But he's just hurt, right? He's going to be okay?"

"He—" Laodice said, and stopped, the words sticking in her throat.

It didn't matter. She saw Hazel read the meaning in her silence, and watched the sudden, brutal understanding shatter her like a hammer.

"No," she said, and stepped back, her skinny arms wrapped around her chest. "No."

Yvette had caught up with her, and Laodice felt a shock of gratitude. "Hazel, come inside," she said. "Come and—"

"No!" Hazel said, twisting away from Yvette's comforting hand. "No, not *you*. You *hated* Jesse. You wanted me to *leave.*"

Yvette's hand fell to her side and she swallowed hard. The police had arrived, and the EMT was stepping up with an emergency blanket and something in a little paper cup, but Hazel twitched away from all of them and hurtled towards the trail, screaming Jesse's name.

She crashed right into Telfer, emerging into the light.

He staggered under the weight, and then caught her at the wrist and waist. She screamed, and tried to hit him with her free hand. Then the police were there. As far as Laodice could tell, they restrained her gently, but her own eyes were blurring with tears.

"Okay, hon, you're all good," the EMT said cheerily, and Laodice realized they were clearing the decks for their next patient, who was being guided towards them, now sobbing so hard she could barely walk.

"Right, thank you," Laodice said, and stumbled away to stand by Yvette. The others were edging out of the building now.

"Someone should go with her," Yvette said, her voice dead.

"Me," Alma said, and climbed into the back of the ambulance to introduce herself to the medics. The ambulance drove away as another police car arrived.

Telfer made it to the little group of spectators and looked at her. He wasn't quite frowning.

"Can we go to our room?" she asked.

"Wait," Yvette said, shaking herself as if she were coming out of a dream. "What's happened? What did you tell the police?"

"Yes, we can go to our room," Telfer said, ignoring her completely. He held an arm out for Laodice, and she took it.

Sarah was waiting for them inside the door, her eyes glittering with barely suppressed panic. "You have a phone, don't you?" she demanded. "You have to hand that in. It was in the terms and conditions!"

"Shut the fuck up, Sarah," Laodice said, and went with Telfer up the stairs.

"Get clean and dry," he said when they reached their room, and gently nudged her towards the bathroom.

Laodice closed her eyes tight as he closed the bathroom door behind her. She couldn't cry until she fell asleep, no matter how appealing that sounded. Showering around the dressing on her arm was a little awkward, but the hot water did her good. And she emerged to find a box of cereal, two bowls, and a carton of milk laid out on their coffee table. Telfer was shaking cereal into his own bowl.

"I went downstairs and bullied Danielle," he said, answering her unasked question. The muscles in his wrists moved as he prepared a bowl for her. He had really nice wrists.

"How's she doing?"

"She's upset."

Laodice dug into the cereal. She ate two bowls, and briefly contemplated a third before pushing her bowl away.

"I was thinking," she said.

"Yeah. I don't think it was a simple accident. Detective Bernard was too interested in whether we might have moved the body."

Laodice thought back to the moment Jesse's mass had shifted under her hand, the moment she'd known without yet knowing that she was touching death, and shuddered. "I wasn't thinking about that," she said. "I mean, actually, I was, and that's the problem. But I was also thinking about sex."

Telfer put his spoon down.

"As a solution to obsessively thinking about finding a dead body, I mean. You know how sometimes when you have sex you just stop thinking at all for a minute? Like your body blanks out your mind so the only thing you can think about is how great you feel?"

"I'm familiar."

"Okay, well, yesterday, you offered, and I understand if you've changed your mind or if this is too weird, but if the offer is still open..." she let her voice trail off and spread her hands.

Telfer was silent for a moment. "Your timing is very peculiar," he said at last.

"I know," Laodice said humbly. "Like I said, I understand that the answer's probably no."

"It's not," Telfer said, stern and unsmiling as he leaned across the table and tipped her chin up. He did loom impressively. "Are you sure?"

"No," Laodice said, in complete honesty, and kissed him anyway.

Chapter Eleven

Never mind finding oblivion in sex. Telfer's brain momentarily blanked out just from *kissing* Laodice.

He'd imagined this in a half-dozen idle fantasies brought to more painful life by her proximity these last few days, but nothing could have prepared him for the softness of her lips, the hot sweetness as she opened her mouth to him. He was off-balance, leaning over the stupid brass coffee table, and immediately dizzy.

The coffee table was a problem. It was a barrier between them, where there should be no barriers, but he didn't want to let go of her long enough to get around it.

He scrambled over it instead without breaking contact, and Laodice squeaked, then laughed against his lips. He didn't care if she was laughing at him, he could *touch* her, he had permission to *touch*. He let his eager hands rove over her body, feeling her shift and sigh as he stroked the curves of her back. He gripped her ass, loving the way his fingers sank in as he pressed her closer against him, and she broke away from his mouth.

"Are you hard already?" she asked, sounding amazed.

"Don't sound so surprised. I've been hard for you all week."

"You have?" Laodice marveled, and then he had to grind against her so she could feel the proof. He had to kiss her again, thrusting his tongue deep so that she could know how much he wanted her, how badly he needed to be inside her. He slid his hands up under that T-shirt she'd been wearing in bed, felt soft flesh press into his palms, and could have stayed there for a while, except Laodice was grabbing the hem and yanking it over her head, wriggling enthusiastically.

Telfer found himself staring at a pair of beautiful full breasts. There were rosy nipples surrounded by soft areolas. There were blue veins tracing through the pale skin. They were *breasts*, which were never disappointing, but in this case were so impressive he felt himself drop several IQ points just looking at them.

"Wow," Laodice said, looking pretty entranced herself. "This pink lighting is doing great things to me."

"I'm going to do great things to you," Telfer promised, and put action to words as he hefted her breasts with his hands and dove in.

"Oh, wow," he heard Laodice say, as his mouth closed over her breast. "Yep, that's—" she squeaked again as his teeth scraped gently over her nipple, and he was suddenly sucking on a hard nub that had tightened against his tongue.

Telfer's experience was mostly in one-night-stands or brief flings, high in desire and low in emotion. Generally speaking, he'd heard, sex was better once you knew a partner's body and rhythms, the things to include and the things to avoid. He'd always shied away from getting to that stage of intimacy, but he still wanted sex to feel great for everyone involved. So he'd studied, and when he put theory into practice, he paid attention to what his partners responded to. Even the most reserved person would betray what they liked and disliked, if you observed closely enough.

And Laodice wasn't the least bit reserved.

"Fuck, yes," she said, and her hands slid into his hair, clamping his head against her chest. "Who taught you that, Terzi?"

He flicked her nipple with his tongue in answer, and she moaned. His hand was busy on her other breast, stroking the soft skin of the underside, his thumb strumming over the nipple.

"Okay, we have to get to *bed*," Laodice said, sounding sex-drunk and dazed, and she pulled away.

Telfer let her go for long enough to shuck his shirt and padded towards where she was scrambling backwards up onto the bed, her breasts swinging with the motion.

Her eyes widened as she took in his shoulders, his abs, the sparse hair that thickened to a dark line pointing straight down his belly. "You have an incredible body," she said.

"Thank you. It's at your complete disposal."

She grinned at him, and beckoned him forward. "Great. Do that thing with your teeth again."

"Your word, my command," he said, and did.

***

If distraction was what she was after, mission well and truly accomplished, Laodice thought. Five minutes ago she'd been aware of every scrape and strain. Now those pains were fading into the background while other, distinctly more pleasant sensations took center stage.

The bed was soft, the covers were smooth, and Telfer was braced over her as he licked and sucked, that thick hair in easy grabbing distance. What a pleasure it was to get her hands in there and direct his attentions.

Not that he needed much direction. She *liked* her breasts, but nipple play had never done much for her, maybe because the sensations had so much boob to travel through. Now it turned out that what she'd really needed was someone to really *go* for it, with a lot of enthusiasm and a little bit of teeth. She jerked when he bit down, and jerked again when he immediately pressed his tongue against the spot, soothing. The tease was going directly to her pussy, where everything was humming and heating up nicely.

And they still had half their clothes on! No one had even got their hands on the really good stuff yet!

"Lose the pants," she ordered, with as much authority as she could summon under the circumstances: sprawled topless on a bed, while Telfer Terzi—*Telfer Terzi!*—absolutely devoured her tits.

He growled against her—oh, wow, the reverberation was really something—and tucked his thumbs into the waistband of her yoga pants. He went backwards on his knees, yanking her pants and panties down her thighs, over her knees, and then out of sight. She had the impression he might have flung them somewhere.

"Um," she said, because she'd meant he should lose *his* pants, but Telfer looked at her splayed in front of him as if he were a starving man offered a banquet, and she decided that this was fine, actually.

"Can I taste you?" he demanded, looking crazed and Laodice realized that all she'd really done was *be there* and that was still driving him this wild.

She could probably lie back and let him do all the work. That sounded *great*.

"By all means," she said sweetly, and his eyes narrowed, all intense focus and desire, and she had enough time to think *uh-oh* before he hooked her knees over his shoulders and buried his face between her thighs, and she stopped thinking much at all. She was only just aware of the bedclothes wrinkling underneath her clutching hands, of the high, muted noises she was making, of the way her head was burrowing back into the pillows as he pushed her up the bed with his sheer drive.

But mostly she was pure sensation radiating from her core, stoked to white hot heat in an instant by his tongue, by his hands holding her open, by the way she could give in and give up.

She came fast and hard, shaking as she tipped over the edge, but he didn't move away. He pressed his tongue against her fluttering pussy and waited until he got some signal from her breathing or her muscles relaxing and began gently, carefully working her up again, this time all slow caresses and teasing strokes. He pulled back a little and blew on her clit, a soft puff of cool air, and she'd never have thought that could do anything, but he went back to that slow tease again, and the third time he pulled back and blew, she felt the orgasm swelling. Not an explosion, this time, but something that flowed up her body and down again in slow shivers as he teased her with the tip of his tongue, an orgasm she felt fill her body and ebb away like the tide.

Telfer sat up and inspected her face.

Laodice felt, dimly, that she should try to be cool about this, but that was hard when her vision was fuzzy and every cell in her body was vibrating to some kind of cosmic rhythm. "Holy *shit*," she said. "That was *amazing*."

Telfer grinned. He would have had every right to give her his trademark smirk, but instead it was a wide, boyish smile she'd never seen before. He looked proud and happy, a man who'd done a great job and thought he deserved some praise for it.

Which he did. His *tongue*, what the hell was happening there, how was he getting so much out of a simple muscle that was really kind of gross whenever you stopped to think about it?

"What are you thinking about?"

"How gross tongues are," Laodice said absently, and when he flinched she sat up and reached for him. "Wait, no, not yours. Your tongue is gorgeous, it gets a gold star, come here."

She kissed him thoroughly, feeling her body hum, not desperate for another orgasm, but definitely willing to explore the possibility. She could taste herself in his mouth, salty and musky.

Telfer himself seemed perfectly happy to keep necking, but Laodice was getting pretty curious about his whole pants situation. She let her hand drift down his body, and from the way his hips jerked forward, pushing his cock into her palm, she thought he was into it too.

But it was worth checking. She kissed her way up to his ear and whispered, "Hey. Wanna fuck me?"

Three seconds later she was flat on her back, while Telfer simultaneously shoved his pants down and produced a condom, looking wild around the eyes.

"Wait, I want to *see*," she said, and he froze. She sat up again and looked him over. The pants situation was—yes, that was an *impressive* cock right there, jutting out of a thatch of dark curly hair. He sure as hell didn't skip leg day. The muscles in his thighs were tight and defined, twitching with harnessed energy as she scanned him.

"Give that here," she said, and held out an imperious hand for the condom. He gave it up, something clenching in his jaw while she carefully—and maybe a little theatrically—tore open the packet and pulled out the little latex sleeve. He grunted when she rolled it down his cock, with a movement that wasn't quite a thrust, and stayed right where he was. Laodice reclined back amongst the pillows, arranging them under her head and hips.

If this was all it took to make Telfer biddable, maybe she should have slept with him *years* ago.

"All right," she said, when she was settled to her satisfaction. "Go ahead."

It was like she'd blown a whistle at the start of a race. He was on her at once, one hand busy at her breast, his mouth on hers as if he'd die if he had to spend another second before kissing her. His other hand was busy between them, aligning their bodies, and then his hips jumped and he was inside her.

"Oh," Laodice said, and wrapped her legs around his lower body. "Yes, that's good."

He rocked into her, eyes fixed on her face. She'd been expecting an explosion of frantic motion, but he was appallingly controlled, sliding in and out with a pace that tightened everything inside.

But he didn't look happy about it. His jaw was still set, his eyes determined… *oh*. The idiot was holding himself back. He was trying to get her there again, when all he really wanted was to let go.

She wrapped her arms around him too, so that she was hanging on with all four limbs, and bit his earlobe.

"Fuck me," she said in his ear, and used the power in her legs to yank him deeper. "Fuck me *hard*."

He grunted, almost as if she'd hit him, lost all control and went for it. He pounded into her, wet slapping sounds and the heady smell of sex rising around them, and she snarled at him to go harder, go faster, *more*. He somehow found a touch more space, seated himself in her body just a little more deeply, and then his eyes, fixed on hers, rolled up into his head and he collapsed on top of her, shuddering as he came.

Laodice held him, stroking his hair with one hand. He kissed her shoulder and the side of her neck.

"That was—" he said, and then shook his head and kissed her mouth.

"It was *very* good," Laodice said. "Nice work, us."

The longest scrape along her forearm twinged then, and she remembered that Jesse was dead. It was a less demanding thought than it had been before. The oblivion granted by sex couldn't last forever, but she couldn't dwell on the chill, pathetic corpse she'd touched when she was holding a warm, sweaty body in her arms, very much alive.

And a bit heavy, honestly. She tapped at his shoulder and wriggled until he got the hint and withdrew, taking care of the condom. Laodice found her yoga pants and panties tangled up together and hanging from a lamp clear on the other side of the room, and hopped into the panties. She considered putting her t-shirt back on too, but was modesty really a consideration here? She climbed back into bed while Telfer hit the shower, and was almost asleep when he came back to bed, snuggling up behind her and wrapping one arm around her waist.

Telfer Terzi was a cuddler. Who knew?

"Laodice," he said, and there was something in his voice, some uncertain note she should pay attention to. He'd said he had to tell her something. Well, they couldn't handle a real conversation now, not after the day they'd both had.

She patted his hand, the one resting lightly on her stomach. "Thank you for the excellent orgasms," she said. "Good night."

***

After Telfer woke, he spent some time wondering what the hell had happened. Last night he'd started out doing his usual great work, with perhaps slightly more attention to detail. Laodice had gone off like a rocket, which had made him feel… Good. Happy. And then she'd drawn him inside her, hot and wet and welcoming, and commanded him to go hard.

And he had. This morning there was a tightness in his left glute that could have come from that scramble down the bank yesterday, but he strongly suspected he'd simply fucked himself into a muscle strain.

It had definitely been worth it, for sex that good. Maybe some of the best sex of his life. Laodice had been on his mind for a long time, much longer than any of his other occasional partners. When the reality of Laodice's generous enthusiasm had been even better than the fantasy, of course it had been impressive.

Reality wasn't usually better than fantasy. That was the appeal of fantasy. You could enjoy it, and tell yourself real life could never be that good.

Maybe that was why he'd woken up so early, his mind whirring in the way that suggested some kind of panic dream in his subconscious. Maybe that accounted for the tightness in his chest as he lay behind her with his hand on her belly, breathing in the scent of her hair and feeling the rise and fall of her sleeping breath.

Detective Bernard had said they shouldn't change their plans, that they should stay until Saturday. Last night, that had seemed like an unappealing proposition. Now he was contemplating the next four days with more equanimity.

True, his initial offer had been for a one-night-stand, and Laodice had taken it up for the explicit purpose of momentarily wiping Jesse's death from her mind...but maybe he could propose a second round. Or a third. A four-night stand wasn't a significant commitment, and the circumstances were surely unusual enough to justify it.

Then they'd go back to Olympus and be colleagues again, and then one of them would get the editing job, which would put an end to the possibility of any further intimate contact. They were both far too professional to pursue a relationship between a manager and a direct report, even if it hadn't been expressly forbidden.

This should have been a reassuring thought, a reminder that even if their liaison was longer than a single evening it had a definite end date. For some reason, Telfer preferred not to dwell on it. He shifted a little closer to Laodice, removed a strand of her hair from his mouth—her hair was magnificent, but it got everywhere—and wondered whether she'd mind if he woke her up.

Fortunately, she stirred before he could give into temptation. And unlike yesterday's waking, she didn't startle awake and then get away from him as fast as she physically could. She murmured something, and then rolled over onto her side, so that they were face to face.

And this time, she was smiling. Looking very pleased with herself, in fact. "Hey."

"Hi," Telfer said. He was aware his answering smile verged on foolish, but it was hard to care. "How are you feeling?"

She stretched, and the sheet fell to her waist, exposing her breasts. They lay stacked on top of each other, molded by gravity into two soft pillows that he, for one, just kind of wanted to snuggle into.

Laodice noticed. Her eyes turned wicked. "*Most* of me feels great, thank you." She touched a wound on her forearm, covered by a long strip of plastic bandage, and winced. "Some of me, less great. How are you?"

Telfer considered this. "No regrets, but I might have strained a muscle in my ass."

"Well, you have so many muscles in there to strain," Laodice said demurely. "Hey, what did you want to talk about last night? I'm sorry I put you off, but I'm not great at conversation after good sex. My brain kinda goes *wheee* and refuses to consider anything else."

Telfer filed that away for later consideration, and refocused. What *had* he wanted to talk about? He'd had the impulse to make some sort of general apology, to ask if they could wipe the slate of four years of petty disputes and stupid arguments and start again. They knew each other better now. He liked her, as a person, and she'd indicated, even in the middle of their latest fight, that she was starting to change her mind about him.

"I think Jesse might have been murdered," he said.

"Yeah," Laodice said, going serious all at once. "Me too. If he'd had both shoes on, or a flashlight..."

"And the cops think the body was moved. Were the bushes broken before you went through them?"

"I don't remember. Maybe."

"I don't remember either," Telfer admitted.

"Well, if it was murder, it was probably someone at Halcyon," Laodice said. "Only about ten percent of all homicides are committed by strangers."

"Sometimes your statistics are morbid," Telfer said.

Laodice shrugged. "I'm just saying. The people in this building weren't strangers to Jesse."

"What did the cops ask you?"

"They wanted to know the last time I saw him, whether he'd seemed all right, whether I'd moved the body." Laodice grimaced. "They didn't ask about whether he had any enemies, but I bet that's coming next."

"Good luck to them going through that motive list. Blackmail, attempted espionage, emotional abuse..."

"Can you really imagine Carrick killing him?" Laodice asked. "Or Patrick, or Samuel?"

Telfer shook his head. "How did Hazel seem? Women who don't see any way out have murdered before."

"Not Hazel. She was destroyed." Laodice sighed. "And she still hadn't gotten around to admitting that maybe he wasn't the best husband. I don't think it was her. But then, Manny would never have thought his uncle capable of killing his dad. Hm. What about if Jesse worked out the wage-skimming and threatened Sarah?"

Telfer considered it. He could see the appeal of the theory, but... "That's a motive for her to buy him off, not murder. She wouldn't want the police looking into this place."

"Which is why she moved the body," Laodice suggested.

"By herself? He'd be a heavy burden for someone her size. And besides, Hazel might have reported Jesse as a missing person. Why would Sarah take the risk?"

Laodice's voice was tart. "You're assuming Sarah makes good decisions."

Telfer shrugged, acknowledging the point. "At any rate, I don't think we should be ruling people out because we like them. You're right, I can't imagine Carrick killing someone, but that doesn't make it impossible."

Laodice's nose scrunched. "Alma would have a motive, if Jesse *did* find out about Erik's secret identity. Honestly, I think she could kill."

"That's pure speculation," Telfer said firmly. "We don't know that he discovered anything of the kind."

Laodice looked at him for a long moment. "But we're going to find out, aren't we?"

"We *shouldn't,*" Telfer temporized. "We're not investigative reporters. We're wedding writers."

Laodice grinned. "Yeah. But we're wedding writers who have been entangled in a story about crime, money, and love. We're going to snoop."

Telfer abandoned himself to temptation and grinned back. "Yes, we are."

Laodice pursed her lips. "Hey, I know we said it was only one night, but—"

"These are unusual circumstances," Telfer said. "I think we can define a one-night-stand as covering the remaining period of our stay."

"Exactly what I was thinking," Laodice said, her voice rich with approval, and Telfer looked at her breasts again. Still there. Still spectacular.

Five minutes later, Laodice was hovering over him on all fours with her incredible ass in easy reach. Her hand leisurely stroking his cock, while her cotton panties dampened under his exploratory fingers. Telfer slipped one finger under the elastic to touch slick, hot flesh, and was rewarded with a gasp.

"Good morning," Sarah's voice said.

Laodice groaned and clambered off him, flopping onto her back. Telfer thumped his head into the pillow, twice.

Sarah's voice was tentative, for once, lacking the determined enthusiasm she normally adopted. "As you know, there's been a terrible tragedy," she continued. "The authorities have asked us to remain on site and there are a few things to discuss. I'd appreciate it if everyone could meet in the gallery room in half an hour."

Laodice looked at the burner phone. "Well, at least she waited for a decent hour," she said.

"I can't say I give her timing much credit," Telfer said. His cock had wilted a little at the sound of Sarah's voice, but all he had to do to regain his erection was look at the astonishing banquet of a woman lying beside him. "Still, we've got half an hour. Not really time for my best work, but if you don't mind a little urgency..."

Laodice looked tempted, but she shook her head. "It wouldn't be appropriate for us to turn up at breakfast looking fucked-out."

"Sure it would," Telfer said, reaching for her, but she slipped out of bed, warm and laughing.

"And I need to wash my hair."

"I could help?" Telfer said, seized by a vision of Laodice wet in the shower, water beading on her skin as he carefully soaped every inch of her.

"Later," she promised. "Can I say? I am very into how into me you are."

"I'd love to be into you," Telfer said, but he said it to the closed bathroom door.

Chapter Twelve

I t was a gloomy breakfast, only slightly alleviated by the waffles and bacon on offer. Laodice did observe that Sarah seemed to have given up on the no-caffeine rule; she was sucking down black coffee herself.

Hazel wasn't there.

"She's under observation at the hospital," Alma said, when Yvette asked. "She was in shock, and they were worried—anyway, while I was there I heard that Jesse's family are on their way. They plan to get a hotel in the Hippocampus, and I guess she'll join them when she's discharged." She scrubbed her face with her palms.

"Are you okay?" Laodice asked.

Alma sighed. "Mostly I couldn't do anything except be there. I was an E.R. nurse for a while, and that can be awful, but at least you can try to treat people. Just sitting with Hazel was hard."

Yvette nodded. "Are they taking Jesse home for services?"

"I'm not sure."

"Mortuary transport across state lines can be complex," Yvette said, and looked to Xavier. "We could help…?"

He patted her hand. "I think they've got it handled, babe."

Most of what Laodice knew about claiming and transporting bodies she'd picked up from the movie *Little Miss Sunshine*, which she didn't think was an authoritative guide. But it was interesting that Yvette, at least, seemed to be behaving under the assumption that Jesse's was a natural death, one where the police would promptly release the body.

Sarah put her coffee down and coughed for attention. "I know this puts a damper on the Halcyon experience," she said.

"You think?" Patrick muttered.

"—but since we have been asked to stay, and the activities have all been organized in advance, you're all welcome to participate."

"We've been *asked* to stay," Patrick said, louder, and folded his arms. "I'm not convinced we should." He turned to Telfer and Laodice. "What actually happened?"

"We went for a walk, and discovered Jesse's body," Telfer said. Laodice admired the neat summary that left out so many pertinent details.

"Do the police think there was foul play?" Samuel asked, looking queasy.

"You'd have to ask them," Telfer said.

Yvette straightened. "Wait, really? What did they ask you?"

Laodice wasn't quite as good at deflection. "They wanted to know if we'd moved the body," she admitted.

Xavier and Yvette exchanged a glance.

"Well, okay," Patrick said, "But even if there was a crime, the police haven't shown up with a warrant, they haven't charged any of us, and they can't *keep* us here."

Sarah grimaced. "If the police decide you've left town to avoid arrest, they can also charge you with unlawful flight. You'd be extradited back here to face charges, and you wouldn't get bail."

"She's right," Xavier said officiously, but Laodice was most interested not in the information but that Sarah had been able to say it with so much easy authority. The added legal peril of people who tried to skip town following a crime wasn't necessarily common knowledge.

"Anyway, regarding the *program*," Sarah said. "It might be better if we can all do something to keep our minds off all this. I'll understand if anyone wants to skip today's session, of course, but—"

"We'll do it," Xavier said, and when Yvette gave him an inquiring look, he smiled at her. "You'll like it, babe. You like when you're busy."

"I do," Yvette said, sounding more sure of herself.

"What's the activity?" Erik asked.

Sarah beamed at him. "It's all about living art as a memento of your love!"

"And what does that mean?" Britt said warily, but Sarah claimed the instructor would be able to explain it better.

The instructor was a tiny, wizened lady with a strong East European accent who could have been anywhere between sixty and ninety years old. She was a sculptor, a painter, a sex therapist—"what?" Telfer whispered in Laodice's ear—a performance artist, a dramaturge, a striptease instructress—"*what?*"—and they were permitted to call her Madame Esme.

The room had been set up with six curtained booths, like those that a pop-up massage kiosk in a mall might use. Madame Esme had taken center stage at the front of the room, standing in front of a table with six black boxes. She was leaning on a cane with a silver filigree head, her sharp black eyes flickering over each of the couples.

"Where are the sixth pair?" she demanded, and when Sarah stammered out an explanation, she took it in stride, apparently unsurprised by sudden death. "Very well," she said. "Twelve would be better, but ten will work." She stared at Sarah until she left, then beckoned the couples closer. "So," she said. "You have all heard of the Belkovsky exercise?"

Nobody had. Madame Esme sighed, disappointed, yet not surprised by the undereducated youth, and explained that it was a theater exercise where the actors, naked in the dark, groped each other with painted hands. It was supposed to build unity and trust among casts.

"We were supposed to know that?" Telfer whispered.

"Shh!"

"As theater, love. As love, art," Madame Esme concluded. She gestured at the table with the black boxes. "Take one. Retire. Explore. Record the results, if you wish."

Xavier raised his hand. It should have been ridiculous, but it was in fact exactly the right move to signify the relative status of the people in the room. Madame Esme gave him permission to speak with a regal nod. "Um, are we supposed to all get naked with each other?" he asked. "I mean, uh, no offence if that's what people are into, but—"

"No. Unless you have welcomed other lovers into your union?"

Xavier shook his head.

"So, then. Each box contains a different medium, which you will explore with your lover. You will have privacy of view behind the curtains, and I will play music, so that you will have privacy of sound. Should you breach the barriers of good taste I shall ask you to leave." This, Laodice thought, meant that sex in the booths was out of bounds, but she wasn't completely sure. Madame Esme struck her as someone who might dismiss a rule like that as American prudishness.

In any case, no one was brave enough to ask her directly. They grabbed boxes and went to their booths. Laodice, who had grabbed a surprisingly heavy box last, was all too aware of the one left on the table and the empty booth beside the one she and Telfer occupied.

"We begin!" Madame Esme said impressively, and a moment later loud orchestral music with plenty of horns and percussion rang through the room.

Telfer began to laugh. "Where did Sarah *find* her?" he asked. Laodice could hear him under the music, but if the others were saying anything, it wasn't audible to her.

"She's my new role model," she said firmly. "I'm going to be just like her when I grow up."

"You could do worse," Telfer admitted. The booth contained a coat stand, presumably for their clothes, two narrow folding stools, and a polaroid camera, presumably so they could record the results. "What's in our box?"

Laodice prised off the lid. "A lump of clay. Some plastic sheets, a bowl, a bottle of water...are we supposed to make something with this?"

"Or smear it on each other?" Telfer suggested, a glint in his eyes.

Laodice touched her freshly-washed hair protectively. "Maybe life-sized models of our naughty bits."

Telfer made a sweeping gesture with his hands that encompassed her chest. "So there'd have to be a *lot* of clay."

Laodice stared pointedly at his crotch. "Right back atcha."

Telfer cracked up. He was actually *giggling*, Laodice thought, astonished and delighted. She reached up to cover his mouth, and he kissed her fingers, then her palms. It was an unexpectedly tender gesture, and she looked away, suddenly shy.

"We should probably do *something*," she said, and spread a few of the plastic sheets on the ground before she settled herself cross-legged, laid another sheet over her lap to protect her dress, and tried to mold the clay. It resisted her efforts at first, but as she added water and pressure, it softened.

Telfer took a lump too.

"So, first angle of attack?" he said, keeping his voice down despite the music.

"Talk to Alma and raise the blackmail theory," Laodice said. "Better yet, maybe you should talk to Erik. I get the feeling he might be an easier nut to crack."

"Erik doesn't really talk," Telfer said doubtfully, but he shrugged. "I'll try."

"I'll talk to Patrick and Yvette. Let's see if we can get a stronger idea of the timeline. If *anyone* saw Jesse after he left Patrick and Samuel's room, we might have a better idea of what happened." She glanced at Telfer's art. He'd created a Venus of Willendorf type with enormous breasts, a full stomach, and massive thighs. Even as she watched, he rolled some thin tendrils of clay between his fingers and added them as hair, coiling them around the head until they met his standards. "Is that supposed to be me?"

"I'm following Madame Esme's instructions," Telfer said. "I'm *exploring*." His face looked stern, even argumentative, but she thought she knew him better now. There was a tilt in the head, a gleam in the eye that hinted at humor rather than offense.

How often had she misinterpreted that face, and taken offense in her turn?

"So you are," she said, and started rolling out her own long piece of clay. She gave it arms, bent to fold over the chest, and a head with an exaggerated nose.

"Hey," Telfer said, so indignantly that she just had to tap his own nose, leaving a clay smear down the bridge.

"If the face fits," she said, and he caught her wrist.

It was a playful gesture, but she caught her breath, suddenly very aware of the long, cool fingers wrapped around her forearm, of the constriction so light it was barely a hold.

Telfer's eyes darkened. His grip tightened, then released her.

She wasn't sure whether he moved first or she did, but they were suddenly pressed body to body, mouth to mouth, protected from the others by the curtained booth and the loud music. He wiped his hands on his pants before he stroked her neck, under the heavy mass of her hair, and that was... it was sweet, it was thoughtful.

But wait, Laodice thought (distantly, because Telfer was doing something fascinating with his tongue in her mouth) it didn't matter if the others caught them doing this. They were *supposed* to be doing this. It was not doing it but pretending to that had been the cover, and now they were doing it for real—

She broke off the kiss, breathing heavily.

"Okay," she said. "And I think you should talk to Carrick too. See if you can figure out what the blackmail material was, and if it was worth killing for."

Telfer leaned his forehead against hers. His own breathing wasn't steady. "Right. Uh, how long do you think this is going to go on?"

"The other activities were a couple of hours."

"Okay," Telfer said, and squished another lump of clay with some violence. "Well, if we're keeping our clothes on, we might as well do something useful. Help me model this out."

***

Telfer regarded the results of their work with dissatisfaction. They had a rough clay model of the creek and the bank, with a little model of Jesse's body. By mutual, silent agreement they hadn't tried to give the face any features—better to distance themselves from the living man they'd known, if they were going to try to figure out his death.

"He was lying like this, I think," Laodice said doubtfully, and made a gesture with her left hand, as if she was pressing down on something. "I touched... I think it was his arm, or his collar. I felt skin and cloth, I remember that." She shivered, and went to wipe her palm on her skirt, then exclaimed in annoyance and wiped it on the plastic sheet instead.

Telfer thought about pointing out that they were both liberally smeared with clay, and it wouldn't make any difference, but stopped himself at the last minute.

They stared at the sad little model. It wasn't to scale, and neither of them had enough artistic skill to make anything realistic. Their memories of the creek had been fuzzy from the start, and were fading fast.

"This is useless, isn't it?" Telfer said abruptly.

"Well, you wanted something to keep your hands busy," Laodice said. "It was useful for that."

Telfer glared at her, wanting to say something sharp about the wasted effort, but she was smiling at him, and he couldn't stay angry.

"Fine," he said, and sat back, listening to the music. The dramatic trumpets and drums they'd begun with had blended into something with lots of violins climbing on top of each other, and then something weird and atonal with an instrument Laodice had identified as a bassoon.

Now the whole orchestra was joining in, kind of raggedly, sometimes playing on top of each other, but out of time.

"What *is* this?" he asked.

"I don't know much about this kind of music," she said.

"Well, it's not my idea of romance. But you're the expert. What do you think?"

She listened for a moment, and then shook her head. "Sexy, maybe. Kind of frenetic." She looked at him for a moment. "What do you mean, I'm the expert?"

Telfer felt an unexpected heat in his face. "You're an excellent wedding writer," he said gruffly.

"Thank you," Laodice said politely. "So are you."

The music did something with cymbals, and Telfer jumped.

"But we both work in Bridal," Laodice continued. "What makes me, particularly, the expert on romance?"

"You know how to do it," Telfer said. He felt as if he were edging over a narrow bridge, while the precipice gaped below. "Date people, and have relationships, and so on. You're good at it."

"Oh," Laodice said. "Thank you for noticing? I worked at it, you know. It's not an inborn thing."

Telfer thought she'd probably started with some natural talent, but he nodded anyway.

"My sisters laugh at me for caring too much about romance," she said suddenly. "Xena once said that I'd fall in love with a mop, if it leaned against the wall in an appealing way. But I think who we love, who we bind ourselves to—that's maybe the most important decision of our lives. People prepare for years for their jobs, they get expert advice on home ownership or personal finance. Why shouldn't we train ourselves to love well? I'm not ashamed to say I want to be in love forever, that I want to marry someone great and be his, and have him be mine. And I want to do it right. It might be the most important thing I ever do."

Telfer swallowed hard. "I hope you get that," he said. "It sounds...that sounds really nice. And very sensible."

Some tension went out of Laodice's face. Her sisters laughed at her, she'd said. Did she think he might laugh at her too? "Have you thought about getting married, one day?" she asked.

"It doesn't seem very likely," Telfer said. "You might have noticed that I'm not the easiest person to love."

"Oh, you're not so bad," Laodice said. Her voice was flippant, and he tried not to take it personally. A week ago, "not so bad," would have been the nicest thing she'd ever said about him. "But I thought you'd be all about the practical side of marriage. You know, the financial and legal benefits. Maybe not so worried about the love part."

"The benefits are substantial," he admitted. "But my parents...you should have seen them. They were so in love. They were perfect for each other. I don't think I could settle for less than that."

Laodice stared at him.

"What?"

"You're a bigger romantic than I am!" she said.

"I certainly am not."

"Yes, you are! You want the *perfect* thing, and you won't settle for less. I bet you believe in one true love."

"Don't you?" he countered.

"No," Laodice said definitely. "I think everyone has many possible true loves, not one fated partner. I've been in love a lot, and sure, some of those loves were doomed from the start, but a lot of them could have worked out. They didn't, but that doesn't mean the possibility wasn't there."

"I'm not sure I've ever been in love," Telfer said. "For a while, I wondered if I might be aromantic. But I don't think so. I think I feel the pull towards it, the possibility, and then...I don't let myself go any further. I *want* romance. But I don't think I can do it right." He stopped, appalled at how honest he'd been, at how vulnerable he'd made himself.

Laodice didn't say anything immediately, and he braced himself for scorn. Or worse, pity.

"Thank you for trusting me with that," she said quietly, and when he looked at her he saw understanding. Sympathy, maybe, but not pity. "Love *is* hard. I wish more people would acknowledge that."

"Or I'm a coward," Telfer said, and Laodice tipped her head, considering.

"Cautious, maybe," she said. "Coward, no."

The music crashed through some strings, offered a flute trill, and ended abruptly on a final brash chord. In the absence of music, they distinctly heard a moan and a giggle from another booth, abruptly cut off.

"So!" Madame Esme said, and rapped her cane on the floor twice. "Dress, and rejoin me! Leave your art in the booth if you wish it to be private, or bring it with you for critique. You have until the song ends."

Telfer had expected more classical music, but instead Beyoncé's honey smooth voice greeted them, and ordered them to start snappin.' Madame Esme, he thought, liked to defy expectations.

He quickly smushed the unhelpful and incriminating crime scene model into a clay lump, and tossed it in the box, while Laodice bundled up the plastic sheets.

"Wait," she said, and went up on her tiptoes, brushing at the clay on his nose. Telfer caught her elbows on her way down and lifted her back up for a quick brush of his lips over hers.

She smiled at him, and ducked out of the booth.

Telfer stood still watching the curtain swish back and forth in her wake. The pull, the possibility, towards the most romantic person he knew. Who wanted him, sure, maybe even liked him. More than that, though? No.

"Not cautious," he said, under his breath. "Just a coward."

He went out to join the others. Laodice could have left the clay smear in place. Yvette and Xavier had chalk dust all over their hair and clothes, and Patrick and Samuel had splotchy paint handprints on their visible skin. Doubtless there were more under their clothes, from the way they grinned and nudged each other.

Carrick and Britt looked tidier, so he wasn't sure what their art medium had been, but Alma and Erik, as they exited their booth and joined the others, were an unholy mess. Alma's hair was matted on one side with something red and sticky, and she was wearing a necklace of fresh strawberry stalks, threaded through each other, with some of the bitten off fruit still clinging to a few of the green leaves. Erik had a white smudge in his golden curls, and the collar of his shirt had some dark stains with a distinctive scent.

Telfer sniffed. "Is that chocolate sauce?" he asked.

Erik grinned at him.

Telfer shook his head. "We got the dud box, honey," he told Laodice.

"Oh, I don't know. I rather liked your portrait work."

Telfer thought of the sexy fat woman he'd rolled out of the clay and had to stifle a laugh. As if anyone could properly capture Laodice's vibrant beauty in a still medium. She was a woman who needed to move.

And he was interested in getting her upstairs for some more movement as soon as possible. He didn't think he was the only one looking for some action, if the flushed cheeks and stealthy glances among the others were any indication.

But as Esme finished her lecture on keeping creativity alive in their union, Sarah came in and announced that lunch was awaiting them.

No one seemed enthusiastic about this. Patrick actually groaned.

But getting some fuel wouldn't be a terrible idea, Telfer decided. If he was going to be keeping up with Laodice he needed to maintain his stamina.

Laodice tugged on his hand, and he dipped his ear toward her lips. If he'd been expecting sweet nothings, he was sorely disappointed. "Sit with Erik," she hissed. "Get him to talk."

Oh, right. The *murder*.

***

Laodice respected the ease with which Telfer cut Erik out of the herd when they stepped into the lunch line. Apparently mindful of the need to keep her guests happy, Sarah had added a salad bar to the sandwich and fruit platters, and a chafing dish held a fragrant rice and prawn concoction. Kyle had obviously been sent to some more upmarket places in town.

"Oof, cilantro," Alma said. She'd watched Telfer take Erik away for some guy chat without alarm, so she either had nothing to worry about, or she was an incredible actress.

"Have you got the soap taster gene?" Laodice asked, piling rice on her plate.

"No, it doesn't taste like soap to me. It just tastes bad." She grabbed a sandwich instead, and then scanned the other offerings without enthusiasm. "Okay, not to be a bitch at a bad time, but isn't it kind of weird that literally nothing has been à la carte? We keep getting buffets or meals served without any choice."

"I guess," Laodice said. Should she let Alma in on the wage-skimming scam? No, Alma didn't have her need to watch the story unfold, and she didn't suffer fools without reason. She was totally capable of telling Sarah off, reporting her to her employer, and sweeping Erik away to a hotel in the Hippocampus for the rest of the week.

"The buffet is kind of fun, though," she added, as they sat down. "Like summer camp, but tasty."

Alma, as she'd hoped, took the diversion. "What kind of camp did you go to? I was a theater kid, so it was drama camps all the way for me."

"Really! I would have thought you'd have been more science-oriented."

Alma laughed. "I mean, that too, but we didn't have the money for space camp, which was what I *really* wanted. And drama camp gave me an audience, which I desperately needed, but didn't get a lot of. My sisters' dramas tended to take up most of the room at home." She rolled her eyes companionably. "Listen to me, trauma-dumping my way to friendship. I should save this for therapy. I truly am interested, though, what kind of camps for you?"

"Xena did outdoor adventure camps and Cassie did creative writing, and I did anything which wasn't those, so I wasn't stuck between them," Laodice said, with an honesty that startled her. Too late, she remembered that Elle Evagora didn't have a famous influencer sister with a unique name. Well, Alma already knew she wasn't Elle, and the others didn't seem to be paying attention to them.

Alma took a bite of her sandwich and made an encouraging noise.

"I love my sisters, but it was nice to have a few weeks a year when we weren't all over each other." She thought. "Actually, this week has kind of been like that, too. Usually we're in the group chat every day. I feel like I have more room to do my own thing without the peanut gallery."

Alma coughed. "I get that," she said.

"It's just... I tell them everything. Maybe I don't need to."

At some point, she supposed, she'd tell her sisters she'd slept with Telfer. Was going to continue to sleep with Telfer until Halcyon was done, all things going well, because *wow*, even hours after the sex, her body was still singing with it. But if she told them now, Cassie would be not-saying a lot of advice, and Xena would be aggressively enthusiastic about it and...she didn't want that. She wanted it to be this thing between her and Telfer, this surprisingly honest, extremely hot thing where they were both into each other, and didn't need to mediate that through anyone else.

And as a bonus, she wasn't going through her usual mental checklists about whether he was meeting her romantic needs and whether this might be a more permanent arrangement, because it so clearly couldn't be. It was weirdly relaxing, to not have that on her mind.

Alma's coughing fit had gotten worse.

"Are you okay?" Laodice asked, reaching for the carafe of water to pour her some, but Alma clutched her wrist, her eyes going wide.

"Nuts," she forced out, the word forced from her throat, her breathing hoarse. She pointed at the sandwich she'd taken two bites from.

"Oh, fuck," Laodice said, and stood up. Alma didn't have a purse with her. "Erik! Do you have an epi pen?"

Erik turned from where he was talking to Telfer, and his face was lit with horror as he rushed to Alma's side. He yanked an epi pen from his pocket, muttered something to himself, then stabbed it into Alma's thigh.

The room was full of gasps and wide eyes.

"Call an ambulance," Laodice snapped at Sarah, and helped Erik ease the stricken woman to the ground. You were supposed to keep people still and quiet, she remembered, to slow the allergic reaction.

"I—" Sarah said, staring at her. "I—"

"Now!" Laodice said, but Telfer had pulled out their burner phone and was already dialing.

"Hey, you're not supposed to have that," Xavier said indignantly

Laodice was about to explode at him, but Yvette actually snapped, "Not the time, Xavier!" as she hurried over. "I did a first aid course, can I help?"

"I think it's working," Erik said, watching Alma's face anxiously. Her eyes were closed, but she had a grip on his hand, and her breathing sounded more measured. "What was it? What was the nut?"

Yvette poked through the sandwich. In between slices of cold smoked chicken and juicy tomato was a tiny brown smear. "Peanut sauce, I think."

Erik went white around the lips. "That's the worst one. Maybe we should get the second pen from upstairs."

"I think I'm okay," Alma said, her voice raspy, but audible.

"The ambulance is on its way," Telfer said, sounding wonderfully calm and composed. He wasn't crowding the three of them where they were crouched over Alma, and Laodice caught the look he gave warning Patrick back when the other man would have come closer. He was so good in a crisis. He'd checked Jesse's pulse to make sure, when she'd still been freaking out, and he'd seen that Sarah wasn't capable of action. Now he was keeping the space around Alma clear and calm, without calling attention to himself or what he was doing.

Laodice did like a reliable man.

Alma managed to walk out to meet the ambulance, holding Erik's arm for support. The rest of them watched from the lobby, and Laodice wasn't the only one who sighed with relief when the EMT fitted the oxygen mask over her face and closed the door on her, whisking Alma and Erik away.

"Well!" Sarah said. "That was unfortunate. Um, it's siesta time now, so please feel free to rest and relax…"

Laodice had had enough. "Can I speak to you for a minute?" she snapped.

Sarah's eyes darted around the audience. "Sure! Can it wait until—"

"No," Laodice said, and took off towards the staff door behind the bar, waving Telfer off when he made a motion to follow. Sarah scurried to keep up with her, apparently deciding that discretion was the better part of Laodice shouting at her in front of eager listeners.

The staff door opened onto a white-painted back room with a cluster of empty office cubicles and industrial carpet. It was nothing like the lavishly decorated guest spaces, but pretty much what Laodice had expected, down to the dusty desks where more staff should have been. There were a few dark office spaces towards the back, and one lit-up—Sarah's office, presumably. A server cupboard hummed to one side, peculiarly loud in the silent room.

"Now, what's this about?" Sarah asked, forced sweetness in her voice.

Laodice whirled on her. Confronting a potential murderer without witnesses was probably stupid, but she was betting on herself winning any bare-knuckle physical confrontation, and there wasn't room in Sarah's sleeveless black shift dress for a weapon.

"Did you kill Jesse?" she demanded. "Did you try to kill Alma?"

Sarah's jaw dropped. "No!"

"Oh, really? You knew she was allergic to nuts, and now there's peanut sauce in her sandwich. And you've been hitting on Erik since the moment he arrived. Did you see an opportunity to get Alma out of the way?"

"No! It was a *mistake.* Kyle must have forgotten to check all the ingredients when..." She hesitated for a moment. "When he talked to the chef," she finished.

"When he ordered them from the restaurant, you mean," Laodice said. "Do you think we're *idiots*? You don't have a chef."

Sarah reared back. "We certainly do," she said. "Halcyon prides itself on—"

"Show me."

"What?"

"Show me your kitchen. Introduce me to your chef. And your housekeeper, and your night manager."

Sarah's mouth opened and closed again.

"Right. That's what I thought."

"Well, you're wrong!" Sarah said. "I didn't try to kill Alma, and I don't know anything about Jesse. I've never *killed* anyone. It was a mistake."

And that had the ring of truth, with some genuine outrage to boot.

But Laodice wasn't willing to let her wriggle out of all responsibility. "It's a mistake that wouldn't have happened if you had a professional kitchen, with a chef and a safety plan."

"Professional kitchens make mistakes all the time!" Sarah protested.

"That is *not the point.*" Laodice pointed at her, wishing she was taller. Xena would look properly imposing in this moment. "You're a grifter, Sarah. It's obvious that you're siphoning wages for imaginary staff into your own wallet. And in the process, you nearly killed Alma. Not to mention you've been trying to latch onto Erik from the moment he arrived. Did you see him as your next meal ticket?"

"Meal ticket?" Sarah demanded. "I make my own money, thank you."

"Then why the non-stop flirting?"

"Are you insane? I wanted to *fuck* him. That is the hottest man I have ever seen in my *life*. He's totally wasted on that mousy nurse."

"And you're indifferent to his millions, I'm sure."

Sarah looked interested. "Millions?"

Oh, hell. It had been a while since Laodice's investigative and data journalism elective, but she was pretty sure you weren't supposed to give information *away* to the subject.

"Well, I'm assuming," she said, trying to sound dismissive. "I mean, we've all got enough money to be here."

Sarah's eyes narrowed. "Oh, really? Do you, Elle?" She said the name with a heavy dose of sarcasm, and Laodice instinctively recoiled. "Because I did a little snooping myself. Your fiancé, he's for real. Telfer Terzi, son of the Filiz Flowers fortune. He should come into a nice little nest egg when his uncle kicks the bucket. But you—you don't exist. No social media profile, no mentions in the legacy media society pages."

She waved dismissively at Laodice's lacy sundress. "You dress the part. But you don't act quite right. Sometimes you sound like an airhead heiress, and sometimes you sound like a smart woman. I'll give you some credit; you know how to keep the drama alive. You pick fights with your fiancé and flirt with the bartender to make sure you keep his attention." She gave Laodice a patronizing look. "Honey, take it from me. Depending on a man to be your money is the wrong move. You can't rely on them. You think you've got them completely snowed, and then they pull out the prenup. Run your own game, that's my advice."

Laodice stared at her, thinking rapidly while she pretended a shock too great for words. Sarah thought "Elle" was a grifter too. Actually, it wasn't a bad conclusion to draw, although a real con artist would probably have a better cover identity. Laodice sometimes acted towards Telfer in ways a normal fiancée wouldn't, she turned conversation about herself away, she had that burner phone... Hell, right at the beginning of the stay, Sarah had been expecting someone named Eli to accompany her. The sudden replacement had to have raised some mental alerts.

Also, Telfer had money? He'd never mentioned it.

"But you didn't try to hurt Alma," she said, needing to be sure.

"For the nine millionth time, it was an accident," Sarah said, exasperated. "You think I want deaths or suspicious events here? The last thing I need is the police poking around. And I don't think *you* did it either, for the same reason. You don't seem like a dummy to me." She eyed Laodice. "You keep quiet about the staff, and I'll keep quiet about your game, okay? I don't think either of us want to spoil a good thing."

"Yeah, okay," Laodice said. Playing along with Sarah might get her more insight. "Did Jesse find out about the wage-skimming?"

Sarah snorted. "I doubt it. He stole a master key, though. Did something go missing?"

Laodice shook her head, and Sarah relaxed. "I wondered if he might snoop around or steal shit from the other guests. He seemed like a perv to me. I figured I could sting him for that later, or that Hazel might pay to cover it up." She smiled at Laodice. "That's another piece of advice. Always have more than one deal going. That way, you diversify your income streams *and* you don't depend too much on any one job. That's important. You've got to know when to get out."

Laodice smiled back. It wasn't hard. For some reason, Sarah as an open criminal was easier to like than Sarah as an insincere guide to love. "I'll keep that in mind," she said, and then added, "I mean, Telfer's not the only egg in my basket."

"Good!" Sarah looked speculative. "Actually... I've got something else going on. But it's big. I could use a reliable partner."

"The manifesting business?" Laodice hazarded.

Sarah laughed. "Hell, no. That's totally legal. You can life coach people into anything, as long as you never promise results. Even better if you can put the blame on them for not visualizing prosperity hard enough or whatever bullshit. But that's all chump change. The job I'm talking about is *real* money. Retirement money."

"I thought Kyle was your partner."

"Like I said, honey, you can't rely on men."

"And Danielle?"

Sarah looked amazed. "Danielle? She's not part of the job. She's the help—she came with the building. She's not even that helpful. It's been nonstop tears and headaches since you found Jesse's body. Look, are you any good with computers?"

"Sure," Laodice said. It was an outright lie. She knew enough to navigate the Olympus systems and didn't bother IT more than most people in the building. "I mean, you know I do cars, right? I started out as a driver. But that's risky. I upskilled in tech instead."

Instead of calling her out on this outrageous bullshit, Sarah actually seemed impressed. "You were a driver?"

"Yep," Laodice said, frantically trying to remember the details of every heist movie she'd ever seen. "Small jobs. Stores and stuff, no banks or museums or anything. But you don't get shot at in tech." She risked a patronizing look herself. "That's why Elle Evagora doesn't exist online. I don't want to be searchable." And, thanks to that early encounter with some of Xena's less fun followers, Laodice's own social media accounts were locked to friends and family. Laodice had never thought she'd be grateful to that cesspit of fatphobic self-hating incels, but being forced to control her online visibility had just paid off.

"Could you hack a server?" Sarah asked.

Laodice thought that might be a question that revealed Sarah knew even less about tech than she did. "Piece of cake," she said confidently. "What's the job?"

Sarah's eyes narrowed, but Laodice decided she was thinking, not suspicious. "I'll get back to you," she said. "Let's finish—"

Kyle banged through the door. "Cops are here," he said, with no preamble, and then did a doubletake at Laodice. "Uh, hi, Elle."

Sarah beamed at him. "Elle has decided it's best for everybody if she doesn't ask more questions about the staff. In case someone asks more questions about her."

"Oh," Kyle said, and looked at Laodice with a more personal interest. "So I was right? You're on the job with that Telfer guy? I figured you had to be, stuffed shirt like that."

Laodice raised her eyebrows, inwardly nettled by the jab at Telfer. "Sometimes business is a pleasure."

"Yeah, right," Kyle said. "Call me if you want a real good time, babe." He turned back to Sarah. "They want to talk to everyone privately, one by one."

"Fuck," Sarah said, and massaged her forehead. "That's all we need. Okay, well, you know the drill. We don't need to lie, because we don't fucking know anything. There's no security footage, because the guests need their privacy. And we're each other's alibi for the night in question."

"And when they ask to talk to the rest of the staff?" Kyle persisted.

"Send them to me, and I'll explain that we have a small staff to keep costs down."

Kyle looked unconvinced. "What if they get in touch with our backers, and they're like, 'what do you mean, there should be eight people there?'"

Sarah shrugged. "It's a loose thread, sure, but they won't pull it for a while. Not when they've got all these suspect statements to trawl through. And we only need a few more days."

Laodice cleared her throat. "So Jesse was definitely murdered?"

Sarah blinked at her. "Sure. Cops don't waste their time on questioning people about accidental death."

"You sound like you don't care."

"I don't," Sarah said. "My door locks tight. Nothing you want to share with us, Elle? Your tall, dark and handsome didn't shove Jesse down the stairs and drag him out into the woods?"

"And then led me right to the body?" Laodice said, surprised at how dry her voice was. "No, I don't think so."

Kyle looked disappointed, but Sarah was already moving towards the door. "My money's on Carrick," she said. "Ten bucks says he fesses up before dinner."

Chapter Thirteen

Telfer resigned himself to not being able to whisk Laodice up the stairs for a quick bang. If a seriously injured woman and a distraught fiancé hadn't been enough to dampen everyone's desires after the naughty art sessions, the cops turning up had been a total cockblock.

Patrick flatly refused to speak to the detectives. He was polite about it, and Telfer figured he'd had a similar talk from his parents to the one Telfer had gotten from Uncle Burak, because he clearly didn't want to give them cause for charges of obstructing justice or interfering with an officer in the pursuit of their duty. But he held firm, citing his right to remain silent, and asking, pointedly, if he was under arrest.

"We were hoping to avoid that, Mr. Orwin," Detective Bernard said, equally politely. "It would help us a lot if we could speak to you. We're trying to rule people out as much as anything."

"So I'm not under arrest or charged with any crime?"

"No, sir."

"Then I decline." Patrick gave the others a long look, as if he wanted to warn them too, but wasn't sure whether that was all right.

"None of us are obliged to speak to the police, but it would probably help if we did," Xavier said, sounding pompous.

"Of course *you'd* think that," Patrick said, and shook his head when Xavier opened his mouth. "Don't— I'm heading upstairs. Samuel?"

Samuel hesitated, and Telfer winced at the momentary pain that flickered across Patrick's face. But he went to join his future husband, and they went upstairs, talking quietly to each other.

Bernard turned to Xavier next. "Then you, Mr. Westlake," he said. He didn't look particularly enthusiastic. Finding out that Xavier and Yvette were lawyers had probably been as fun for Bernard as learning that Telfer and Laodice were journalists.

No one else refused an interview, but there was nothing to stop them going upstairs or chilling out in the hot tub while they waited. Instead, cowed by the silent expectations of the police, everyone waited in the lounge area while they were called in one at a time. Telfer was unavoidably reminded of badly organized job interviews.

He thought it was too late to stop people conferring on alibis or confusing their witness statements via conversation, but a uniformed officer sat with them anyway, presumably in case anyone felt like letting something slip. Telfer desperately wanted to know what Laodice had gotten out of Sarah, but instead he had to pass the time trying to figure out how the interviews had gone by the expressions people made when they left.

Kyle looked annoyed, Sarah glassily unreadable. Xavier looked ruffled and Yvette upset. Danielle was in tears as she left, and the female detective had actually escorted her out, looking sympathetic. Carrick had been sweaty and uncomfortable. The detectives spent a long time talking to Britt, and then called Carrick back in again. They left together, Britt patting his shoulder, and Telfer hoped he'd come clean about the blackmail.

The detectives called Telfer in last. Laodice had looked thoughtful going upstairs, but made a flat-palmed gesture Telfer thought was meant to be reassuring.

The first thing Bernard said was: "Ms. Troiades has informed us that she's undercover here for a story, and would prefer us not to advertise that to your fellow guests unless it becomes necessary."

Right. They were setting the stakes for the interview. Now Telfer and Laodice had incentive to cooperate.

"That's correct," Telfer said.

"Can you explain to me the nature of your relationship?"

"We're co-workers."

Bernard smiled. "With special benefits?"

Was he guessing, or had Laodice told him? No way to know for sure. "If you want to put it that way," Telfer said. "Is this relevant?"

"We're trying to get a feel for the dynamics." Bernard checked a notebook. It had some scribbled notes on it, but Telfer wouldn't lay any bets that they had anything to do with the next question. For all he knew, it was a grocery list. "You're also friends with Carrick Balshaw, is that correct?"

"I'm not sure I'd say friends. We were friendly in college, and have reconnected here."

"Ah. When was the last time you saw Jesse Heller?"

Since Telfer had already given Bernard this information, it seemed like an obvious test. He was asked several more questions of a similar nature ("And what made you decide to take that particular route on your walk? Mm. And how did you say Ms. Troiades happened to fall into the ditch again?") and then Bernard, turning over a piece of paper, casually asked, "What did you think of Jesse?"

"I didn't like him," Telfer replied, and cursed himself when Bernard brightened and leaned in.

"Really? Why not?"

"He was a dick."

"Any specific examples?" Bernard probed.

"Sometimes you just don't like people," Telfer said.

The female detective, who'd introduced herself but stayed silent up until this point, broke in then. "We've heard that Mr. Heller was aggressive towards his partner."

"I heard him shout at her," Telfer said. "And he said some unkind things, both to her face and behind her back." He grimaced, remembering. "He also tried to make Elle—Laodice, I mean—drink to excess when she'd been clear she didn't want to, and he told me that you had to keep a close eye on women because otherwise they cheated."

"Do you think he suspected his partner of cheating?"

"I think he probably accused her of that as a way to keep her in line."

"Do you think he was right? Was she cheating? Did you sleep with her?" The questions came rapid fire, so quickly that Telfer couldn't control his response. He stared at the detectives, who were looking politely interested.

"I did not sleep with Hazel," he said, slowly and clearly. "I don't think Hazel would cheat, but you'd have to talk to her. I imagine you *have* talked to her."

The female detective sat back. Detective Laurens, that was her name. "We appreciate multiple perspectives," she said calmly.

"She's a fragile little thing," Bernard said. "Brings out your protective instinct."

Telfer rolled his eyes. "I also didn't try to be her white knight and murder Jesse for her, if that's your next angle."

"Or help her out, once he was dead?" Bernard asked, and waved off the stink-eye Telfer gave him. "Come on, Mr. Terzi. You know how this goes."

"So the body *was* moved," Telfer said. Maybe Bernard thought the information gathering should all go one way, but he didn't have to go along with that. "And by someone strong enough to move it, which rules out Hazel, and probably Patrick and Yvette." He ran through the rest of his mental list. "And Danielle and Sarah, I suppose. Maybe Britt." Although on further thought, Britt did look strong. She could probably fireman carry a body a reasonable distance. Alma was a nurse and used to moving bodies, even if they were usually alive. Erik, of course, would do anything for her.

"You don't rule out yourself or Ms. Troiades," Bernard observed pleasantly.

"Not physically, no. In terms of motive or opportunity, we didn't have one."

"What if he discovered she was a journalist and threatened to expose her?"

"Did he?" Telfer countered.

"Hypothetically, if he had, would she have reacted poorly? I understand she's working towards a promotion."

"Hypothetically, you would have to ask her," Telfer said, and when the detectives went silent and looked at him expectantly, he sat still and stared back. He knew how silence worked. And unlike him, the detectives couldn't afford to waste their time waiting out someone who couldn't be a likely suspect.

"Right," Detective Bernard said. "If we can go over your movements on Monday night, please."

Telfer, who had been expecting a question like, "where were you between the hours of x and y," mustered his reserves and detailed his movements as honestly as he could, given that he really wasn't certain about many of the times. The lack of timekeeping at Halcyon had to be frustrating the cops.

Bernard asked him a few more questions about the other guests, poking in a desultory way at why Patrick might have refused to speak to them, but Telfer stuck firmly to, "you would have to ask him," and the detectives cut him loose with polite and unenthusiastic thanks for his cooperation.

He went upstairs, thinking hard, and found Laodice wrapped in the feather and velvet hotel robe, tapping furiously on her laptop.

"Getting notes down?" he asked.

"Arguing with my sisters," she said, face flushed, and snapped the laptop closed. "How was it?"

"I don't think I'm a real suspect. But would I know if I was?"

Laodice grinned. "They asked me if I'd ever seen you get angry."

"What did you say?"

"That I'd once argued with you for forty minutes about whether an article was too obvious a piece of SEO, but that the only thing you'd ever murdered were good pitches."

Telfer sat down on the edge of the bed. "I think we should discuss your belief that I shoot down good stories without reason."

"You have reasons. They're wrong, but you have them. Did you get anything from Erik?"

Telfer refocused, thinking about that lunchtime conversation. "He said Jesse barely talked to him, much less asked about his secret identity. The first time he and Alma met Jesse and Hazel, Erik shook Hazel's hand. Jesse made some joke about stealing his girl that wasn't a joke. Erik avoided him and Hazel as much as he could after that."

"You believe Erik?"

"He tried not to tell me about that first encounter, but he can't lie worth a damn. I have no idea how he's kept the author thing secret for so long."

Laodice shook her head. "It must have scared Alma, when she could see he was lying to her, and didn't know why. In other news, Sarah thinks I'm a gold digger marrying you for your money."

"What?"

Laodice's eyes were very bright. "But in the interests of women supporting women, she wants me to join her on a big job with my elite hacking skills."

"Do you have those?" Telfer asked, trying to keep up.

"She thinks so. Also, that I used to be a getaway driver. I couldn't believe what was coming out of my mouth." She paused. "I didn't actually know you had money."

"I have a trust, but it's mostly invested in my uncle's business," Telfer said. His mind was busy with a vision of Laodice wearing something short, tight and red, driving her convertible at breakneck pace up a winding mountain road while hundred dollar bills flew away from the stacks piled behind the seats. "You'd be a very sexy criminal."

"Thank you. But the short answer is I think Sarah didn't kill Jesse. She's not particularly cut up about his death, but she's mostly annoyed that it brought the cops in. And Alma seems to have been a genuine accident."

"Bernard gave me the impression he's looking for someone strong enough to have moved Jesse to that ditch."

"Someone. Not two people?"

"I don't think so. Maybe there's crime scene evidence we don't have, one set of footprints or something."

"This is fun," Laodice said, frowning. "Is it wrong that it's so fun?"

"A lot of wrong things are fun," Telfer said, thinking about Laodice as a criminal mastermind again.

"Speaking of," Laodice said, and undid the belt of the velvet robe.

Underneath, she was wearing something hot pink and silky. There were ruffles. There were straps. There was...

"Is that crotchless?" Telfer asked, his throat tight.

Laodice propped one foot up deliberately. "For convenience. Now, if we narrow the list down to people capable of carrying Jesse, who does that leave us?"

"You're killing me," Telfer said, and she pouted and closed her knees. "Wait, no, I can do this. Ruling us out, Xavier, Carrick, maybe Britt, maybe Alma, Samuel, Erik, and Kyle."

Laodice licked her lips. Telfer didn't think they were dry. "Not Patrick?"

Telfer tried to summon some blood back to his brain. "I think he's too small. Maybe Patrick murdered Jesse, and Samuel moved him—look. You're insanely hot and I'm losing my mind, but mixing murder discussion and sex feels wrong. And not the fun kind of wrong." He blew out a breath. "Sorry."

Laodice had wrapped the robe around herself again and abandoned the sex kitten pose. "Don't be sorry," she said earnestly. "You set a boundary. That's totally okay. And we think no on Erik and Alma having a motive?"

"Yes."

"And Sarah and Kyle are each other's alibis."

"Huh. Are they sleeping together?"

Laodice shrugged. "Maybe. So, Xavier, Carrick, Britt, and Samuel. Or Patrick and Samuel working together."

"And as far as we know, Xavier has no motive either."

"No." Laodice was silent for a moment. "I don't like who we're left with."

"Me either," Telfer said.

"Sarah thinks it was Carrick."

"Why?"

"I don't know. Vibes, probably."

Telfer grimaced. "I'll try to talk to him after dinner."

"I'll talk to Britt." She paused. "So...are we done with the murder discussion?"

"I think so."

"Great," Laodice said cheerfully, and untied her robe again. "Because I've got all this lingerie I haven't been wearing, and I'd like to get some use out of it."

"I'm not sure how long you'll be wearing that," Telfer said, and started taking off his shirt.

***

233

Despite his suggestion, Telfer seemed to be happy for Laodice to keep wearing the teddy, especially when he discovered that playing with her nipples through the satin made her eyes roll back in her head. For her part, Laodice thought it was fair that she put more work in this time, and Telfer's reaction to her mouth on his cock was extremely satisfying.

He made a strangled noise as she hollowed her cheeks and dragged up, letting his cock spring from her lips with an obscene popping sound. She watched the head swell and darken, then teased it with the tip of her tongue.

"Get up here," Telfer demanded.

"But I'm having so much fun," Laodice said, pretending that the order didn't turn her on.

"If you keep—" Telfer said, and then groaned as she bobbed down his cock again, taking him as deep as she could manage. Pretty deep, actually, and if she had more time and was a little more patient, she could—

"I'm *serious*," Telfer said, sounding like a man on the edge, and she let him slide out of her mouth and hovered, looking up at him. She was aware that her mouth was swollen and her hair was tumbling wildly over her shoulders, pooling over his belly and thighs.

"Hello," she said, and touched her top lip with the tip of her tongue.

"You're the sexiest woman I've ever seen," Telfer said, and it wasn't playful banter, he *meant* it, and that slammed straight into the pit of her stomach.

She accidentally-on-purpose let his cock drag between her breasts as she slithered up his body, and he groaned again, and then she was kissing his mouth, and he was grabbing her, muttering delirious nonsense between kisses as he got the condom on and guided her hips back and onto his.

They both gasped when she took him inside her body, and Telfer's eyes were riveted on the pink fabric between her legs, the gap he was splitting open. Laodice bounced a little, getting used to the stretch. "Tell me how much you want me," she invited.

"Fuck," Telfer said, which was probably more of an exclamation than an instruction, but she settled a little deeper on his cock anyway. "What do you want to know?"

"You said you'd wanted me for years. What did that look like? Did you fantasize about me?"

"That would be wrong," Telfer said, his eyes locked on hers. "Us working together, me thinking that kind of thing..."

"Mm-hmm. Did you, though? Did you see me walk around in a long dress and wonder if I was wearing panties?"

Telfer's hips jumped up. "That one," he strangled out. "Definitely that one. Sometimes, we'd argue and I'd think, this is why shouting at someone and then kissing them is a cliche..."

"It is!" Laodice said, delighted. "The *worst* cliche, so rom-com of you. What if I grabbed you by your tie and dragged your mouth down to my tits?"

"What if you sat naked in an office chair and I ate you out?"

"What if," Laodice said, and lost track of herself for a second, as Telfer jumped his hips up and hit something *really good*. "What if we were both working late, and you—oh, that's perfect."

Telfer's abs flexed as he sat up, his arms going around her. "And what?"

"Huh?"

"We're both working late," he said, punctuating every word with a thrust. "And I do what?"

"You sweep everything off your desk, and you say, that's it, I can't take it anymore, I have to have you."

"And you're into this?"

"It's a *fantasy*," Laodice said, and wriggled, seeking the friction she needed. "I'm like yes, take me, right here, right now. Oh no, wait—"

"I absolutely can't," Telfer ground out, and she laughed, taking his face in her hands and kissing him, because he was *funny* and *sexy* and this felt *so good*.

"We do it on the top floor," she said. "Hera's office, only it's *my* office, I'm the CEO of Olympus, and I tell you to strip me naked and turn me around and fuck me against that big glass wall. I look out over the whole city, and I can see you reflected behind me, looking at me the way you're looking now, like you could just eat me up, like you could never get enough—"

"Fuck," Telfer croaked, leaning his forehead against hers, his breath puffing over her lips. "Please tell me you're close."

"Nearly there," she said. "Oh. Oh, there, yes, that's it, please, please, that's it, don't stop, oh—" she broke, in long, quivering waves of pleasure, and he held her through it, rocking his hips in relentless rhythm, and before she could express her gratitude properly or even catch her breath, he closed his eyes and shuddered, and she felt him pulsing inside her.

They sat there, entangled in each other, while their breathing eased and their heartbeats slowed, then Telfer kissed her again, slow and gentle.

"I could never get enough of you," he said, and then his eyes widened, as if he really hadn't meant to say it.

"Oh," Laodice said, and felt a prickling in her eyes, because all right, she was awash with hormones right now, so everything made her emotional, but that was actually kind of *sweet*. "Thank you. That's an amazing compliment."

"Not a compliment," Telfer said gruffly. "It's a statement of fact."

Laodice flushed. She carefully extracted herself from the embrace and went to clean up, thinking about the next steps in their investigation, but wanting to be respectful of the limit he'd set. No mixing murder talk and sexy times.

She'd just managed to wriggle out of the teddy and get in the shower when Telfer stepped in with her. There was easily room for two, and the flexible shower head had some excellent settings, and it turned out they had to delay the murder talk for a little longer.

***

Dinner was fish and chips. Danielle brought out their plates, looking sad and pale, and then placed two giant bowls of green salad in the middle of the table for the guests to serve themselves. Kyle moved around the room, offering a variety of white wines to go with the battered cod.

"A Hippocampus specialty!" Sarah said brightly, which might even have been true, but Telfer was willing to bet the fancy restaurants by the waterfront provided more options. He dolloped tartare over everything, and sat beside Carrick.

Carrick looked unwell. His usually ruddy face was pale and his forehead clammy.

"Are you okay?" Telfer asked.

"Sure. I mean, no. The murder and all."

Telfer glanced casually around the gallery room. Xavier and Yvette were sitting at one end of the long table. Britt and Patrick hadn't come down for dinner, and Laodice had joined Samuel at the other end, leaving Carrick to him.

If he lowered his voice, they should all be out of earshot.

He took the chance. "I thought you might be relieved."

Carrick stared at him. "Relieved? What do you mean?"

"Because he was blackmailing you," Telfer said bluntly. "I overheard you talking about it."

Carrick pushed his plate away with a violent motion, his knife clattering to the floor. The other couples turned to look, and Telfer bent to retrieve the knife. When he came back up, Carrick was doing a pretty reasonable attempt at looking casual, but his eyes were wild.

"Did you tell the police?" he demanded, his lips barely moving.

"Not yet."

"Don't," Carrick said, more earnest than pleading. "It won't do you any good."

"Do *me* any good?"

"I didn't hurt Jesse. But I...I can't talk about this, man."

"We can go somewhere else."

Carrick shook his head. "I can't."

"Are you in trouble?" Telfer asked, feeling a surge of unwilling sympathy. "Carrick, whatever it is, shouldn't you come clean? Honesty is the only defense against blackmail."

Carrick looked...sympathetic. As if *Telfer* were the one who needed comforting. "I didn't do anything to Jesse," he repeated. "I know it looks bad, but I promise it wasn't me."

Against all odds, Telfer believed him. Whatever had put Carrick in a flop sweat, he didn't think it was murder.

But he and Laodice had agreed not to rule people out because they liked them.

"Where's Britt?" he asked, trying a different angle.

Carrick didn't noticeably relax. "In our room. She wanted to get some work done."

"What does she do?"

"Analysis," Carrick said shortly.

"Whoa. Everything okay with you two?" Telfer said, trying to keep his voice light.

Carrick scowled at his plate. "No. Not really.." He grimaced, apparently at his own tone. "I don't think Britt and me are going to last."

"What? Why?"

"She could do so much better than me."

Telfer blinked. "But you're getting married."

Carrick shrugged, and ate a fry. It had to be cold. "Maybe."

Telfer wished he'd never sat down. He had to be the person in this room least equipped to offer anyone romantic advice, maybe even including Sarah. "Have you talked to her about this?"

"No," Carrick said.

"Maybe you're just getting cold feet."

Carrick stared at him. "You think—oh. No, Telfer, I'm not worried about how I feel. I love her. I'm going to love her until I die." He said it with easy conviction, then sighed. "But she doesn't feel the same way."

Telfer glanced at Laodice. "How do you know, unless you talk to her?"

"I just do." Carrick made a reasonable attempt at a smile. "Anyway, don't let me put you off. I'm shitty company today. Go sit with Elle."

Laodice, with consummate timing, had chosen that moment to get up, excusing herself from the table. She shot Telfer a look on the way out, her eyes brimming with suppressed excitement.

Telfer diagnosed that since she couldn't get anything out of a Britt who wasn't in attendance, she was going to snoop.

"At least you two are great for each other," Carrick said, cheering up. "Look at you, grinning like an idiot. I never thought the ice man would melt. You were a one-night-stand legend in college."

"Oh, well," Telfer said, and ate a few fries himself. The cold grease coated his tongue. "I guess appearances can be deceptive."

Chapter Fourteen

L aodice had internally debated between sneaking into the staff area or knocking on Britt's door. She really wanted to talk to Britt—the self-possessed woman would be hard to shock or shake anything out of, but it might be possible to appeal to her better nature, and see if she knew or suspected anything about Jesse's blackmail attempts.

However, Kyle and Sarah were both in the dining room, and if previous patterns held true, they'd be there until the end of the meal at least. That meant Danielle was the only person in the staff spaces, and she'd overheard the young woman asking Sarah if she could go nap in her room. Sarah had dismissed her with irritation, but it was good news for Laodice. She might never get a better time to snoop.

The foyer was still and silent, and Laodice shivered as she headed for the bar and the door behind it. It was weird; she knew there weren't any security cameras and that nobody in the gallery room could possibly hear her, but she was still moving quietly, her ears straining for any sound.

And just as well, because as she neared the staff door, she heard the unmistakable noise of someone turning the handle, as well as an exasperated huff.

Laodice took two steps backward and ducked behind the bar. It was partial concealment at best, and she held her breath as Danielle shoved the door open, but the younger woman didn't look behind herself as she strode towards the main entrance. Laodice caught the flash of a phone screen in her hand.

"Hello?" Laodice heard her say. "Yes, it's urgent."

And then Danielle was out the front door.

Okaaay. Well, that was weird, possibly even suspicious. Hadn't Telfer said Danielle wasn't allowed to have a phone? On the other hand, if she'd been employed here, Laodice would have totally broken that rule too. And if Danielle had decided on getting a breath of fresh air and talking to a friend instead of taking a nap, Laodice wouldn't fault her for that either.

There was no keycard scanner on the staff door, and though there was a deadbolt, it wasn't engaged. Sarah obviously didn't care about making the others keep up any kind of security protocol. Laodice slipped through the door and wondered what the police had made of the lax security. If they'd bothered to ask, of course, and if Sarah had told the truth. She couldn't help thinking of Olympus, with its security gates and guard station on the ground floor, of the keycard that got her to the sixth floor and Stephanie at the Bridal reception desk, screening all visitors. In comparison, Halcyon appeared to be running on the honor system, which would be all well and good if one of the inhabitants wasn't a murderer.

The lights were still on in the administration area, which probably meant Danielle planned to come back soon. Laodice would need to work fast.

Unfortunately, Sarah's office door *was* locked. Laodice poked around a couple of the other offices, but there was nothing in them but furniture.

Brand new office chairs sat behind unmarked desks with empty drawers and filing cabinets, everything with a patina of dusty neglect.

Remembering what Sarah had said about her hacking a server, Laodice tried the humming cabinet next, but that, too, was locked. She turned into the hallway off the office space, feeling like an idiot. Only about fifty-four percent of murders were ever solved, and that was by the professionals. She wasn't a police officer or a spy, and it was sort of silly to behave like one.

On the other hand, something strange was happening at Halcyon, and the police might not be the best people to work it all out. There was the murder, of course, but also the job Sarah had mentioned. Something big, she'd said. Retirement money.

Laodice was fairly certain Sarah meant to retire in comfort.

The hallway had several doors. She found a small staff lounge behind one, with a kitchenette and a new couch. The next two doors were locked, but she went on, doggedly trying them all while she listened for the sound of Danielle's return. She'd already marked several hiding spots.

The next door opened onto a small, obviously unoccupied bedroom, with a single bed holding a bare mattress and two pillows without cases, a nightstand, and a clothing rack. A smaller door inside the room opened onto a sink, toilet, and closet-sized shower. Laodice envisioned the luxurious bathroom she'd enjoyed upstairs, and felt a pang of guilt.

Hm. If this was the live-in accommodation for staff, then the two previous locked doors were probably also bedrooms. She went back to the hallway and tried the door opposite.

This one opened on another bedroom, empty of an inhabitant, but definitely in use.

The bed was neatly made with a patterned duvet, and a pair of shiny black shoes were under the clothing rack, which held white business shirts and black slacks. There was more furniture, too: a plastic set of drawers that probably held more clothes, and a narrow bookshelf, leaning haphazardly from the weight of the hardcover books crammed into it. Laodice squinted at the titles in the light coming in from the door, and spotted *The Encyclopedia of Cocktails, Spirited, Meehan's Bartender Manual*, and *Cocktail Codex*.

Kyle's room. She slipped inside and closed the door, turning on the nightstand lamp for light.

Then she paused. Up until now, she hadn't done anything really bad. Keeping information from the cops wasn't a crime, and walking into a restricted area might get her kicked out of Halcyon, but didn't *feel* illegal. Searching someone's private possessions felt criminal. And was, you know, wrong.

Laodice waited for the voice of her conscience to chime in, which it usually did sounding uncannily like Cassie. Not a whisper.

Okay, then. She grabbed a couple of tissues from the nightstand, in case fingerprints became a thing, and pulled the top drawer open.

Underwear, socks, and a handgun.

She sucked in a breath.

Come to think of it, what *was* Jesse's cause of death? Based on what she'd seen of the body, she'd been assuming a blow to the head. Something had definitely split his scalp, and there'd been blood all over his face. Wouldn't she and Telfer have noticed a bullet wound?

Her memory of heist movies and the occasional crime drama weren't helping her out much on this topic. She'd have to do some searching online when she got back to the room. In the meantime, it might be useful to know that Kyle had a gun.

She made quick work of searching the rest of the bedroom and the bathroom, both of which were annoyingly normal and didn't have anything like a secret panel that concealed a briefcase full of a million dollars and several passports, Jesse's missing shoe or laptop, or a signed confession note that outlined exactly what Kyle had done and for what reasons. It was the room of a man who didn't spend much time in it and hadn't brought many possessions to Halcyon. The collection of mixology and cocktail books were the closest things to personal items. They'd obviously been read, with narrow highlighter tabs bristling from the top of *Cocktail Codex* like a neon-colored cityscape. She opened it and thumbed through. There were some pencil notes printed in a strong hand, indicating different amounts or noting substitutions. He'd highlighted a lot of the introduction.

Laodice recognized the signs of a true obsessive, and replaced the book with more respect than she'd previously had for Kyle.

Time was running out. She scanned the room one last time, decided she hadn't disturbed anything too much, and went back to the hall. Two more empty bedrooms, a laundry room with two washers and dryers, and at the end of the hallway, the kitchen.

It was a beautiful space, with gleaming stainless-steel benches, a full complement of pots and pans, and several oven and grill stations. Her own kitchen was usually used for heating takeout leftovers, one-pot pasta dishes, or the occasional lazy breakfast, but she'd seen the test kitchens at Olympus. This kitchen was smaller, but it had the same feeling of ruthless efficiency in the service of art. The only notes of discord were a dirty cutting board and knife, with a few lettuce scraps clinging to the blade, and the deep fryer in the corner, still smelling of fish. So the salad had been prepared onsite, and the fish and chips at least cooked here... She opened the doors to the enormous fridge and found two heads of lettuce waiting their turn to go under the knife. The freezer next to the fridge had a giant bag of frozen french fries, three-quarters empty, and a popular brand of battered fish fillets.

More confirmation of what Sarah had already all-but-confirmed. But nothing new, no revelations into the dual mysteries of who had killed Jesse and what Sarah thought was going to be her last big job.

This whole spying venture had been a bad idea, risky *and* stupid. She went into the walk-in pantry, closing the door behind her. It was barely stocked—boxes of cereal and kitchen basics. She closed her eyes, annoyed, and opened them again.

Then she went still. At the top of her eyeline, nearly out of sight on the top shelf, she could see the corner of something smooth and black.

A laptop, maybe.

Maybe *Jesse's* laptop.

She needed something to stand on. A stepladder, or a stool, or even a box. She opened the pantry door, and nearly fell headlong into Britt.

They stared at each other in mutual shock and suspicion.

Britt recovered first. "What are you doing here?" she said, in a harsh whisper.

"What are *you*—" Laodice began, and cut off as they both heard the sound of footsteps in the hallway, getting closer.

Britt grabbed her arm. "This way," she said, almost inaudible, and Laodice let herself be hustled through another door, into another short hallway, which spat them both out in the room that Laodice had thought was probably meant to be a gym, right next to the hot tub room.

Britt let out a breath she might have been holding the entire time, and Laodice wrenched her arm free. It hadn't escaped her that she might have been walking with a murderer. She'd made the decision to go with her in an instant, and had had to follow it through. Now she was thinking.

"Upstairs," Britt said, her voice tense, and they went back through the foyer and past the gallery room, where Laodice could still hear voices in quiet conversation. It seemed like years since she'd been in that room, but her whole spying adventure had probably taken a grand total of fifteen or twenty minutes.

Laodice followed Britt, eyeing the woman's broad back. She was putting some pieces together. The walk, the steady authority, the practical watch she hadn't removed…

Britt opened the door to the room she shared with Carrick, and for a moment Laodice lost her train of thought. The suite was decorated in clean white and chrome grey, with strip lighting glowing softly on the walls. The bed was low and white, with subtle trapezoidal shaping. But it was the ceiling that drew the eye, shaped and painted to suggest a geometrical observation dome, with stars not just painted on the roof, but twinkling LED lights brightening, then fading in a complex pattern.

"A spaceship room," she said. "Cool."

Britt smiled, her eyes softening a little. "Carrick loves it." She motioned with her chin to the door. "Closed, please."

Laodice obeyed, but before Britt could start talking, she leaned casually against the wall and looked her up and down. "So, you *are* a cop."

Britt's eyes narrowed. "Who said that?"

"None of your business."

"I am not a police officer," Britt said, too carefully.

"Isn't this the thing where if you're a cop you have to tell me?"

Britt rolled her eyes. "That thing wouldn't apply, and also doesn't actually exist."

"Really?"

"Think about it. Undercover officers would be made in an instant. Anyway, I'm not, strictly speaking, a cop."

"Uh-huh. So as far as I know, you were snooping around, exactly like me, and I have no obligation to do anything you say."

Britt regarded her. "I'm a law enforcement agent with different responsibilities and a jurisdiction outside the local police force. For reasons I am not able to discuss, I need you to not mention to anyone that you saw me in the staff area."

"Are you FBI? CIA?"

"I'm not going to tell you."

"NSA?"

"Laodice, I'm not going to tell you. I wouldn't even be telling you this much if I didn't need you to keep your mouth shut. Can I trust you?"

"I'd need to see some sort of ID," Laodice said, and then registered that Britt had used her real name.

Britt waited a beat, to make sure she'd gotten it, and shrugged. "I don't have my ID on me."

"Well, that's convenient."

"Not right now," Britt said, dryly enough that it took Laodice a second to recognize it was a joke. "Okay. Give me a minute." She reached under her pillow, and Laodice tensed, but Britt's hand came back holding a phone, not the weapon Laodice had abruptly feared.

Britt noticed her tension. "At least you have some survival instincts," she said. "I was beginning to wonder." She held up one finger and placed a call. "Hello. Yes, sir, that's correct. Would you be able to confirm to someone that I'm a member of an unspecified government agency?" A pause. "An accidental encounter in the course of my investigation." Another pause. "No, sir. Nothing relevant to your case. Here." She handed the phone to Laodice.

"Hello?"

"This is Detective Bernard of the Hippocampus PD."

Laodice had more or less expected that. "This is Laodice Troiades."

A pause. A sigh. "Ms. Troiades, I can assure you that I have personally checked Ms. Evans's credentials, and she is indeed a member of a government agency. I have spoken to her superior officer, and was informed that exposing this information would endanger both Ms. Evans and her current case."

"But you told her who I was," Laodice said. Unless Alma had spilled the beans, it was the only explanation.

"I did." Bernard waited a beat. "Is that all?"

"So you don't know what she's working on either, huh?"

"Ms. Evans is outside of my jurisdiction, Ms. Troiades," Bernard said, and yeah, he didn't know and he didn't like it. Having some kind of federal agent—Britt had to be, if she was getting cooperation from the local police—interfering in his case must be intensely irritating.

Britt held her hand out for the phone. Laodice ignored her.

"Was it the blow to the head that killed Jesse?" she asked, trying her best to sound casual.

"I'm not able to discuss—"

"So he wasn't shot?"

"Shot?" Bernard said. He sounded startled for a beat, then his voice slid smoothly back into weary patience. "What makes you say that?"

"Just wondering!" Laodice said cheerily, and hung up.

"You're a menace," Britt said, as Laodice handed back the phone. "Are you happy now?"

"I won't tell anyone except Telfer. And he can keep a secret."

Britt grunted, as if that was more or less what she'd expected. "No one else, please. I'm not kidding when I say this could be life or death."

"Does Carrick know?"

"Yes. You can confirm that with him if you like, but don't discuss it further."

"And you know that Jesse was blackmailing him?"

"For fuck's sake," Britt said, looking genuinely angry for the first time. "How much have you managed to ferret out? Anything else you want to tell me?"

Laodice thought of the laptop, hidden on the top shelf of the pantry, and held her tongue. Britt wasn't there for Jesse's killer, and if it did turn out to be Jesse's laptop, Laodice would, naturally, hand it over to the police. But she wanted a look at it first.

"Okay, yes," Britt said. "Jesse was trying to pressure Carrick to get him a new job. Jesse's family are high-flyers—politicians, big funds—and Jesse was supposed to graduate summa cum laude, go to law school, and become a senator by the time he was 35. What actually happened was that he partied through college, graduated without honors, and smashed his car into a preschool fence while he was on coke."

"A *preschool*?"

"It was at night. No one was hurt."

Laodice raised her eyebrows. "But none of that looks great on your law school application."

"Nope. He might have gotten in somewhere, provided he pleaded rehabilitation and his dad wrote a big enough check." Britt shook her head. "But *then* he paid someone else to take the LSAT for him. And that, the schools don't tolerate. He was red-flagged. No law school pipeline to politics.

"My guess is that his dad called in a few favors to get him a place at a buddy's office, but Argive Holdings is a bigger place, a bigger name. That's why he was pressuring Carrick. He thought blackmail would get him in faster than actually working for it, the lazy asshole."

"He's dead," Laodice said doubtfully. She wasn't sure if not speaking ill of the dead should really extend to Jesse, but her mother's voice was sounding in her head anyway.

"He's a dead lazy asshole," Britt said, unmoved.

"Did Hazel know? About any of this?"

"I'm not sure. I do know that it was a whirlwind romance. He met her through friends last year. She's got a sizeable trust fund, and stands to inherit substantially more."

"She'd already married him," Laodice said.

"And how did you know that?"

"I overheard her telling Yvette."

"I should put you on payroll," Britt said. "Well, what's your take? Who do you think took out Jesse?"

"I—" Laodice said, and then stopped. If it wasn't Carrick or Britt, that meant the last real suspects she and Telfer had left were Samuel and Patrick. She and Telfer hadn't told the police about Jesse trying to bug them, and Britt probably didn't know about it either. And the timeline worked. Patrick could have killed Jesse in reaction to his snooping—by accident or self-defense, it had to be, she couldn't see him committing murder—and then he'd gone downstairs, pulled Samuel away from the cocktail thing, and later that night, when everyone else was sleeping, Samuel had taken Jesse into the woods and hidden him.

And the next morning—what? They'd hidden Jesse's laptop in the kitchen pantry for...some reason? They'd kept pretending they wanted to talk to Jesse, showing Laodice and Telfer the bug and pretending to be worried about Hazel, all the while knowing that Jesse was dead and his body was lying in a creek?

Laodice let go of her skirt and smoothed the fabric she'd crumpled with her hands. "I don't know," she said. "I don't know what the police turned up or what everybody's alibis are."

Britt was watching her shrewdly. "But you have an idea, don't you?"

"Up until ten minutes ago, you, Carrick, or both of you working together were my top suspects," Laodice said, with perfect truth. "I didn't *want* to think it was either of you, but blackmail's a good motive."

And she couldn't help noticing that Britt hadn't told her anything about the blackmail, other than to confirm Carrick was being pressured. Instead, she'd ruthlessly spilled the sordid details of Jesse's background. Was she hoping Laodice would bite at juicier meat if it was dangled in front of her nose?

There was a shuffling noise outside the door, and she must have reacted somehow, because the next moment Britt had glided towards her and was opening the door for Carrick.

"Hey," he said, smiling at her, and Laodice saw his whole heart in his eyes.

She sort of wished she hadn't. Whatever Britt's investigation was, he seemed to be a part of it, which meant she and Telfer weren't the only people who'd started the week in a fake relationship.

Carrick's feelings, it seemed, were all too real.

*✱✱

Telfer had unearthed a pack of sticky notes from his satchel, and sat at the dressing table-cum-desk, doing his best to make some sort of coherent order of the firm evidence (rare) and guesses (many) he and Laodice had put together.

"Hey, I think we can—" he said, turning to Laodice when she came in, and then he saw her face. "You got something?"

"I got a *lot*," Laodice said. "In order, Danielle has a phone, Kyle has a gun, I think Jesse's laptop is hidden in the kitchen, and Britt's a Secret Service agent or something. Oh, and I'm pretty sure the cause of death was head trauma, because of the way Bernard reacted when I mentioned shooting."

"Okay," Telfer said, and leaned back in his chair. "Explain."

Laodice did. It took over half an hour, with a lot of backtracking and, "did I tell you about that? What about this?" and he wasn't aware if she knew she was grinning through most of it, revved up by her success and the adrenaline rush of what sounded like a couple of nerve-wracking encounters with law enforcement. She did stop smiling towards the end, when she brought up the increased likelihood of Patrick and Samuel as perpetrators.

"I was thinking about that," Telfer said, and pointed at his sticky notes.

"Cool, a murder board," Laodice said, leaning over his shoulder. "All you need is some red string."

Telfer had thought the same thing, but he was using arrows instead. "We've been thinking that if it was more than one person, it had to be a couple, but that's not necessarily true. Patrick could have killed Jesse and bribed Kyle to move him. Or Hazel could have done it—"

"Not Hazel," Laodice said.

"We're not ruling people out because we like them, remember?" Telfer said.

"This isn't because I like her. I saw her realize he was dead. She didn't do it."

"Logically, though, she had the best motive and the most opportunity." He pointed to the line of green notes that detailed the timeline. "We only have her word that Jesse didn't come back that night. What if he did? What if he said something or did something—hit her for the first time, maybe—and she realized that she was trapped, that divorce would give him half of everything. Maybe he came at her and she panicked and smacked him with something."

"Like what?"

"Like anything. There's a ton of blunt instruments in this room. You could murder me with that lamp."

"Don't think I haven't considered it," Laodice said, but her heart clearly wasn't in it. "And then she got someone else to get rid of him?"

"Yes. She could have gone to Yvette for help—she already knew Yvette had promised to do anything to help her."

"Yvette probably couldn't carry a body that far."

"She spends hours in the gym every week," Telfer said triumphantly. "She's thin, but strong. And even if Yvette didn't take on the task herself, what are the odds she could talk Xavier into it?"

"High," Laodice conceded. "But this is all pointless, Telfer, because I'm telling you Hazel didn't do it."

Telfer frowned. "And what evidence do you have?"

"Again, I was looking right at her when she learned he was dead," Laodice said, too patiently, as if he was the one being obtuse. He must have done something to express his disbelief, some movement or expression, because she reached out and grabbed his shoulder. "Hey. I'm serious. It doesn't fit neatly into your chart, but I was there. I know."

Telfer shook his head. "Intuition isn't evidence. Haven't you ever been wrong about people before?"

Laodice hesitated. "Occasionally, but not often," she said. "And I'm right about this. Can't you trust me?"

"I can trust *you*," Telfer said. "But I'm sorry, no, I can't take Hazel's innocence as a matter of fact based on your feelings." It was true, and he had to say it, but he tried to soften it the way Laodice might, with a smile and a softer tone.

She looked at him thoughtfully, with no instant switch into confrontation. "Okay," she said. "We'll agree to disagree."

Telfer clutched his heart in an effort to play down his real surprise. "We're *not* going to argue?"

"Not this time," Laodice said cheerfully, and bounced onto the end of the bed. "What else did you get?"

"Not much, other than Carrick being head over heels for Britt, and certain she doesn't feel the same way. Which makes more sense now." He thought about it. "And now I understand why they didn't look mussed up after the art event. I suppose they must have sat there and listened to the music. Oh, and he was jumpy about the blackmail thing. Said looking into it wouldn't do me any good, and he couldn't talk about it. That has to be Britt's case, right?"

"Yes," Laodice said. "I'm dying of curiosity, but she's not going to tell us anything about it, and she and Detective Bernard were both serious about us not telling anyone else."

"Not even your sisters?"

"I *can* keep secrets from my sisters." She gave him a sly look.

"Ashamed of me?" Telfer asked lightly, and barreled on before she could answer: "So our next priority is that laptop. I'll wait for things to quiet down and get it tonight."

Laodice blinked. "*You* will?"

"I will. I don't see why you should have all the fun." He reached above his head, making a plucking gesture with his hands. "Besides, unlike some people, I can reach the top shelves."

"Rude," Laodice said, and stretched, looking sly again. "In the meantime, how should we entertain ourselves?"

"Have you paid any attention to the handholds in the bath?" Telfer asked politely. "If not, I have a few ideas I'd like to propose."

Laodice was already walking towards the bathroom, peeling her dress off over her head. "I had a few thoughts myself," she said over her bare shoulder. "Let's see how far they coincide, hm?"

***

The strained muscle in Telfer's butt was vigorously complaining about all the use he was putting it to. The rest of his body was shouting it down and demanding more, as soon as possible. He couldn't remember the last time he'd had this many orgasms in close succession, much less with another person. Orgasms were *good*. Sex was *good*.

Sex with Laodice, in particular, was *really, really good*.

She was dozing on him now, while he waited for the minutes to tick by. 1 a.m., they'd decided, would be the best time to launch what Laodice insisted on calling "the mission," when everybody would be, if not safely asleep, at least likely to be in their own rooms and unwilling to wander.

Telfer lifted a lock of her hair from his chest and let it drift through his fingers. Smooth, soft and warm, like the woman herself. The curl wound about his finger, apparently unwilling to let go. That, sadly, didn't apply to Laodice, he reminded himself. This was an interlude. An extraordinary, precious interlude, but an interlude nonetheless.

The burner phone clock showed 1 a.m., then 1:05, then 1:07. Telfer lay there, wondering why he couldn't move. Laodice was drooling on his chest, forming a small wet patch that should have been disgusting.

Thinking that she was cute when she drooled was probably not a good indication that this interlude would be easy to leave behind.

When the phone clock hit 1:11, he put his hand on Laodice's shoulder and shook gently. "Hey," he said. "Time to go."

"Blerf," Laodice said, and pushed herself upright, making a face and wiping at her mouth. "Oh yuck, was I—"

"Let's get moving."

"You know, what I appreciate about you most is the small talk," she said waspishly, but she got up without further drool-based questions.

In these early morning hours, with the emergency lighting strips and the dim flashlight of the burner phone to guide their feet, Halcyon was a much more convincing murder scene. Their shadows slanted across the floors. They'd both foregone shoes, preferring to pad silently through the dark halls.

It was so quiet that Telfer kept holding his breath, and then had to consciously control the sound as he exhaled. He couldn't hear Laodice's breathing at all. He looked down at her face, thrown into sharp relief by the harsh light of the phone in her hand. Her eyes were focused, all her generous, exuberant energy narrowed to this point.

Her other hand was holding his, soft warmth in the cool dark.

Telfer felt his heart turn over in his chest and silently surrendered to the inevitable.

They didn't speak or signal each other as they went down the stairs, through the lobby and into the small, empty room next to the pool. The staff door that led to the kitchens was still unlocked. Laodice handed him the phone and stood aside.

Telfer had argued that only he had to go.

Laodice had argued that if he was going to sneak into a restricted area and commit a probably-crime in the early hours of the morning, she could at least serve as a lookout.

She'd won.

The kitchen was right where she'd said it was, down a short hallway. He hadn't quite been prepared for the size of it. The phone light couldn't illuminate the whole room, and he had to inch his way along the sides, keeping a sharp eye out for anything that might slip or fall and make a noise. When he came to the pantry, he let himself sag in some relief, and then opened the door.

Too confidently, it turned out; the door creaked loudly, and he flinched so hard he nearly crashed into the bench behind. At the last moment he found his balance, with nothing but a scuffle of socks on the floor and an involuntary gasp to mark it.

There was the laptop, exactly where Laodice said it would be. It was in finger-tip reach, if he stood on his toes and stretched.

They'd had a brief conversation about fingerprints—checking out possible evidence before they handed it to the police was one thing, but accidentally destroying evidence that might point to the killer was another. As he'd hoped, there were several boxes of food prep gloves in the pantry. They were unopened, which made him think dark thoughts about Kyle's haphazard food safety, but he tore through the perforated cardboard and plucked out a pair.

Then he stood on his tiptoes, held his breath, and reached. The tips of his questing fingers touched hard, cool plastic.

A furious shout tore through the quiet night.

Telfer jumped several inches straight up, adrenaline surging like an electrical shock. The laptop tipped and slid, and he caught it, fumbling. There were more shouts, the sound of sirens—what the hell was going on?

He fled into the kitchen, no longer trying to be slow and silent. There was a muffled thump and sharp-voiced questions from the hallway opposite his entrance point, where Laodice had said the staff bedrooms were. Everyone was waking up. The lights came on as he bolted for the exit. Laodice was waiting outside the gym, bouncing on her toes in anxious motion. Red and blue lights were flashing across her tense face.

"Got it," Telfer said, and hastily looked over his booty. There were no marks of ownership on it, no distinctive stickers or scuff marks. It was a regular, mid-market black laptop.

The shouting was getting more distinct, resolving into words. He could make out Patrick's voice, cursing, and a fierce bellow he thought was Samuel. The logical thing would be to wait until whatever was happening was resolved and then sneak upstairs when it got quiet again. Telfer looked at Laodice's eyes, alight with the need to know, and knew that neither of them were going to do the logical thing.

"We snuck in here to have sex," Laodice said quickly. "That's why—"

"In the hot tub," Telfer said, looking at the bare walls and unappealing room. "I have *some* pride."

"Then why are we dry?" Laodice demanded. "Nope. Empty room, sex on the floor, guess we're just weirdos. Come on." She hurried down the hall to the lobby, where the red and blue lights were coming in from the cars parked outside.

Telfer took a moment to strip off the gloves and stuff them in his pocket, then held the laptop at his side, trying to touch it as little as possible. There was no way to hide it on his body, and he didn't want to leave it here—the only thing he could do was pretend it was his and hope no one could say differently. He followed Laodice and paused with her at the point where the small hallway opened out into the lobby. Here, on the periphery, they might evade notice for a while.

Halcyon's lobby was swarming with uniformed officers. Sarah was clutching a piece of paper and arguing with one of them, looking absolutely furious. Danielle was crying into Kyle's shoulder. He absently patted her back.

The shouting was mostly coming from upstairs. Telfer caught his breath as a uniformed officer walked from the staircase to the front door, solemnly holding a plastic evidence bag with a brown loafer in it.

"Jesse's shoe," Laodice said quietly.

Telfer wondered if she felt as sick as he did. Detective Bernard came down the stairs next, looking tired. He was followed by Patrick and Samuel, both of them cuffed, both of them hustled along by uniformed officers. The shouting had stopped. Samuel's mouth was a grim line. Patrick's eyes, trained on Bernard's back, glittered with fury.

Based on that look alone, Telfer had no doubt that Patrick was capable of murder.

But had Patrick actually killed *Jesse*? The shoe pointed that way, but wouldn't a guilty man have tried to ingratiate himself more with the police? Or would a *smart* guilty man have refused all cooperation, hoping that due process might help protect him?

Patrick and Samuel were being moved towards the exit. Patrick was still staring at Bernard, but Samuel's gaze roved over the space, caught Telfer's eye, and held it for a long moment.

Telfer couldn't read his face. He couldn't see guilt, or regret, or even anger, now that the yelling had stopped.

Xavier and Yvette came down the stairs, fully if hastily dressed.

"We're acting for you," Yvette told Patrick. "Say *nothing* unless one of us is in the room."

"I have lawyers," Samuel said, looking faintly astonished.

"Are they here?" Yvette asked pointedly.

Detective Bernard coughed. "No offense, Ms. Long, but are you even licensed to practice in this state?"

The look Yvette gave him could have stripped paint. "Of course I am. And so is Mr. Westlake. Shall we?"

"Just so you know," Laodice said, barely audible to Telfer's ear, "I'm in love with Yvette right now."

Detective Bernard and half the uniformed officers disappeared with the arrested men and their impromptu lawyers. A few people in paper hazmat suits came in, presumably forensic crew. Britt and Carrick came downstairs. Carrick seemed jumpy, and Britt unfazed. Knowing what he knew, Telfer watched her closely, but she didn't give any sort of collegial glance to the police. Instead, she asked Sarah if they could get hot drinks and stay in the lobby lounge.

"The police said they'll let us know when we can go back upstairs," she said.

"Is the search warrant for the whole place?" Kyle asked uneasily.

Sarah glared at the crumpled paper in her fist. "The premises of Halcyon Pre-Wedding Services," she said viciously. She looked up as Telfer and Laodice approached. "Where were you two?"

Laodice managed a creditable blush. Telfer looked at the ground, trying his best to seem embarrassed. "We were, um, exploring the recreational facilities," he said.

Carrick chuckled, but the sound was hollow. "With your laptop?"

"Inspiration," Laodice said, the blush deepening. Telfer nearly ruined the deception with involuntary outrage—he didn't need porn to inspire him, not when he had Laodice right there—but Carrick looked sorry he'd asked and the subject was dropped.

Danielle excused herself to make hot drinks, and Kyle went with her to help. Sarah sat with them on the lobby sofas and stewed. Telfer couldn't remember if he'd left the pantry door open in his flight from the kitchen, or for that matter if he'd left any trace of his passage there. Laodice was sitting beside him, and he didn't think he was imagining the tension thrumming through her body. After a while, she tucked her stocking feet up under her, tugged his arm over her shoulder and nestled into his side.

Carrick chewed his lip. "I didn't think it could be Patrick," he said.

"The police will be acting on evidence," Britt told him.

"Yeah," Carrick said, and scratched his unshaven jaw. "Still."

Telfer watched the police go back and forth. He had some serious doubts himself.

***

From the shelter of Telfer's arm, Laodice was watching Sarah.

For a con-artist she wasn't good at concealing her emotions. She was chewing on her fingernails, darting glances at Kyle, and generally acting in a suspicious manner. On the other hand, maybe she was being a very *good* con-artist. Taking a police invasion on the chin might be a lot to expect of even an experienced hotel manager.

Laodice thought of Manny, Cassie's partner, who *was* an experienced hotel manager. What would he be doing in this situation? The answer was obvious as soon as she'd thought the question. Manny was a natural caregiver. He'd be offering blankets and snacks and reassuring words to the guests, whatever was needed to make them feel better. He'd cooperate with the police, but he'd *care* for the guests. He wouldn't be sitting up straight on the end of a sofa, worrying at a rough spot in the upholstery with bitten-down nails.

"Do you know how long we're going to be down here?" Laodice asked her.

Sarah took a moment to realize she was being addressed, then shook her head. "They didn't say."

"Could we get some blankets or something? It's a little chilly."

She hadn't even looked at Telfer, but he immediately pulled her in closer, and rubbed his hand up and down her arm, carefully avoiding the bandage. Laodice had to seriously resist the urge to go gooey-eyed at him.

"Sure," Sarah said indifferently. "Danielle?" Then her face sharpened, and she looked intently at Laodice. "Actually, Elle, would you mind helping me fetch blankets?"

"Sure," Laodice said, and slid out from under Telfer's hold with some reluctance. But she could catch a hint when it was hurled directly at her head.

"I can—" Danielle began, but Sarah cut her off.

"Nope! You rest. We've got this."

The police officer in the foyer barely stirred when Sarah told her where they were going, but Laodice could feel his eyes on their backs as they went through the door behind the bar.

"I'm going to trust you," Sarah said, the second the door closed.

Your mistake, Laodice thought, though she didn't think Sarah actually meant it. "With this big job?" For a moment, she was worried that Sarah was going to ask her to hack Jesse's laptop.

"Yeah." Sarah pulled a key out of her pocket and opened the humming server cabinet. Inside were...wires and circuits and little LED lights. Things were plugged into other things. Laodice would be prepared to suggest there might be a cooling system in there, and probably the internet.

"Can you hack this?" Sarah asked.

"Piece of cake," Laodice said. "But I'll need a few more details."

"Hack it first. Then I'll tell you the rest."

Laodice folded her arms, trying to look sure of herself and her skills, and not at all like someone who was in well over her head and sinking rapidly. "So I commit a crime, and *then* you tell me what it's for? No dice, babe. Besides, I'm not doing anything when the cops could walk in any minute."

Sarah actually looked insulted. "I didn't mean right now. When the cops are gone, come back and hack it."

"And you'll tell me what the job's about before I do," Laodice said.

"Sure, fine," Sarah said, which wasn't all that convincing, but was at least a step in the right direction. Laodice had no computer skills, but she had plenty of experience in asking questions that got her good answers. And once she'd learned about Sarah's "big job", she could always claim the server had some special protection or needed extra gear she didn't have.

The door behind them opened. Laodice didn't jump, but it was a near thing.

"What is it, Danielle?" Sarah asked, closing the server cabinet.

"I remembered that we moved the spare blankets to the upstairs supply closet," Danielle said, looking curiously at both of them.

"Well, that's why we couldn't find them," Sarah said brightly. She slipped the key back into her pocket. "Be a pet, Danielle, and see if the police will let you go upstairs to fetch them. Thanks for helping me look, Elle."

As Danielle went back through the door, looking confused, Sarah grabbed Laodice's arm. "Meet me here at 5 a.m., if the cops are gone by then," she whispered. "We have to act *fast*."

The police kept them in the lobby for a couple more hours, and Laodice worried that Sarah had been too optimistic. But eventually, they were permitted to go back to bed.

Jesse and Hazel's room, and Samuel and Patrick's, had been closed off with strips of crime scene tape, and, presumably, locked. Laodice couldn't see any signs of entry into their own room. Telfer and herself probably weren't that interesting to the police. From what she'd been able to glean from nonstop eavesdropping on the officers downstairs, the shoe was circumstantial, but compelling evidence.

Telfer put the laptop carefully on the dressing table, and they both stared at it.

"It's bound to be password-locked," Telfer said.

Laodice suppressed a burst of irritation. He was probably right, but it wasn't as if he'd mentioned it earlier. "Maybe we can guess it," she said, and levered it open.

"Fingerprints," Telfer protested, and Laodice frowned. She should have thought of that, too. It was so late…maybe they should sleep and try this in the morning with fresh minds.

But Patrick and Samuel had been arrested, and she couldn't shake the sense of urgency. She resented every second it took Telfer to pull the nitrile gloves out of his pocket, every second it took to squirm her hands into them before she could press the power button.

The laptop *wasn't* password-locked. Jesse had apparently turned off the automatic prompting. It didn't take much to imagine him as someone who was too impatient to wait through even the minor inconvenience of a lockscreen.

But it was definitely Jesse's laptop. Laodice felt a tension at the back of her neck release.

"It can't have been Patrick," she said. "Patrick wouldn't hide a shoe in his room and the laptop in the pantry. That wouldn't make any sense."

"It's a good sign," Telfer said cautiously. "Unless he was trying to divert suspicion?"

"Then why keep the shoe?" Laodice demanded.

"People make dumb mistakes under pressure."

Laodice made a face at him, since she couldn't actually argue otherwise, and started looking through Jesse's files. Unfortunately, he hadn't done anything useful, like stick a virtual note to the desktop with a name and "Might kill me later", or create a folder labeled "Blackmail Opportunities: Pursue."

"Where would you put something you didn't want people to find it?" Telfer asked.

"Porn folder," Laodice said immediately.

Telfer looked doubtful. "Would there even be one? I think these days it's mostly streaming."

"Speak for yourself, thank you. My porn is smutty e-books about faeries." She clicked through a few folders labelled "Pics" "Pics(1)" and so on. It *was* mostly image files, and the few she clicked on were completely innocuous—a picture of a latte with stylish foam art, a few pictures of buildings, a photo of Hazel in a bikini at the beach, wet hair sticking to her face, smiling up at the camera with so much joy and love that Laodice had to pause and stare at her, blinking hard.

Telfer didn't say anything, but she heard his breathing change.

The next folder, Pics(4), didn't contain any images. It was all plain text files, but when she opened a few, they were gibberish—long lines of letters, numbers and symbols.

"That's encrypted data," Telfer said, suddenly sounding wide awake.

"How do we decrypt it?"

"We'd need whatever program he used, and the key. May I?"

Laodice passed the laptop over, and watched Telfer work. His hair was flopping over his face, his eyes were bloodshot and puffy, and his facial hair was growing in stubbly patches around his chin and jaw. He was undoubtedly, objectively, in the least attractive state she'd ever seen him.

But his long fingers moved swiftly over the laptop, and his bloodshot eyes were determined to solve the mystery and find the truth. She'd never liked him more. It was a pity that this thing they had was going to be so brief.

"Okay," he said, a note of triumph in his voice, and then blinked at her. "What?"

Laodice shook her head. "Nothing. Daydreaming."

"Well, I found the program. It's buried pretty deep, which is some indication he wanted to hide it. The key to unlock the encrypted files will be in there. But the program, unfortunately, *is* password-locked. This is as far as I can go."

Laodice sighed. "So I guess we should hand it over to the police." She checked the phone. It was nearly 5 a.m. "Right now, I have to go talk to Sarah and pretend I know how to hack a mainframe or whatever."

"I believe you're supposed to type very fast and then say 'I'm in,'" Telfer said, but the light words didn't conceal the worry in his eyes. "Are you sure you should go alone? If it *wasn't* Patrick, then there might still be a killer here."

"I'll be fine," Laodice said. "Besides, I can hardly take you with me. She thinks you're my mark." She patted his shoulder. "You stay here and have a nap."

There was a brief pause. "While you're walking into the unknown?" Telfer said at last. "No. I don't think I'll do that."

"Okay, stay awake and fret about me then," Laodice said, and she wasn't sure which of them moved first, but suddenly they were kissing.

It was soft and sweet, the barest brush of tongue, and then she had to pull away and say, "All right, I have to go be a cybercriminal now. I'm taking my laptop for verisimilitude."

"If you're not back in half an hour, I'm coming after you," Telfer said, and she was sure he wasn't joking. It should have been annoying, for him to present that kind of ultimatum, but it was actually reassuring. He'd do it. He was reliable like that.

Creeping silently through the hallways of Halcyon was beginning to feel like an everyday kind of activity. She went down the stairs by feel, with the moonlight outside to guide her, and reached confidently for the door handle of the door behind the bar.

It didn't move.

Laodice frowned, and tried again. Nope, definitely locked. She contemplated knocking quietly, or calling through the door, and was about to try the former when car lights flashed through the courtyard windows.

She went still, and listened hard.

The slam of car doors, people moving towards the front door in quiet conversation... Oh shit, of course, Yvonne and Xavier would be coming back to Halcyon for the night. Okay, Plan B. She gave up on the bar door, and scuttled through the foyer towards the back of the building, moving as quickly and quietly as she could and feeling like a cockroach trying to avoid discovery.

The big front door creaked open, and she heard quiet murmurs as she escaped into the short hallway at the back, heading for the exercise room door Telfer had snuck through a few hours before.

Had it been only hours? The night felt like it had stretched over a month. She went through the door and down the hall towards the kitchen; some light was glimmering through the glass panels of that door.

She pushed it open cautiously, but while a few lights were on over workstations, the big room seemed empty.

"Sarah?" she whispered cautiously.

There was no response.

Laodice bit her lip. Sarah had probably lost track of the time and fallen asleep. Laodice was going to have to sneak through the kitchen, down the hallway where the staff bedrooms were, and hope that she picked the right bedroom door.

For a moment, her courage failed her.

Then she squared her shoulders, and stepped forward. The workstation lights were dim blue, turning her exposed skin ghostly. Laptop tucked under one arm, she edged around the big island in the middle of the room.

Sarah was lying at the far end, face down in a puddle of blood.

Laodice clapped her free hand over her mouth to force down the scream.

Telfer was right. She should never have come alone. There was a killer in the building and they'd killed again and she had to get out *right now*.

There was a low murmur of voices on the other side of the big kitchen doors, coming towards her. Laodice's mind jolted out of the frozen fear and spun, faster than she'd ever thought before.

She wouldn't make it to the far door without being spotted.

Hiding behind the island was a temporary solution and would leave her too exposed.

The pantry was several yards away. She cleared them in a second of frantic, silent motion, yanked the door open, and hurled herself inside.

At the last moment, she didn't close the door completely behind her. Beneath the terror, beneath the self-castigation, she was still herself; still curious, still determined, still dying—perhaps literally—to finally know the truth.

She crouched on the floor of the kitchen pantry and peered through the gap, waiting to solve the mystery at last.

Chapter Fifteen

Telfer lay on his back, fully dressed, and stared at the wavery reflection of himself in the polished tin ceiling.

He wished Laodice had let him accompany her, at least as far as the foyer. Realistically, he couldn't be of much assistance, and Laodice seemed confident she could get what she needed to know out of Sarah and then make an excuse to get away without difficulty, but he wasn't sure. Sarah had proved to be unpredictable and emotional.

It felt strange that he'd previously applied those labels to Laodice. Who was, of course, still unpredictable and emotional, but in a way he'd come to appreciate.

Laodice would be in the office by now, talking to Sarah. If they'd got her wrong, or if she had an accomplice…

Telfer got up. For once, he was going to listen to his own instincts.

He opened the door, and blinked. Yvette and Xavier were in the hallway outside their door, looking exhausted, and Samuel was with them.

"What are you doing here?" he said, without thinking.

Samuel glared at him. "I'm out on bail," he said, biting off the words. "Since I'm only an *accessory*. Xavier and Yvette have kindly offered me the use of their shower and a change of clothes, and then I'm heading back to the station."

Telfer's instincts spoke again. "You didn't move the body."

"Don't answer that," Xavier said quickly, but Samuel was already snapping, "Of *course* I didn't."

Telfer believed him.

There was no logical reason to do so. He didn't trust the police, but Bernard seemed to be an intelligent, careful man who wouldn't make an arrest without at least some evidence. Jesse's shoe had been in Patrick's room. The police had whatever physical evidence had made it clear that one person had moved the body.

But Patrick almost certainly couldn't have moved the body by himself, and Samuel was the only person he'd ask for help in that situation. If Samuel hadn't dumped Jesse in the woods, then Patrick hadn't murdered him.

It was a tenuous, emotion-based, totally irrational chain of beliefs, and yet Telfer was sure it was true.

"Wait a second," he said, and went back to his room to retrieve the laptop, barging into Xaiver and Yvette's room without knocking. "This is Jesse's," he said. "Laodice and I found it in the kitchen."

"Who's Laodice?" Xavier asked.

"Elle, of course," Yvette said. "Is that really her name? I'd go by a nickname too."

Samuel was staring at the laptop, hope rising in his face. "Are you saying... We have to tell the police!"

"You can do whatever you need to do with it," Telfer said. "I hope it helps. But we found some encrypted data on there, and I wondered if you might be able to crack it."

"I advise that you don't interfere with—" Yvette began, but Samuel had already opened the device and started typing, his fingers dancing over the keys. She sighed, and sat down on the edge of the bed. After a minute, Xavier sat beside her and looped his arm around her waist.

"Huh," Samuel said. "Jesse had already got into the hotel wi-fi. That's interesting."

"The encrypted data is in Pics (4), and the encryption program is—oh, you found it."

Samuel spared him a single, withering glance, and returned his focus to the screen.

"Why are you looking up Jesse's social media?" Telfer asked.

"Because regardless of what you see in the movies, brute-forcing 2048-bit RSA keys is effectively impossible. I can try a remote connection to my office for a dictionary-style attack with key names and dates. This is a third-party encryption program, so I can keep guessing." He paused. "Actually, wait. Jesse was lazy."

"Yes, he was," Telfer said, remembering Britt's revelation that Jesse had tried to cheat his way through the LSATs.

"I wonder if..." Samuel opened the downloads folder and scrolled down, eyes moving rapidly. Then he stopped. "Oh, man."

"What?"

"This is the first time I've ever been grateful for sloppy security. Those are the keys. He used them, and he didn't delete the file after. Let's see what we've got." Samuel apparently liked to talk through his work. "Notes. Numbers. Names. Lots of audio here, some video... It seems like blackmail and extortion are things he'd been doing for a while." He looked up at Telfer, moisture sheening his eyes. "This is going to give the cops any number of people with motive. *Thank* you."

"Except that you, a suspect, are interfering with that evidence, making it harder for them to convict," Yvette put in.

"That will be the police's problem," Samuel said sharply. "I only care about Patrick."

Oh shit. There was probably something about *Carrick* in those files, and Britt had been very clear that looking into it further wasn't something he and Laodice should be doing. She was going to be pissed if Samuel accidentally stumbled across some pieces of the puzzle.

"Let me check the most recent files," Telfer suggested. "Then we can both swear under oath that you didn't even look at that evidence."

Samuel hesitated, then thrust the laptop at him.

Telfer could feel Samuel judging his typing speed, but he brought up the files with the most recent dates.

"Where's Elle?" Yvette asked suddenly.

"Um, looking into something," Telfer said. Yes, there was the file on Carrick, which he closed before he could make out much more than the name. And there was a file about Halcyon. A complaint, noting interference in the bugs he'd tried to set up, and then a cryptic note: "AH c.f. CB."

CB might be Carrick Balshaw, he supposed. The bug interference was apparently from something else operating on a similar frequency. Did that mean a similar device?

Had they been bugged by someone *else*, this whole time?

A shiver ran down Telfer's spine. He looked at the corner of the ceiling, where the small speaker was innocuously mounted.

"What?" Samuel said.

"When you checked for bugs, did you check that?" Telfer asked, pointing.

Samuel spun and stared at it. "No," he said, and dragged the dressing table chair over.

"What bugs?" Xavier asked.

"Surveillance," Samuel said, and twisted the casing open. "We thought Jesse had—oh, fuck. This is the real deal."

"Not like Jesse's?"

Samuel craned, poking at something. "No, this is *serious* equipment. It's hooked into the power system and transmitting to something. Possibly a black box server."

"A server," Telfer said, and jumped to his feet. "Laodice."

"What the hell?"

"It's Sarah," he said, panic jolting through his body. "It's Sarah and Kyle, and Laodice went to *meet them*." And before anyone could ask questions or delay him any longer, he raced out the door and down the hall, pausing only to thump twice, very hard, on Carrick and Britt's door.

***

Laodice felt as if every cell in her body was tensing as she strained to see through the narrow crack in the door. There was more than one set of footprints approaching, and she stifled a whimper when she heard Kyle's voice.

But he sounded alarmed, not murderous, and he bit off several curses. "Oh shit," Kyle said. "Oh shit, what happened?"

Laodice half-expected the next voice by now, but it was still a shock to hear it.

"She slipped," Danielle said, every word drenched in sarcasm.

"You killed her!"

"Wow, check out Sherlock Holmes. Yes, Kyle. Come on, keep up. This isn't the first body you've helped me get rid of."

"You said Jesse attacked you," Kyle said, his voice strangled. Laodice shifted, and caught a glimpse of his face, staring at Danielle in abject horror. "You said he'd attacked you! You said you'd pushed him away in self-defense…You were *crying*."

"Yeah, well, don't think I'm happy about it," Danielle said. "Men are always so patronizing when you cry at them. It works, though. If it makes you feel any better, he did grab my arm and make some threats. He was walking away when I hit him with that wrench."

"You said he fell down the stairs and hit his head!"

"Oops," Danielle said cheerfully. "Guess I lied."

Kyle made a strange noise, part gulp and part sob. "But why did you drag *me* into it?"

"Because I couldn't move the body myself," she said impatiently. "A missing person causes way less fuss than a murder victim. And I was really hoping scavengers would have enough time to take him apart, but you couldn't even hide a body properly, could you?"

"Why Sarah?"

"Because she was too fucking *nosy*, Kyle," Danielle said. "You two were so embarrassing, with your stupid invisible employees bullshit. You have absolutely no idea what's really going on here, and you were going to get *me* caught." She poked Sarah with the tip of her shoe. "And that would piss off my bosses. They don't like people poking into things that are none of their business, and they *really* don't like cops asking questions."

"Your bosses? Who?"

"Kyle, I literally just told you Sarah was too nosy, take a hint. Are you done with the shock yet? We're going to get rid of Sarah, and tidy up a few loose ends, and then we can get out of here. I've got the go-ahead to cut and run."

Kyle made a snuffling sound. "You're going to kill me too."

"Aw, no," Danielle said, her voice soothing. "I won't do that unless I have to. I like you, Kyle. You've always been nice to me. You helped me out with Jesse, and you didn't say a word. I know I can trust you. Do what I say and everything will be okay."

"Really?" Kyle said, sounding hopeful.

"You bet. I'll bring you in to my bosses, explain that you helped me in a tight spot. They're serious people. They know how to reward loyalty."

"But Sarah—"

"Sarah was not a serious person," Danielle said firmly. "You're better off without her. Now, we're going to do it right, this time. There are gloves and black trash bags in the pantry. Go and get them."

Laodice moved backwards, as stealthily as she could. She couldn't hide anywhere. All she could do was get deeper inside, out of Danielle's view, and hope that Kyle wouldn't give her away. She clutched her laptop, with the vague thought of using it as a shield. Did Danielle have a gun? Did laptops stop bullets?

Kyle opened the door.

Laodice made immediate eye contact, putting all her pleading wish to live in her gaze.

For a moment, Kyle didn't even seem to recognize the fact of her presence. His face was blotchy with tears, his mouth slack. Then he blinked twice and stared at her.

Laodice held her finger to her lips and shook her head. She could feel tears prickling in her own eyes. Was this how scared Cassie had been, when Manny's uncle held that gun on them? Was she ever going to see her sisters again, or trade stupid memes with her brother, or play Scrabble with her parents after Sunday night dinner? Would she drink too many cocktails with Diana again, or pitch a story to Miriam?

Or kiss Telfer?

Surely, that brief moment upstairs couldn't be the last time she'd kiss Telfer.

The thoughts ran through her head in a moment that seemed to last an eternity, as comprehension and fear flashed across Kyle's face.

"Kyle!" Danielle said, her voice harsh, but still quiet.

"Found them," Kyle said, sounding almost normal. He reached right past Laodice's head to the shelf behind her, grabbing a box of gloves. "Um, trash bags?"

"Bottom shelf," Danielle said, and Kyle's eyes dropped to Laodice, who scrabbled behind her. She felt a cardboard box that had the right weight and yanked it out. She was handing the box to Kyle when Danielle appeared in the doorway.

"It's not that—" she said, and then her mouth fell open as she registered Laodice, crouched at Kyle's feet.

Danielle *did* have a gun, a small, deadly-looking thing with a long tube on the front—a silencer?—but she was holding it at her side, a latent rather than a present threat for Kyle. Laodice had been picturing her dressed in tight pants and a black leather jacket, typical assassin chic from the movies, but in fact she was wearing what she normally did; a knee-length black skirt and a plain button-up blouse.

The air seemed to thicken around them, Danielle's eyes narrowing, her mouth opening, her gun hand rising, all in slow motion.

Laodice threw the box at her head.

It was clumsy: a left-handed throw and the angle awkward, and it didn't even make contact. The box flew right by Danielle's head.

But she flinched, and Laodice used that moment to surge forward. She didn't try to get up. She dropped her laptop, launched herself across the pantry floor, and took Danielle out at the knees.

Danielle had a gun, but Laodice had mass, momentum, and the adrenaline of terror zinging through her body. Danielle hit the ground hard, and Laodice lunged up her body and grabbed her wrist. She was vaguely aware of Kyle scrambling out of the way in the close confines, but every other part of her was focused on Danielle and the gun in her hand. She banged Danielle's hand on the ground twice, elbowing her in the face for good measure, but the other woman hung on grimly.

And Laodice was bigger and stronger, but she didn't know how to fight. Danielle abruptly slid both hands along the floor, above her head, and Laodice's center of balance went with them. There was some kind of motion of Danielle's legs, and then Laodice was hurtling forward, tumbling helplessly across the floor and crashing into the kitchen island. There was something cold and sticky on her leg, and she refused to think about Sarah's blood, because she had to *move*.

But her head hurt and she couldn't figure out which way to go.

There was a bang—silencers apparently weren't all that silent—and a thump, and then Danielle appeared above her, gun muzzle pointed at her head.

Laodice looked up, defiant.

"What are you even doing here?" Danielle demanded. "Why is this place such a clusterfuck? This was supposed to be an easy job!"

"It'll take a little while to explain," Laodice said, proud that her voice didn't tremble too much. For a moment, she thought she might actually get away with the delay. Telfer had said he would come for her in thirty minutes, and he'd be true to her word. Danielle looked frustrated and curious. If Laodice could only fill a few more minutes...

But apparently Danielle wasn't going to let curiosity get in the way of pragmatism. She grimaced. "I don't have time for this."

Laodice said something she didn't remember afterwards: "wait!" or "stop!" or "no!" A one-word denial of the death hurtling towards her.

The sound of her protest was swallowed up by Telfer's urgent yell as he ran into the kitchen.

Danielle, without hesitating, swung her gun towards him, and Laodice kicked out, a convulsive action without any aim that managed to connect with Danielle's shin. Danielle staggered, and the gun went off again. She stepped away. "You fucking—"

There were more voices, more shouting. The lights in the kitchen all came on at once. Yvette was yelling, "I'm calling the police!" and Samuel bellowed, "You framed Patrick!" Laodice, looking right at Danielle's face, saw the moment where she registered that the situation had gone irredeemably to hell.

Even then, she didn't panic. "Stay back!" she said, moving the gun in a smooth arc across the room. She was stepping backwards, towards the staff bedrooms, holding them off with the threat of the weapon. "No one needs to get hurt."

"No one *else*, you mean," Telfer said. He sounded furious, wild in a way Laodice had never heard before. "Laodice!"

"I'm all right," Laodice said, finding her voice with difficulty. "But she killed Jesse and Sarah. And Kyle, she shot Kyle."

There was a groan from the pantry.

"And if you *don't* want to get shot, you'll stay back," Danielle said. "I'm leaving. No need for heroics." She reached for the door behind her.

Or the space where that door had been.

Britt, with neat efficiency and theatrical timing, snapped one handcuff around the wrist of her reaching hand, slammed the gun hand into the door jamb, got the other cuff around *that* wrist, and kicked Danielle in the back of the knee. That put the other woman on the ground, both cuffed hands wrenched up behind her back and effectively immobilized. It took no more than two seconds.

"Danielle Harris, I am arresting you on suspicion of murder, attempted murder, assault, and conspiracy to pervert the course of justice," Britt said conversationally. "And this isn't a charge, but I'm personally pissed that you've fucked up my day, so don't try anything stupid."

"You *are* a cop!" Samuel said, and Britt spared him a tight eyeroll as she read Danielle the rest of her rights.

Laodice crawled out from behind the island, and found herself being hauled to her feet and fervently hugged.

"I'm all gross with blood," she said, half-sobbing.

Telfer kissed her hair, her cheek, and ran his hands frantically over her arms, apparently not sure whether he should be hugging her or checking for injuries. "I don't care. Are you okay? Are you hurt?"

"Not really," Laodice said, for a moment unsure about which question she was answering. She was doing her own share of frantic motion, touching his face and shoulders. "I can't believe you ran in like that!"

"Of course I did."

"So irrational," she said, and her voice wobbled.

Telfer embraced her. "I don't care," he said, and his voice shook too. "You're safe. I don't care about anything else."

She pulled back a little to stare at his face. Kyle was groaning on the floor while Yvette and Xavier applied pressure to his wound, Britt was instructing Carrick what to say to the police on the phone she'd handed him, and Samuel was stalking around the kitchen, his face livid with rage. It was the worst possible time for Laodice to have an emotional epiphany, but that seemed to be what was happening.

"Will somebody *please* explain to me what's going on and why my fiancé is still in jail?" Samuel said.

"Ambulance," Kyle said, his voice weak.

"The ambulance is coming," Carrick assured him.

"He moved Jesse's body," Laodice said. "But Danielle told him it was an accident, and she'd really hit Jesse with a *wrench*." She wriggled loose of Telfer, who showed no inclination to let her go, and bent down to Sarah. "I'm sorry," she told the dead woman. "I didn't like you, but I'm sorry you're dead."

"Carrick, tell Bernard we need two ambulances," Britt said.

Laodice blinked at her. "I'm fine," she said, wondering why her tongue was so heavy. "I just need to rest."

Telfer caught her before she hit the ground.

***

Laodice came around before the ambulances arrived, but Telfer and the EMTs both insisted she get checked out at the hospital, and after some frankly adorable grumbling, she agreed.

Telfer didn't even ask if he could go with her. He swung into the back of the ambulance and held Laodice's hand. Kyle's gunshot wound had rated an ambulance of his own, which took off with sirens blaring, lights flashing, and a police escort, but Telfer and Laodice got to travel more sedately.

"Did I tell Britt about Kyle hiding the body?" Laodice said anxiously.

"Yes."

"Did I tell her about the server?"

"No, but I did that. Britt took it with her when she and Bernard took Danielle off to the station."

"Britt went too? I guess her cover was already blown."

"That, and she really didn't want Danielle talking to anyone. Not that Danielle looked like she was going to. She didn't say a word after the arrest."

"I can't believe we never considered Danielle. She was just always *there*."

"We're not very good detectives," Telfer agreed. "Good thing we're writers instead."

"Does everyone know that now?"

"Oh yes. Yvette threatened to sue us, but I think it was mostly affectionate."

The EMT riding with them in the back wasn't even pretending not to listen. Telfer glanced at her bright and interested face and decided to keep some of the other information he'd gleaned to himself for now. If he was right, it was definitely something for limited exposure.

The ambulance slowed, then pulled over.

"That was fast," Laodice said.

The EMT frowned. "Unscheduled stop, folks. Sit tight." She jumped out of the back, and left the door swinging.

A few minutes later, a swearing Britt, limping heavily, was helped into the car. She stared at the two of them, and then closed her eyes as she sank back against the bench seat. "Why?" she demanded of the air.

"What happened to *you*?"

"Squad car was sideswiped. Two gunmen. Shot Danielle and took the server."

"She's *dead*?"

"Extremely dead," Britt said grimly. "And I would be too, if Bernard hadn't been quick with his piece. He winged one, I think. Anyway, they took off, my cover is blown, and this is the worst fucking night of my life."

She lapsed into a baleful silence and refused to say anything else on the way to the Hippocampus hospital. Laodice and Telfer held hands all the way down the hill.

Chapter Sixteen

A police escort apparently got you through E.R quickly. The doctor who examined Laodice wasn't happy about her hitting her head, but after running through an exhaustive list of questions, she concluded Laodice probably didn't have a concussion.

"We'll keep you in for observation," she said. "Fluids, a mild painkiller, and rest."

A nurse gave her pills and a large bottle of water. Then he cleaned Sarah's blood off her, helped her into a hospital gown, and got her into bed.

"Mostly you need sleep," he said. "Let your body do the healing."

The morning was well and truly started. She could see daylight edging around the pulled curtains, and the hospital was full of beeps and murmurs as staff and patients moved around their days.

"I don't think I can sleep."

The nurse smiled at her. "Then lie there and close your eyes for a bit," he suggested.

Laodice thought about reminding him that she was a grown woman, not a four-year-old insisting she wanted another story, but instead she closed her eyes.

She woke up hours later. Telfer was in the chair beside her bed, head thrown back, snoring with impressive volume.

Laodice looked at him fondly for a moment.

He snuffled, made a truly revolting noise in the back of his throat, and let another snore rip. Well, the angle his neck was at couldn't be good for him. She'd be waking him up for his own benefit, as well as hers.

"Telfer," she said.

He woke. She watched awareness flow back into his eyes, that moment when personality entered the picture, and wondered how she'd ever thought him unreadable. You just had to know how to look.

"How're you feeling?"

Laodice mentally cataloged her injuries, starting with the nearly-healed slice along her cheekbone, counting up the bruises and scrapes from falling into the ditch, and finishing with the tender bump on the back of her head. "Good," she said cautiously. "Considering."

"I wasn't sure if you wanted me to get in touch with your family."

"Did you?" she asked, alarmed. On consideration, this was a dumb question. If he had, there'd be a lot more people in the room.

"No."

She beamed at him. "Good call. I want to get back to the city first. And I need to write the story before I have to process a lot of feelings about it. Are the local news on it already?"

Telfer looked smug. "Yes, but most of what they have is 'more details to come.' We were embedded in the story. Plus, we're going to be let back into Halcyon under police supervision, to pack our stuff and get your car."

"Oooh, that inside touch. Our room isn't part of the crime scene?"

"No. Though your laptop is, downstairs. You're welcome to use mine."

"*Thank* you."

"I made some notes," he added.

She laughed. "Of course you did. Honestly, I'm a little surprised you haven't already filed something."

"I figure I get dibs on the follow-ups." He stood up and closed the door to her room. "Britt wants to see us," he said quietly.

"Do you think we can get anything out of her?" Laodice said.

"Maybe. I've been thinking about what could be on that server. The bugs Jesse found were wired into the speakers. Samuel thinks they were installed with the rest of the system."

"Was someone listening to everything we said? No, can't have been. They'd have stopped us sooner."

"Right. I think everything was being *recorded*, but not transmitted anywhere offsite, not yet. I was thinking about the kind of people who could afford Halcyon. People with money. Lawyers, tech people, finance guys. People with sensitive information, maybe people vulnerable to blackmail—that's obviously why Jesse wanted to go. Isolated, forced into artificial intimacy, not in their usual environments or with their usual defenses."

"Danielle was talking about her bosses being a big deal. She was running something else the whole time." She met Telfer's eyes. "And Halcyon is owned by Argive Holdings."

"Yeah," Telfer said.

"Okay," Laodice said, and swung her legs off the bed. "Let's go meet Britt."

Britt wasn't alone. Carrick was looking rumpled and anxious. He was arranging her pillows when Telfer and Laodice came in.

One of Britt's legs was propped up in a cast. "Torn ligament," she said, when Laodice's eyes went to it. "Surgery later today." She coughed.

"Do you need some water?" Carrick asked immediately.

Britt's eyes softened slightly. "Thank you." She sipped from the glass he poured and looked at Telfer and Laodice. "Sit down. Let's go over what you can and can't say."

"Is this the fun kind of censorship?" Laodice asked brightly. She stayed standing, with Telfer upright beside her.

"You can call it whatever you want."

"So you're investigating Argive Holdings," Telfer said.

Britt glared at him and said nothing.

"Off the record," Telfer said. "I need to know. We *deserve* to know." He sounded wonderful, absolutely unrelenting in his search for the truth.

Britt's mouth was a firm line.

"Argive Holdings is an international money laundering hub," Carrick said.

Telfer smacked his thigh. "*Yes,*" he said.

"Carrick!" Britt protested.

Carrick looked stubborn. "If we don't tell them, they'll try to work it out on their own."

"For how long?" Telfer asked, jumping in before Britt could speak again.

"Decades. I got brought into it slowly, little by little. Only small things to start, safeguards I was told to skip or hand over to someone else. Big bonuses, if I just kept my mouth shut. Then I was asked to do something way over the line." He sighed. "And then I knew how deep I was. It was so much money that I wasn't sure I could survive saying no. I shut my mouth and kept working.

"Jesse found out about one of the small things, I don't know how, and tried to blackmail me." He grimaced. "He had no fucking idea who he was dealing with. If I'd passed his name up the line, I think it would have been taken care of. Permanently."

"And you didn't want to do that," Laodice said, leaning in and smiling at him.

"I thought about doing it," Carrick admitted. "And then I thought about how I'd have to *live* with it afterwards. I didn't want to be a murderer. Not even by proxy. The next day I called the tip line for the money laundering guys at the Treasury Department. They were very interested in what I had to say."

"You're a whistleblower," Laodice said, impressed. She wouldn't have thought Carrick had the guts.

Britt sighed. "Confidential informant."

"And you're his handler," Telfer said. "You're with Treasury? I didn't know they had law enforcement."

"I'm on loan," Britt said. "Look, this is all *incredibly* need-to-know. And they don't need to know, Carrick!"

"They do," Carrick insisted. "This way they know why they shouldn't write about it."

Britt looked dubious. "I was planning some patriotic threats."

Telfer snorted and Britt eyed him. Carrick apparently took this as permission, because he continued: "Anyway, Treasury gave me the money to pay Jesse off, and I started doing more for the shady side of Argive. Then I got 'engaged' to Britt, and she helped me work myself deeper in."

He gestured out the window, in the vague direction of Halcyon. "This whole retreat thing was a gift for the last 'favor' I did them."

Telfer hummed thoughtfully. "And you're getting Britt entry to Dammond's inner circle?"

Britt shot Carrick a look, but he missed it. "Well, I'm trying," he said anxiously. "It's kind of hard to keep up with Dammond, but he likes that we went to school together."

"So Dammond *is* directly involved in the money laundering," Laodice said. "Is Adrestus Argive? Are the Argives in charge?"

"Yes," Carrick said, at the same time that Britt said, "Carrick, shut up, *I mean it.*"

Carrick subsided, giving her a guilty look.

Britt rubbed the bridge of her nose. "Fuck," she said, with feeling. "Right. This is a federal case we've been building for years. Do you two know anything about the conviction rates of federal prosecutions?"

"Something like ninety percent of the accused don't even go to trial," Laodice said. Telfer gave her a warm look, probably because she was being a statistics nerd again. "There's so much evidence against them that they usually just plead guilty."

"Right. And if people do go to trial and plead not guilty, mostly we convict them. The moral of the story is, if we get to the stage of laying charges, you probably committed the crime."

Telfer made a face at that, but Britt ran over the top of him. "But nearly ten percent of cases get thrown out of court, because of mishandled evidence or failures in process. Guys like this—rich guys, powerful guys, celebrity lawyers on tap—we don't pull the trigger on a case until we're *certain*, you get me? Not only certain they did it, but certain we can nail them on it."

"And you can't nail them yet."

"No," Britt said. "Not yet. And in the meantime, if either of you says a word to *anyone*, I will have you both charged with obstruction of justice and interference in an investigation, and whatever else I can make stick. I've already had to talk to the others about keeping quiet about the bugs in the speakers, but you two are my biggest concern."

"We'll have to write *something*," Laodice said. "A series of murders at a fancy retreat for engaged couples? Not writing the story would be even more suspicious."

"Fine. But you cannot mention the surveillance, or the server, or Argive Holdings. Danielle killed Jesse and Sarah for unknown reasons—feel free to speculate, as long as you don't get anywhere close to the truth. And she died in a car crash on the way to the station."

"What does Bernard think of that story?" Telfer inquired.

"Detective Bernard knows how to weigh immediate gains against the greater public interest. Do you?"

"Yes, ma'am," Laodice said.

"All right. Fine. Yes, we think the Argive family is ultimately in charge of the whole operation. Adrestus Argive is a cunning son of a bitch who does everything through minions and managers, but Dammond's more careless. He was our best bet of breaking the whole thing open and making it stick. But thanks to Halcyon and Danielle and that fucking server, my entire cover is blown. If the Argives haven't heard I'm law yet, they will soon."

"Are you going to be safe?"

"We're both going into witness protection," Carrick said. "Honestly, I'll be happy to get away from it. But I hate that everything I did was for nothing.

Britt patted his hand, her eyes softening again. "You gave us vital information," she assured him. "When it's possible for you to testify, you'll be a huge prosecution asset."

Telfer grimaced. "But for now, they get away with it?"

Britt's face went grim. "Various organizations are pursuing various angles," she said. "And that's the last thing I'm telling you."

Laodice's brain had jumped tracks, putting together what she'd heard from Cassie about her would-be-murderer Theo having too much money, about his house being burned down after he'd been arrested, about Cassie running into Dammond Argive in Weeping Rock, which he apparently always visited on the first day of spring... "Were the Argives laundering money through Tantalus Vineyard?" she asked. "Is that what Manny's uncle was so desperate to cover up?"

Britt was good. Her face barely moved. But Laodice was looking straight at her, and she saw the flicker of recognition in the depths of her eyes. "As I said, I have nothing further to tell you."

"Fine," Laodice said tightly. She wanted to run to Cassie immediately, wanted to tell her that she had the key to unlocking the mystery that had plagued her sister this past fifteen months. But she couldn't. If Dammond Argive was going down—and she really, really wanted him to go down—then Britt was right. She couldn't tell anyone, and neither could Telfer. They couldn't endanger the case.

"One last question," Telfer said, and Britt looked furious, but he held up his hand. "For Carrick. If you knew Argive was dirty, why did you keep trying to recruit me?"

Carrick looked abashed. "It was getting kind of lonely, being the only good guy. You're smart. I figured you'd work it out, and then there'd be two of us." He made finger guns. "Partners in anti-crime!"

"Oh."

"Plus, the salary and bennies are great. You can't be making much at Olympus."

"Probably not comparable, no," Telfer said, and looked at Laodice. His eyes were dark and unfathomable. "But as it happens, I'm happy where I am."

***

Once Laodice was discharged, they went back to Halcyon, for what Telfer fervently hoped was going to be the last time. The police had retrieved their phones from the locked box—the batteries were fully drained, naturally—and allowed them to go upstairs and pack. Their escort had obviously been told that they were media; even Laodice's most innocently phrased questions didn't get any traction, and Telfer didn't bother to try.

He swung their cases into the trunk of Laodice's Spider with a sense of vast relief, and slammed the lid down.

Laodice was sitting in the passenger seat, his laptop open on her knees.

"Um?" he said.

She looked at him severely. "You are about to be privileged as no man has ever been," she said, and tossed him the keys. "Don't fuck it up."

Telfer cocked his head at her. "So you're assuming I can drive stick."

Laodice's jaw dropped. "You *can*, right?"

"As it happens, Uncle Burak insisted," he said, and folded himself into the driver's seat, carefully testing the pedals, which were way too close for comfort. "Let's get the hell out of here."

For the first twenty minutes or so, Laodice barely typed a word, tensing as he approached every corner and obviously biting back commentary. But she didn't voice any of it, and after a while there was the steady tap of keys and the occasional mumble as she tried a phrase out loud. Telfer put in a sentence or two, and halfway to the city they had an excellent argument about split infinitives, but the lion's part was definitely Laodice's work.

Telfer wanted the journey to last forever.

But afternoon faded into evening and light drained from the sky, and as they hit the outskirts of the city, Laodice cleared her throat and said, "Can I read this to you?"

"Please."

She did. Telfer listened. He had to consciously keep part of his brain focused on stoplights and corners, moving with the—fortunately slow-paced—traffic around them. Laodice had turned the messy, bloody chaos of the actual events into an elegant story of love and murder, juxtaposing the bonds of the couples with Danielle's apparently senseless murders-for-murder's sake. Jesse's true character was only lightly sketched, and Sarah was depicted as a self-made woman on the rise. Not accurate, perhaps, but merciful.

It was told from Laodice's point-of-view, which was to say that of a journalist undercover who had stumbled into an entirely different story. In that sense, it was unashamedly biased, but it captured very well the confusion and determination of those days, which already seemed weirdly distant.

"What do you think?" she said at last.

"It's good," Telfer said. "It's really good."

"No comments at all?"

"Some of your adjectives are a bit flowery, and the comparison to a monastery is too much."

"There he is," Laodice said, and when he risked a glance at her, she was smiling fondly. "I was thinking I'd pitch it to *Vanguard*."

"*New Argus* might be a better shot, if you want follow-ups. They have a budget for fact-checking. Is this... Is this maybe the kind of story you want to do more of?"

"No," Laodice said. "I'm glad I could write this one. But I want Bridal."

"Right," Telfer said, and they both stopped talking. After the easy, working quiet of the journey, this silence felt strained.

"So, um," he said, at the same time Laodice said, "I was wondering—"

"You go first," she said.

"No, you."

"I was wondering," Laodice said, staring straight ahead, "If you would ever think about breaking your no-dating rule. On a trial basis. With me."

Telfer's lungs emptied out. He felt joy zing through his body.

But it was immediately swallowed by a rush of fear. "I— I have to think about it."

"Sure."

"There's the job and everything. It would be complicated." He could barely believe the words coming out of his mouth. Laodice had asked him out. Or next to it. He should have been delighted that she wanted to extend their time together.

Instead, he was terrified. He was at the top of a cliff, with dark water yawning below, scrambling for the safety of the edge.

Another moment of silence.

"No worries," Laodice said brightly. "Can you turn off here? Great." Her voice sounded light, but when he glanced at her, he saw her hands were clenched in her lap, rumpling the fabric of her skirt.

"I'm sorry," he said.

"Don't be. You were clear from the start." She loosened her grip and gave him a cheery thumbs up. "Excellent communication skills, Terzi. Okay, the parking entrance is up there, on the right."

"You have a building with parking?"

"Uptown life has its charms. Plus the super gave me a deal on his second space, because he likes me."

"Everyone likes you," Telfer said. His lips felt numb. He followed her instructions and parked in the narrow basement space next to a white van. "Okay. Great story. Really."

Laodice peered at him. "Come inside," she suggested. "Charge your phone, have something to eat. It's rush hour, the subway will be packed. You don't want to take a suitcase on the train right now."

Telfer hesitated, then cursed himself for his weakness. "All right," he said. "But I can't stay for long."

***

Okay. She'd been shot down.

Laodice considered that metaphor and decided that after being up close and personal with a gun in her face, she didn't like it.

Fine. She'd asked Telfer out and he'd rejected the idea. Technically, he'd said "I need to think about it," but that was *no*, especially combined with the panicked look he'd given her.

It was a shame, but that was all. It wasn't *devastating*, she wasn't feeling a sense of deep loss, and she absolutely wasn't regretting the weakness that had made her invite him in, stretching out their unlikely union for even one more hour.

The story was good. The story was *great*. On top of that, she'd had a wild week, with some excellent sex, and she could probably count Telfer as a work friend instead of an antagonistic colleague. All of that was positive.

So why did she feel so terrible?

"Nice building," Telfer said, as they rounded the sixth landing and mounted the last flight of stairs.

"Good for my cardio," Laodice said, trying to sound flippant. Why on earth had she offered to feed him? What did she even have? Half a loaf of frozen bread and the scrapings from the peanut butter jar weren't much of a last meal for a lover.

There was music coming from her apartment. Terrible whiny-boy pop-punk she recognized all too well.

"What's that?" Telfer asked.

"My fucking *ex*," Laodice snarled, and opened her door with a secret relief. Finally, someone she could yell at.

Eli was sitting at her breakfast bar. Laodice's ceramic frog was on the bench, badly patched together with hot glue. The mouth was mis-aligned, gaining an edge that was distinctly demonic.

Eli's own face, surprised and welcoming, faltered when he saw Telfer. "Who's this guy?" he demanded.

"Telfer Terzi. We've met."

"None of your business," Laodice said over top of him. "What the fuck are you doing here, Eli?"

"I wondered if you might be back early, considering." Eli said. "Look, I fixed your frog."

Laodice parked her suitcase with some force. "I broke up with you, Eli."

"I really think we need to talk about that," Eli said.

"We don't. We're done. Give me your key, take your stuff, and go."

Eli glared at Telfer. "Could you give us some time alone?"

Telfer glanced at Laodice, who shook her head. "Nope," he said, and held the door open. "Looks like you're leaving."

"Unbelievable," Eli said. He was actually pouting, and Laodice was finding it difficult to remember why she'd ever thought him handsome. Next to Telfer, he looked like a whiny little boy. "What is this, Laodice? We have a fight, so you immediately fuck someone else to get back at me?"

"We *broke up*," Laodice said. "I *dumped you*. After that, I could have fucked ten thousand guys and it would be nothing to do with you. Get the hell out of my home, and never come back." She paused. "Wait. What did you mean, you thought I'd be back early? Considering what?"

"Considering what happened to Xena," Eli said.

Laodice wasn't sure what her face did, but a second later Telfer had her in a dining chair with her head forced between her knees, his hand on the back of her neck.

"Breathe," he said, sounding calm and authoritative, and Laodice sucked in a deep gulp of air and felt the blood return to her brain. She came up again and stared at Eli, who was staring at her, wide-eyed.

"*What happened to my sister?*" she demanded.

"Nothing bad!" Eli said. "I mean, pretty bad. But no one's dead!"

Laodice gripped her skirt and willed her heartbeat to slow down. "What happened?"

Eli fumbled for his phone, searching for something. "Look, you know I like Xena, great girl, but she really shit the bed on this one."

"Give me your phone," Telfer said, striding over to him, and when Eli didn't move fast enough he simply plucked it out of his hand.

Rude, Laodice thought, as he tossed it to her. High-handed. Kind of hot as hell.

Laodice found Xena's channel. There wasn't anything terrible there, just her usual mix of inspiration, fitness investigation and sponcon, but the latest video had tens of thousands of comments, all of them talking about something else altogether and half of them berating Xena for deleting it.

This was the internet. Everything was there forever.

She searched Xena's name and got dozens of recent links. There was a hashtag. There were memes. There were reactions and commentary and of course, there was the video that had served as a catalyst, replicated over and over. Xena's deletion must have been sheer panic.

Xena had thrown...oh no. She'd thrown a livestreamed surprise engagement party for her boyfriend, Zac. This was the cool thing she'd teased in the sisterly group chat.

But she clearly hadn't discussed the proposal with Zac at all.

Because he'd turned her down.

Live.

Oh, this was *bad*.

People were mocking Xena's own previous videos about consent and communication. There were thousands of comments from disgusting trolls, but worse than that was the commentary from her own fans. Or rather, her previous fans.

Xena was being cancelled, live and raw and in progress. Her reputation was being tarnished, her sponsorships were vanishing, her entire *career* was disappearing.

"Oh no," Laodice said, and looked up at Telfer. "I'm sorry, I can't, I have to—"

"Your phone and charger are in your purse, keep my laptop for now, and I'll see you at work," Telfer said, calm and reasonable, and she wanted to hold him and have him hold her for the agonizing minutes it was going to take until she could get hold of Xena.

But she couldn't. He wasn't hers.

"Here," she said, and handed Eli's phone back to him. "You can leave now."

"It's all right," Eli said soothingly. "I can stay."

Laodice looked at Telfer. "I don't have time for him," she said.

Without a word, Telfer grabbed Eli by the scruff of the neck and marched him out the door. At the last moment, he turned back to look at her.

"Good luck," he said.

Laodice wished, with all her heart, that it didn't sound so much like "goodbye."

Chapter Seventeen

"**W**hat is *wrong* with you, man?" Eli demanded.

"Shut up," Telfer suggested. He let go of the man's collar. Physical violence wasn't part of his normal repertoire, but watching Eli pester Laodice was enough to bring out the bruiser in him. "Where's the key?"

"What?"

"The spare key she gave you. Hand it over."

Eli looked like he was thinking about some form of protest, but Telfer took a step closer, and he fished the key out of a pocket. "My stuff's still in there."

"I'll have it couriered to you." Telfer glared at him. "Don't go near Laodice. She told you to get lost, so you stay lost."

"What are you, her *boyfriend*?"

Telfer wasn't sure what his face did in response, but Eli actually recoiled. "If you pull this again, she'll have you arrested for stalking," he said, in a voice he didn't quite recognize as his own. "And if that doesn't stick, *I* will beat the shit out of you. Understand?"

"You're welcome to each other," Eli said. "You're both fucking crazy." He took off, not quite running down the stairs, and Telfer sat on the top step and rested his head against the railing. Laodice was back there, hurting because her sister was hurting, and he couldn't go to her. He'd stumbled at the final hurdle.

"What *is* wrong with me?" he asked himself.

He didn't have any answers. After a while, he got up and went home.

***

Laodice was a little surprised by the fuss awaiting her return to the office on Monday morning. Objectively, of course, she'd been through something terrible, and she fully expected to pay for it in therapy bills later, but she hadn't even made it to her office before she was waylaid by people in the lobby and elevators who wanted to express their sympathy.

Stephanie, the Bridal receptionist, was usually unflappable, but even she gaped at Laodice's entrance.

"What are you doing here?" she demanded.

"Coming to work?" Laodice said. "My leave is over."

"Insane," Stephanie said flatly. "Go home. Sleep. Knit things."

Laodice sighed. "I guess you read the article?"

"Are you kidding me? Everyone in the building's read it."

Laodice's story had been accepted roughly ten minutes after she'd submitted it on Wednesday evening and published online Thursday afternoon. The *New Argus* editor had been as unsympathetic as Telfer on the subject of adjectives, but she'd been allowed to keep the monastery metaphor. Laodice *had* slept most of Friday. She'd heard from most of the other Halcyon attendees over the weekend, via email to her work account—effusive thanks from Patrick and Samuel, a stiff compliment on the article from Yvette, the promised dinner invitation from Alma.

303

That one assumed a double date, and she hadn't replied yet. Nothing from Britt and Carrick, of course. Nothing from Hazel.

Nothing from Telfer.

Now, Stephanie was staring at her critically. "How are you so calm when someone tried to literally murder you only days ago?"

"I'm screaming inside," Laodice said, and when Stephanie rolled her eyes, she added, "Honestly, I've been a little distracted. I don't know if you follow my sister Xena—"

"Oh man, yes, how is she?"

Laodice winced. Xena had lost her long-term boyfriend and watched her entire career crumple in about six hours. And then, after she'd cried it out over the phone with Laodice, she'd sniffed and asked, "So, what's up with you?"

And Laodice had had to tell her. As much as she could, anyway.

The sisters chat had been busy, despite the fact that there wasn't much to say. She and Cassie had privately agreed that Xena had messed up, but from everything Xena had said, she'd never even imagined Zac turning her down. From her point of view, the engagement had been a foregone conclusion, and one she'd been delighted to share with her fans.

"It's been a rough couple of days for all of us," Laodice said. "I'll tell you over coffee later?"

"It's a date."

When Laodice walked past her into the office, her eyes went automatically to Telfer's desk. He wasn't there. Instead, her other colleagues greeted her with questions and expressions of concern, and it was twenty minutes before she could sit at her own desk and log in.

And Telfer still hadn't arrived.

Miriam appeared in her office doorway. "Laodice," she said, beckoning her in. "A word?"

Laodice sank into the chair she was offered. "I'm sorry I couldn't get you the cover story you wanted," she began, and Miriam laughed.

"My dear girl, you've no need to apologize for that. What a terrible coup you scored."

"I guess."

"I wanted to discuss two other things entirely. First, I'm afraid that the Bridal department will be severing its business relationship with Polyxena."

"I figured," Laodice said gloomily. "Thank you for telling me in person."

"She's young and determined," Miriam said. "She'll work something out. Honestly, if the young man had accepted, her virtual stock would have risen through the roof. Everyone loves a successful romance."

"Emphasis on *successful*."

"Precisely. Which brings me to my second point." Miriam steepled her fingers and gave Laodice a severe look. "What on earth did you do to our Telfer?"

To her intense embarrassment, Laodice burst into tears.

"My word," Miriam said, and jumped to her feet. She bustled around, fetching tissues and a glass of water and the whiskey bottle from the bottom drawer of her desk: "Medicinal, you know, drink up."

"It's 9 a.m.," Laodice protested, but she took a cautious sip.

"So," Miriam said. "From my point of view, this all started when my hardest-working and most reliable journalist asked me if he could swan off to a couple's retreat with you with no notice."

Laodice sniffed. "He said he had leave approved."

"He did not. Though I was curious enough to grant him some. Then, after the ordeal you both went through, he called me in the weekend—and I am not sure how he had my home number—and proffered his resignation."

"*What?*"

"I refused to accept, of course," Miriam said airily. "But in the ensuing conversation, I managed to glean that you two had... formed a connection, shall we say?"

Laodice gave her a suspicious look. "We could say that."

"And what an enormous relief that must have been," Miriam said. "I have been watching you two spark off each other for four years. I was beginning to think you'd never consummate that attraction."

"I hoped it was more than attraction," Laodice said forlornly. "I asked him out. And he said no."

"Did he?"

"He said he'd have to think about it."

"Well, that was sensible of him," Miriam said. "You'd both gone through something terrible together and then you came home to discover your sister's romance had spectacularly and publicly exploded. A brief time apart to consider the matter is only rational."

"It didn't feel rational. He looked scared. It felt like I pushed him too far and he ran. Like I do with everyone, I push them too far, because I want too much, too fast—"

"Stop," Miriam said sharply. "I will allow for a moderate amount of self-pity, but self-doubt is poison. You are wonderful, Laodice. Telfer is a darling. I cannot think of two people better suited to each other, and I'll be damned if I let you condemn yourself for taking a risk."

"But we fight all the time!"

Miriam's clear blue eyes went misty. "I fought at least once a week with my second husband, and he was the greatest love of my life. Tell me this, and be honest. If Telfer were to walk into this room right now and say that he wanted to be with you, would you tell him to go?"

Laodice straightened. "No."

"Good. Come with me, please."

She led a mystified Laodice back through the main office, past reception, and stopped at a small door next to the elevator. "Enter."

"Enter...the maintenance closet?"

"I wasn't given sufficient notice to prepare something more suitable," Miriam said, and sniffed. "Nevertheless."

Laodice was beginning to form some suspicions. She opened the door, and was largely unsurprised to see Telfer standing between the shelves of cleaning supplies, holding a large bouquet of orchids.

She *was* surprised by his expression. He looked shocked. Awed, even. And nakedly vulnerable, all of his usual defenses lowered as he stared at her.

"Really?" she said. "You weren't expecting me?"

Telfer cleared his throat. "I thought you'd be Miriam, telling me that you'd changed your mind."

Laodice stepped into the closet. "Goodbye, Miriam," she said over her shoulder.

Miriam let out an unrestrained cackle. "I expect you both back at work tomorrow," she said blithely, and then Laodice closed the door and stared at Telfer.

He stared back. They were so close she could feel the heat of his body. The sweet, subtle fragrance of orchids rose around them.

"Something to say, Terzi?"

"Do you want to be my girlfriend?"

"*Yes*," Laodice said, and yanked his mouth down to hers. The orchids got a little crushed, until Telfer shelved them so that he could put his arms around her.

"How are you doing?" he asked. "How's Xena?"

"Fine, not fine, and why didn't you *call* me? What were you doing all weekend?"

"Taking stock of myself," Telfer said. "I had a long talk with my uncle. I visited my parents' grave and talked to them too." He shrugged. "That was a one-sided conversation, of course, but it made me feel better."

"But why the flowers and the closet?"

"I thought you deserved something more romantic than a phone call."

"That's sweet," Laodice said, feeling her throat tighten.

"Plus I've never asked anyone to be my girlfriend before," Telfer added. "I wasn't really familiar with the protocols." He looked at her anxiously. "I'm probably going to be pretty bad at this, at least to start."

"That's okay," Laodice assured him. "I have *lots* of practice. The important thing is, do you like me?"

"Yes."

"Do you want me?"

"Very much."

"Do you want to be with me?"

"More than anything," Telfer said, and kissed her again to emphasize the point.

***

After a mutual, slightly regretful decision that while kissing in a supply closet was okay, sex at work in the middle of the day was right out, Telfer successfully argued Laodice into coming back to his place.

He could hardly believe she was there at all. His heart-to-heart with Miriam had been unexpected; that Laodice still wanted him seemed impossible.

But she would never lie about that. It had to be true.

"I have some opinions on your decor," she said, glaring at his black and chrome furnishings.

"We'll fight about it later," Telfer promised, and walked her backwards to his bedroom, getting some decent groping in on the way. She laughed and curved against him, her hair tickling his neck as she kissed him.

"I'm going to buy you an orange shirt," she said, and tackled his buttons. "That's boyfriend stuff, if you were wondering."

"I'll wear it at least once. Want to listen to my nerdy podcast with me?"

"*One* episode, and if I hate it, I'm out," Laodice said. She yanked her dress over her head in one fluid motion, and bounced backwards onto the bed, in a red bra and black bike shorts. "Get up here."

"I'm enjoying the view. I've been meaning to ask, why the bike shorts?"

"Thigh rub. Chafing's no fun."

"Your thighs are perfect," Telfer said, and proved it by kissing the dimpled flesh as he yanked her shorts and underwear down. Laodice shivered and lay back in the pillows, and Telfer lunged in to taste her, so happy he was nearly blind with it. Laodice's hands tightened in his hair as he devoted himself to mapping out her path to orgasm. She was so responsive to his mouth and hands, so unashamedly vocal in her pleasure.

He could have stayed there all day, but she pushed him away. "I want you to come *with* me," she said, and there was an awkward scramble and a great deal of laughter as they rearranged themselves to lie side by side, Laodice curling up her legs and Telfer curving into her from behind.

"No guarantees," Telfer warned, and groaned as he sank into her warmth.

Laodice guided one of his hands to her breast, and the other to her clit, intertwining her fingers with his until he got the rhythm. "I'm not going to last long," she said breathlessly. "Touch me. Oh yes. You're so good at this. Fuck me, fuck me hard."

Telfer did his best. His hips thrust furiously as he drove into her, every stroke reaching deeper. She clenched around him, her body and voice both driving him on, demanding more, more, now. At the very end, he lost the rhythm on her clit, but it didn't matter, she was gone, tightening around him in that delicious squeeze, and he let go, mind and body both emptying out with pure bliss.

They lay there, panting, and then Laodice turned in his arms to face him. "Okay," she said. "What's this about you quitting?"

"You're going to be Bridal editor, and I obviously can't work for my girlfriend," Telfer said. "I'm going to transfer, though, not quit. Miriam said *Money Matters* might be interested, and if not, Odysseus Turner gave me a standing invitation to join the Finance team two years ago."

"He did? You never mentioned that."

Telfer kissed the tip of her nose. "I'm mentioning it now. To my girlfriend."

"You're not going to resent this?" Laodice said anxiously. "I don't want to be in the middle of a fight with you in three years, and you suddenly pull out the 'I could have been Bridal editor if not for you' line."

"Nope," Telfer said. "I won't say I didn't want it. I did. But not only do I want you more…"

"Excellent, very hot."

"… I wouldn't do a better job than you will. It should be you. I was always going to be the also-ran."

"You're definitely starting this boyfriend thing on the right foot."

"Great, but I have no intention of resting on my laurels," Telfer said, and wriggled down the bed. "Now, where were we…"

***

"One more thing," Laodice said, some time later.

"I thought you weren't good at conversation after sex," Telfer said sleepily. He was stroking her hair with one hand.

"Too bad, you bring out the best in me," Laodice said cheerily. "I was thinking that we did all this backwards. We got engaged, then we had sex, *then* you asked me to be your girlfriend."

"Huh," Telfer said. "I suppose our first date is next. Want to go to dinner with me?"

"Yep. And then we should organize some kind of meet-cute. Maybe I'm doing some seasonal decorating and you slip on fairy lights and get amnesia?"

"I don't want to wait until winter for our meet-cute," Telfer protested.

"Okay," Laodice decided. "I'll be late to an important meeting and you'll be a busy dog-walker."

"You get caught in the leashes and your papers go everywhere?"

"Yes. Of course you help me pick them up, and you say 'I know this is crazy but can I buy you a cup of coffee?' With a shy smile. Can you do a shy smile?"

"I think the bigger problem is going to be me getting my hands on a dozen dogs. Why don't we go with the classics? We could take turns driving halfway across the country, arguing about whether men and women can ever be friends."

"If you spent that long in the Spider you'd ruin your back. And anyway, it took Harry and Sally twelve years to get it together. We managed it in four."

"Go us," Telfer said, and pulled her closer. "Now, about this no-conversations-after-sex..."

"How long do you think it took Hildy and Walter?"

"Hm?"

"From *His Girl Friday*. When we meet them, they're already divorced and she's getting married to someone else. How long do you think it took them to realize the first time?"

"Why are we competing with fictional characters?"

"Come on, guess."

Telfer made a thoughtful sound. "I'd say...about twenty minutes. He made a pass and was terrified when she took him up on it."

"Terrified? Really?"

"Scared to death." He rolled Laodice onto her back and hovered over her. "Good thing she knew what she wanted."

"Smart woman, Hildy," Laodice said, and pulled him in for a kiss.

"Okay," Telfer said after a minute. He seemed to be having some trouble breathing. "I think we're missing one thing from this reverse relationship scenario."

"Yes?"

Telfer's voice trembled. "When's the appropriate time to tell you that I love you?"

Laodice had a moment where her own lungs didn't seem to be working right. "Well, traditionally, after you run across the city in a rainstorm," she managed after a moment.

Telfer nodded. "So not right now."

"No. But soon." She pushed his hair back and gazed into his eyes, so warm and honest. "I mean it. Very soon."

"Soon's good," Telfer said, and kissed her again. "I can work with that."

Next From Olympus Inc.

Polyxena Troiades used to be somebody. Now's she's struggling to figure out her future.

Cressida O'Brian used to be somebody else. Now she's struggling to free herself from her past.

When the two women team up to take down their common foe, they risk danger, and even death. But the greatest risk of all might be to their hearts...

Order *XO, Xena*, the triumphant final book in the Trojan Women arc of Olympus Inc!

Afterword

Laodice of Troy doesn't have the fame of her sisters Cassandra or Polyxena. Homer describes her as the most beautiful of Priam's many daughters, but there's not much about her in the Iliad, and she doesn't turn up in *The Trojan Women*, my favorite play by Euripides. Her story and fate are variable. There's a story that she fell in love with a diplomatic visitor to Troy and bore him a son. According to Homer, she was married to Helicaion. According to Hyginus, she was married to Telephus, the king of Mysia, a region in modern day Türkiye.

After the fall of Troy, Laodice was captured and made a slave to Odysseus. No, she was set free, because her husband was a guest friend of Menelaus and Agamemnon. No, she was swallowed by the earth as she was being chased by Greeks intent on capture and rape—because she fell into a chasm, or because she was *such a good wife* that she couldn't bear to shame her husband, and prayed for the earth to swallow her instead, and Hera, goddess of marriage, took pity and granted her wish.

Sure. Yep. Okay.

But this is Olympus Inc, and I get to write happy endings for classical ladies in contemporary romance. *My* Laodice is beautiful and romantic. She wants to love and be loved. But she is not going to be punished for it. She might fall into the earth, but she climbs out again, and the death she finds there is not her own.

Acknowledgements

As ever, I am grateful to my wonderful editor Robyn Fleming, to fabulous cover designer Alison Cooley, and to my sister Gina, for gleefully picking out every typo and sending me screenshots in the chat. Alex Casey accompanied me to a weird wedding expo for research purposes, Casey Blair did stellar keyword investigation, Esme Brett provided sexy moral support, the Spout Lore discord dispensed supportive emojis, and the Crit Show discord gave me in-depth detail on trash bag dispensers.

I am now and forever grateful to the friends and colleagues who let me blurt story at them and give me the grace to drag my brain back from whatever I've been making my imaginary people do. Thank you also to everyone who told me their proposal stories; I ended up going in a different direction, but I loved hearing them!

About the Author

Kate Healey lives in New Zealand and writes spicy contemporary romance and urban fantasy. Karen Healey, who looks suspiciously similar, lives in New Zealand and writes less spicy fantasy romance, science fiction and young adult fiction. They both drink a lot of coffee.

Sign up for Karen's newsletter at http://thathealeygirl.com . You'll get the first news on new books, weird research rabbitholes, and occasional freebies!

Also by Kate Healey

Olympus Inc. Series:

Penelope Pops the Question (a series prequel and newsletter freebie, available when you sign up at http://thathealeygirl.com!)
The Love Labyrinth (standalone novella)

Arc One: The Olympians (now available on Kindle Unlimited!)
#1 *Persephone in Bloom*
#2 *Aphrodite Unbound*
#3 *Hera Takes Charge*

Arc Two: The Trojan Women
#4 *Ask Cassandra*
#5 *Love, Laodice*
#6 *XO, Xena*

As Karen Healey:

The Movie Magic Series:

"Jingle Spells" (a newsletter freebie, available when you sign up at http:
//thathealeygirl.com)
Bespoke & Bespelled
Savory & Supernatural

The Hidden Histories Series (with Robyn Fleming):

The Empress of Timbra
The Spymaster's Apprentice

Young Adult Works:

Guardian of the Dead
The Shattering
When We Wake
While We Run